W9-ACM-764

TRIPLE SHOT

ALSO BY ROSS KAVAN

Schmuck
Tigerland (screenplay)

ALSO BY TIM O'MARA

Raymond Donne Series
Sacrifice Fly
Crooked Numbers
Dead Red
Nasty Cutter (*)

ALSO BY CHARLES SALZBERG

Henry Swann PI Series
Swann's Last Song
Swann Dives In
Swann's Lake of Despair
Swann's Way Out (*)

Stand Alone
Devil in the Hole

(*) Forthcoming in 2017

ROSS KLAVAN,
TIM O'MARA,
CHARLES SALZBERG

TRIPLE SHOT

DOWN&OUT
BOOKS

Thump Gun Hitched copyright © 2016 by Ross Klavan
Smoked copyright © 2016 by Tim O'Mara
Twist of Fate copyright © 2016 by Charles Salzberg

All rights reserved. No part of the book may be reproduced in any form or by any electronic or mechanical means, including information storage and retrieval systems, without permission in writing from the publisher, except by a reviewer who may quote brief passages in a review.

Down & Out Books
3959 Van Dyke Rd, Ste. 265
Lutz, FL 33558
www.DownAndOutBooks.com

The characters and events in this book are fictitious. Any similarity to real persons, living or dead, is coincidental and not intended by the author.

Cover design by James Tuck

ISBN: 1-943402-32-9
ISBN-13: 978-1-943402-32-8

THUMP GUN HITCHED

ROSS KLAVAN

To Mary

Part One

This is not the place you want to be, not now, not at night.

This is right on the mangy, flea-dog outskirts of L.A., out there where there's no lights and nothing left of the aircraft plant except this one piece-of-shit building, a low, gray, dead concrete animal. Sitting inside, in that enormous empty space, sitting there at the table all the way back in the darkened corner across from Tonjay, Dane's not so glad he left his piece in the car.

"You know what a detective thinks about when he heads out the door to fight crime," Bobby Dane says. "He's thinking, sweet Jesus, don't let me do something to screw up my pension. I can't do nothing to screw with my twenty years in."

Tonjay slides the brown paper bag with the money across the table. It looks like a brick. Maybe the three long scar lines that run from Tonjay's cheek-to-nose-to-cheek, like tribal scars, maybe they turn color, maybe not. Bobby Dane can't tell.

"You know what else they're thinking?" Bobby Dane says. "Most cops? They really want to do a good job. Most cops. They want to be one of the good guys."

Bobby Dane takes the brick of cash and stands up. The two guys behind Tonjay, both bruisers, shift just a little, from foot to foot.

"That's why you're lucky," Bobby Dane says. "I'm not that kind of cop."

Outside, he moves fast, watching.

Across the abandoned parking lot and under the spider web shadow of the wire fence, listening to his steps crush gravel in the moonlight, the sway of the trees, Bobby Dane's almost happy now, getting away.

Down the road to where he's parked his car, just a little bit hidden, off the dirt path near what remains of a grove of eucalyptus. He can smell them. When he gets the driver's side door open, he tosses the brick of cash inside and goes on high alert for a moment, curses, as the brick pops off the passenger seat and rolls onto the floor. That's what's got his attention. That's when Bobby Dane gets hit.

The blow catches him hard on the side of the neck. His knees give way. The world goes underwater. But not before Bobby Dane's partly back inside, scrambling, bent forward, grabbing his 9mm from under the driver's seat. He's still got enough going to stand and swing around.

When he does, the automatic disappears suddenly, ripped out of his hand and the last thing he feels is the soft/hard shirt covered elbow that sweeps in and cracks across his ear. Dane's out for just a moment, but that's all it takes. Lying in the dirt beside his car, he stares up as the man above him says, "Liar. Thief. Fucking traitor." Then in Spanish, "*Chorro. Ladron.*"

"Fuck, man, okay, okay. Jesus. You hit me hard."

"I could kick your head to jelly," the man says. "And that's: 'You hit me hard, *Captain Haran.*'"

Bobby Dane keeps his mouth shut. He fights it, he might cry.

"Now, Bobby," Haran says. "What are we supposed to do about this?"

* * *

They go to the hole-in-the-wall bar that's a half mile away. A dive that used to serve the aircraft factory and now barely makes it on strays and losers. The place stinks. The toilets are across from the bar, separated by saloon-style swinging doors so you can see the shoes below and keep an eye on what goes down.

"You owe me," Haran says, "an explanation. I figure I got that much coming."

"How long have you been tipped off?"

Bobby Dane can't hold the gaze. Haran's got the gunfighter look, rawboned and mean, gray hair slicked back a little. He commands respect and gets it.

"I've known long enough," Haran says. "And you don't know as much as you think you know. You want to sell us out? The unit? Okay. But what you're passing to Tonjay and those clowns, all that info is shit, amigo. All of it. Made up and fed to you. I let it go that way."

Bobby Dane can feel his breath coming fast.

"If that's true, Ty, then I'm not gonna need a lawyer. I'll be lucky to live through the week."

"I treated you better than family," Haran says. "Not only that. You're top man on the team and you make me drink out of the toilet."

"I needed the money."

"Bullshit. That's never the real reason." Haran puts his phone down on the table. "What did I do that made you think you needed to screw me?"

"*You*," Bobby Dane says quietly. "Fuck you."

Haran wants to hit him.

"Go ahead. Call your buddy," Haran says. "Tell

Tonjay you've been sussed. Tell him you didn't mean to, but you gave it to him up the ass. Go ahead. Do it. I want to listen."

Bobby Dane doesn't move.

"Go ahead, Bobby," Haran says. "Save your bootless skin, son. Call. Maybe your buddy Tonjay will just bust some of your teeth or take one of your fingers."

"He's not my buddy," Bobby Dane finishes his beer and tries to sound heroic. "Okay, that's it, I guess."

Then Haran says nothing for so long that Bobby Dane starts picking at the table, the jarred and rotten wood, until he feels a shard stick him under the fingernail. For a little while he plays with the pain until he can't stand the silence and he says, "You gotta help me, Ty. Okay, I fucked up. But it's too much. I'll get sent away and they'll probably kill me inside. Maybe I don't matter anymore, okay. But what about Kira? They'll probably kill her, too."

"I oughta take you to IA in shanks, you piece of shit."

"Yeah, okay. So, I'm not you and I never will be," Bobby Dane breathes in like it's the last time he'll ever get the pleasure of the air. "What difference does it make? I'm fucked now," he says. "Jesus, Ty. At least don't take me off the unit. Let me go in on this one. Shit. I'll disappear after, I swear to God."

"Sure you will," Haran says. "We make you look like the hero who put it over on Tonjay? You gotta be shitting me."

Haran stands. Lets his shadow fall across Bobby Dane and likes the effect. "You fuck me big time and I pull your ass out of the fire, is that it?"

"Aw please, Ty," Bobby Dane says. "We've been

through it, you and me, haven't we? You know we have. I don't know what happened. Maybe I'm cracking up, I don't know, I don't know what I'm doing anymore. I need help, man."

Haran grabs his phone from the table, pockets it. "You report to the unit on time, you piece of shit," and harder than he intended, Haran shoves Bobby Dane's head to the side. "You owe me, Bobby."

Bobby Dane sits there slumped until he hears Haran's car pull out. For the rest of the night and up until the moment of the raid, he tries not to panic.

The raid goes perfectly until it doesn't.

Cloudy, moonless night, a warehouse on the edge of downtown. Industrial stairs to the second floor and the lookouts on the roof already handcuffed and face down on the concrete. The unit puts four men up the stairs on one side, four men up the stairs on the other, everyone in black, flak jackets, helmets and M-4's. Haran leads one squad. Bobby Dane takes the other.

All the way up the stairs, Haran is thinking about Bobby Dane, even though he knows that break in attention is a mistake, it's a good way to get killed.

The windowless, stinking room is wide as a desert but when they burst in it shrinks right down to size and fast. There are Tonjay and five men in cheap suits standing there around a stack of wooden crates in the center of the room, talking, bullshitting with each other until a jaw-drop silence slaps them quiet as the two squads of cops move inside.

The crates are labeled "Blood Oranges" and "California Fruit Growers Exchange."

It's Haran who yells "Police!" and "Hold it!" and not all the men in suits pay attention. One of them puts his hands in the air and drops to his knees. Another goes for a handgun at his waist. In the silence of the big room, the crack of Haran's M-4 sounds like the walls are splitting open and the man who went for his piece jackknifes and spins away at the same time, tumbling into the pile of crates and then onto his face. The crate topples. The oranges bounce out onto the floor. And under the oranges, the hidden, perfectly round hand grenades bounce out, too, and lay there in the room squat and deadly.

That's when Tonjay runs. The big, scar-faced man—nobody's paying particular attention to him until now, they're too set on securing the room—but Tonjay bolts towards an open door at the rear of the space.

Haran's face dips towards his lapel mike to the team waiting outside: "We got a runner. Southeast exit."

And then, Haran turns to stare at Bobby Dane, as in, *There goes your fucking friend*, but when he does, another man in a suit scoops one of the grenades off the floor. And pulls the pin.

Some of the cops shout. Doesn't matter. Even with that noise, all of them can hear when the grenade pin pops off the floor with a metallic ring. Then, they're all looking at the bad guy in a suit who's now holding the live grenade.

"If you want this to end with smiles," Haran says to him, "you'd better, very slowly, hand that motherfucking thing over to me."

He's been around this before. Six years in the service, Infantry, Rangers, the cool metal skin of a grenade doesn't rock his world. Everyone can see that. Bobby Dane, though, he's shaking and trying to get a grip.

"I'm just going to come a little closer," Haran tells the grenade man, "and I'm going to put my hand on yours. And take that thing. And it's all gonna be just fine."

Haran slides one foot closer. The grenade man tenses, grunts. Raises his hand like he's ready to throw.

And suddenly it's Bobby Dane who says, "Give it here."

"Don't, Bobby," Haran says.

"C'mon now," Bobby Dane says to the grenade man. "Let's be friends. Hand it over."

"You don't need to do this, Bobby," Haran waves him off.

But Bobby Dane won't do it, cuts him dead. "You know I gotta do this," Bobby Dane says quickly and to the grenade man, "no sense in all of us getting hurt." Bobby Dane's sweating, the smell of it mingles with the smell of dust and oil in the room. "Be smart."

The man with the grenade slowly, finally listens. Bobby Dane, now blinking away sweat and edging towards his own crazy fear zone, slowly reaches out and gets a grip on the grenade man's hand, keeping the safety lever depressed with a thumb. The grenade changes hands.

The moment the exchange is made, the former grenade man pulls what looks like a 9mm automatic from the small of his back and jams the barrel into Bobby Dane's forehead. He makes a motion with his head: Go to the door.

Bobby Dane can barely draw breath, it's like he's in a chamber without air and all he hears is a strange, constant hum in his head: *You fucked this up big time.* He wonders if the shame that's now burning in his chest is as obvious on his face. The two of them—with the gunman edging Bobby Dane's head back with the 9mm—now begin inching towards the door at the rear of the room.

"Hey, tough guy," Haran calls, "there's no way out. We've got people outside all over the fucking place."

Haran starts moving close, striding closer, like grenades and automatics and hostages don't really exist in his world. Close enough to make a slow, liquid reach for the automatic, keeping watch on the grenade, saying quietly, "Let's be easy, it's all okay."

The gunman moves. Quick. The automatic rams down on Bobby Dane's wrist and the grenade flies out of Bobby Dane's hand, hits the floor and rolls. The gunman bolts. Haran dives for the deadly metal ball, grabs it, flings it, launches himself forward at Bobby Dane's knees as he shouts, "GRENADE!" more out of some well-worn groove than any thinking concern.

He scrambles across Bobby Dane on the floor, covering him.

And then the blast, so loud it's like silence. The terrible earthquake shake of the room, the sound of shattering glass and that strange, cutting "hissssss" that shrapnel makes when it severs the air overhead, when it lodges deep into flesh and memory.

* * *

Not long after the newspapers get bored with the story and the TV people go back to talking about kids who'd help old people across the street, Bobby Dane quietly leaves the force and noisily enters the Army.

Noisily, because his friends throw him a bash at the Autry Center Western Museum. It's a party like only cops can throw. What Haran sees, as he walks the path towards the cowboy museum, is some of the cops from the raid fooling around near a statue of William S. Hart, the silent movie cowboy star. They're imitating his quick draw. Two other cops are slap-boxing over by a display case of Indian spears. There's a huge banner that reads, "GOOD LUCK PVT. DANE!" and below it, Haran sees Kira, Bobby Dane's wife.

She's made herself look absolutely beautiful which, as Haran says to himself, wasn't all that difficult. They kiss hello and after the usual politeness Haran says, "So. How's he holding up?"

"You should talk to him."

"What's he said to you?"

"You know how Bobby is," Kira says. "When things are great he won't shut up. When things stink he's like being in church."

She knows nothing about Bobby Dane's sellout, about Tonjay, about the money. She can't understand why he's leaving the force for the service. So Haran tells her he'll find Bobby Dane and put some sense into him.

Outside, past the cops who are slap-boxing and screwing around by the Hart statue, Haran sits with Bobby Dane and shares a beer as Bobby Dane goes on and on about how he's just this tiny bit afraid now that he's actually going away.

"Everyone feels like that right before they go in," Haran says.

"That's not what I'm saying," he breathes deep a couple of times. "I know I fucked up bad."

Haran nurses the beer. "Yeah. You did."

Bobby Dane just stares at the cops slap boxing.

"I don't understand why you did it," Haran says.

And after a while, Bobby Dane says, "Neither do I."

Then he's talking very fast. He talks about the past and about all that Haran's done for him and about how he thinks Haran has lived a life, a real life and about how it is when you're trying to live up to somebody else. "You're like the guy that all the little boys and girls want to be," Bobby Dane says.

That's when Haran tells him to stop and says, "This is bullshit."

But Bobby Dane keeps going. "You're a real piece of work, Ty, you know that? The way you've lived. I mean, even in the service, they pin you with enough medals to tear your pockets off. So now, when you talk it's like every word comes down from the mountaintop."

"This'll be the end of it, we're even," Haran says. "Nobody owes anybody, right? C'mon, let's go back inside."

"No, listen," Bobby Dane says. "What I'm trying to get to is...I'm sorry. I didn't know what I was doing. It had nothing to do with you."

Haran knows that's not true but he wants to cut Bobby Dane loose with a clean conscience, let him go away without shame or blame, he wants to say something about what it's like trying to live with honor. But he's afraid. He doesn't want to sound stupid, he can't say it, he fails. Then Bobby Dane finishes his beer, crushes the can, curses and walks away, back towards the Autry Center as Haran yells after him.

The party is now out of control—that's Haran's judgment. He curses Bobby Dane and himself under his breath, loses Bobby Dane in the crowd. Haran walks through, pushing this one and moving that one by the shoulders, standing way above all of them, and he searches the packed room for Bobby Dane and that's when it all changes. He comes up on the cops who were slap-boxing and who are now practicing how to disarm a man who's holding an automatic. Which is exactly what one of them holds in his hand.

"Tell me that's not a real piece," Haran says to them.

"No harm, Cap, just practice," this is Hendricks, from the unit, short, square, tough and drunk. He's been practicing with McCoy, also from the unit, who now says, "He's right, Pete, put it away."

"Give me the weapon," Haran says.

"It's a party, Cap, you don't have to go rule book," Hendricks sways just a little bit.

"Hand it over. Now."

Bobby Dane comes back through the crowd. He stands beside Haran and says to Hendricks, "That's a loaded piece? What the hell's wrong with you? You heard the man."

"I heard the man," Hendricks says. He does a quick, drunk-comic pointing of the weapon at Bobby Dane and that's when anyone standing nearby clears the area. It's just the three of them.

Hendricks eyeballs Bobby Dane. He almost spits, "Now you can say he saved your life twice," and he spins the automatic movie gunfighter style, doing a trick that ends with the butt pointing to Haran. Who takes the pistol.

That only lasts for an instant.

Hendricks suddenly shouts "Whoa!" and throws his hands in the air like Haran's an assailant. Or maybe he only seems to move that way. So quickly that it beats the eye, Hendricks' hands rise up and instead of going straight in the air, they suddenly go for a disarm, grabbing at the weapon. But too much scotch gets in his wires and now Hendricks and Haran are wrestling over the automatic and Bobby Dane moves in hitting Hendricks in the kidney with the side of his hand. Somebody screams. Not loud enough to drown out the blast of the 9mm—just one shot. Hendricks bucks and goes down and from the crowd it looks like there's a moment where Bobby Dane and Haran are grappling but nobody's certain. All they can see is that when the two men separate, breathing heavy, eyes locked, it's Bobby Dane who's holding the gun.

"The DA has a hard-on," Haran says. "Negligent discharge of a firearm. He'll go involuntary manny and ask four years state."

"What do you want, a speech?"

The visitor's area always smells of ammonia and the light seems yellow, like it came from a disease. Haran, for just a moment, feels like he's in a dream. He wishes that was true. Bobby Dane has that far-off, unfocused stare.

"And then there's wrongful death and the civil suit, I'd bet cash money on it."

"I want you to leave," Bobby Dane says.

"Goddamnit, Bobby. I'll go tell them what happened."

"Leave. Or I'll call for the CO."

"You'd do this to Kira?"

"I'm gonna set things straight."

"You oughta learn to let things be crooked," Haran stands. "It's a lot more real. Fucking idiot."

"Don't come to see me anymore, Ty," Bobby Dane says. "If I'm gonna do this, I'm gonna do it alone."

"What's this? More playground courage? You're fucking crazy."

"Crazy is better in here," Bobby Dane says. "And you're the one who was always talking to me about honor."

Haran snorts, pushes himself away and walks over to find the guard and get out.

"You know, Ty," Bobby Dane says from where he's sitting. "You're gonna get yourself killed someday." He's looking down at the beaten up tabletop. "You care too much."

"Hey, Bobby?" Haran says as the guard opens the door. "Bullshit."

The night before he quits the force, Haran sits at a bar on Sunset and has three drinks, scotch, the first drinks he's had in four years.

He begins to have those *three drinks at the bar* thoughts that seem to float in on wings and bless the brain. There is such a thing as honor and it's important, yes, it is and that's the way to be somebody, that's it, and a man has to live that way, goddamnit, that's just the truth and the way of the world. There's what you owe and paying your way. Paying for it. Yes, there is.

By the time he's done, though, Haran's brains are working just well enough so that he knows to take a cab home. Along the way, in the grand comfort of the cab with the lights gliding by and flashing and the air sweet, Haran decides that he was wrong. At the bar. There is no honor. There can't be because he's not going to say anything to anybody. He's not going to find a cop or a lawyer or a judge to tell the whole truth—"It was me holding the gun when it went off"—he's not going to argue or plead with Bobby Dane.

He's not going to help out.

He's not going to prison.

Fuck 'em all, Haran says to himself.

Bobby Dane sees San Francisco Bay and thinks: I may never see that again. He gives them a tough time from the get-go—hits another prisoner, tells one CO to *fuck off*, mouths off to the CO who signs him in. They talk about putting Bobby Dane in Administrative Segregation and then decide to house him in South Block with the rest of the bad asses.

Bobby Dane's been in San Quentin plenty of times but not like this. When the cell door closes behind him, he lets the tomb-echo sound dig into him and lets it shut things off, feels himself begin to go dead.

He tosses his bedding on the bottom rack. Above,

lying on his back, there's a small, wiry old man who's reading a Jehovah's Witness magazine.

"I'm Baker," the old man says. "You the cop who killed a cop?"

Bobby Dane doesn't answer.

"Killing a cop is plus one," Baker says. "Being a cop is minus one." He lays the magazine down across his face. "That adds up to zero. Which is the same as your chances here on the inside."

"And of course, you're gonna help me out."

"Maybe," Baker says. "Maybe we'll help each other."

"How very lucky I must be."

"Yeah, me, too," Baker is now sitting up with his skinny little legs dangling. "But I've been lucky in here a lot longer than you have." He pulls a pack of gum from inside his shirt and offers a piece to Bobby Dane, who refuses. "Aw, look, you little cornhole," Baker says. "We're gonna be smelling each other's shit for a long time in here. Best idea? Let's just try to be friendly."

Bobby Dane nods and starts making up his bed.

It's two weeks later when Kira comes to visit. She's put on ten years and without make-up Bobby Dane has to stare to recognize her. She doesn't touch the Plexiglas when she speaks into the visitor's phone and the first thing she says is, "Ty told me what really happened."

"Ty doesn't know what really happened."

"This is insane, Bobby."

"I need you to listen to me," Bobby Dane says.

"What's my role in all this? What's the fantasy? I'm supposed to say, *Oh, baby, I'll wait for you forever?* Well, it's not gonna happen."

"Don't come here anymore," Bobby Dane says. "I want you to go on and live your life."

"Oh, Jesus, Bobby, that's even stupider."

"You're coming in...the reminder is worse. I won't make four years if I keep seeing you."

There's a long pause before Kira stands up and moves away from the Plexiglas window. Bobby Dane can't hear her anymore but he can read her lips as she stares at him. "Fuck you, Bobby." It's the last thing she says to him before she walks out.

After the second fight, Bobby Dane does three days in Isolation. The fights—both of them—mean nothing to him. He can handle himself. And it's isolation he wants, the silence, the dark, the solitude enforced by steel doors. He sets a routine of pushups, crunches, deep bends and stretches. He does squat thrusts until he thinks his heart will burst. Some karate katas, moving meditation. All of it with discipline. The rest of the time he sits. He makes the decision that every thought he has, every feeling, is really about how he's lived his whole worthless life up until this moment.

In some way he can't express even to himself, Bobby Dane is certain that all of it has been a failure and that he deserves to be locked up. Selling out the unit was only the final act, maybe the way he was choosing to get caught at last, get right with himself. But it's his entire life that's now getting the sum up. He's failed Kira, the unit, he's failed Haran, more importantly he's failed himself. This is the only way to make good on it.

And more: He decides he won't "do time." Bobby

Dane has seen the pathetic lines on the wall, the calendar days crossed off, the marking of moments like a condemned man counting his breaths. He makes up his mind that he'll let it go, that he'll pay no attention to how much time he has left inside and he'll live as though this moment right now is all there is until it changes.

Bobby Dane decides that he'll come out clean.

Three days after he gets out of Isolation—three days according to the authorities, Bobby Dane's not counting—that's when Bobby Dane hears about Mortales and it's Baker who tells him.

"You been to Mexico ever?" Baker says. "Mortales. I mean, hell, you were a cop, you never talked about the place?"

"I don't know how we missed it."

They're in the yard under a clear, warm sky, under the smell of the water, with Bobby Dane pumping iron, a hundred and twenty pounds, as Baker sits by with his copy of *Christianity Today*.

"No con bullshit, you know, it's real, a real place."

"And I do what, now? Start posting pictures on the wall of where I'll be when I get out?"

"I gotta say," Baker says, "I'm glad we're paired up in here. Makes me feel, well, Jesus, I'm glad I'm not you."

"Don't think I haven't noticed how good you have it."

"Uh huh. You know what I hope for when I get out?"

Bobby Dane towels off, sits down beside Baker on the weight bench.

"I hope chow is a little better than dog food and that where I sit down don't make my hemorrhoids bleed too bad."

"And they say you're not a dreamer."

"But, see, now you," Baker says, "you got a lot of life to go, you're a young man. You ain't gonna be no cop no more. So, then. What? Who's gonna want you? Ex-cop, ex-con. Ex, ex. One more ex and you'll be working naked in the movies."

Bobby Dane slaps his towel down in Baker's lap and says, "This is where we are right now, that's all I know," and starts doing another set of curls.

"What I'm saying is," Baker says, "I can get us down to Mortales. Once we're out. It'll be our town, Bobby. No cops, no hassle, no law. Just sunshine and tequila and maybe a little senorita now and then. All protected. Forever. No sweat, nothing to worry your pretty head about. Forever."

"Well now, you've given me something to live for."

And Baker keeps talking about Mortales, this town way down in Mexico, hidden up in the mountains and away from all prying eyes and searching men, run by those who've crossed the line for others who've crossed the line or worse, a place where they can go to live peacefully, pleasurably and forever. Bad Boy Heaven. Bobby Dane barely hears him, the voice is a hum. This is where he is, right here, right now.

If it changes, it changes. He'll get out when he gets out.

Haran drifts.

After he quits the force, he sells his house and all he owns and heads towards Mexico, thinking he'll leave the country, run through his money and just disappear. But he doesn't even have that much push. He rides through Utah, Nevada, Colorado, New Mexico; sometimes sleeping in the back of his pickup and sometimes camping out. He drinks. As he thinks of it, he *goes back to drinking* like this is a way of life he's chosen. He thinks about Bobby Dane and about that last raid and about the night that gave him a drunken cop and a live weapon and about the time he spent in the service and he feels all of it drop down loose and heavy like the sky has fallen.

This goes on for months and then longer. Haran winds up in Arizona not too far from the Mexican border, out in the middle of the desert that the locals know to steer clear of and that the tourists just stare at, far off from the highway, the great American "Out There." Who owns that land? they say. That's where Haran finds a small dive bar, a rectangle of concrete blocks at the ass-edge of nowhere, surrounded by nothing and promising drink and maybe, if the price is right, women.

The place is owned by Jessie Sax, a former whore from Nevada. Older now and retired, this is what she bought with her savings from years of legal work where the sign said "Brothel" just outside of Carson City. "A brick shithouse," she tells Haran. "That's what I worked for, I just didn't know it."

She takes him in.

Haran tends bar, sweeps up, keeps Jessie warm when she needs it and lives in a trailer not too far from the concrete bar. At night, he drinks until he can fall asleep. If Jessie's not feeding him, he takes his Winchester and goes out into the desert, shoots rabbits, skins them and cooks them outside. Sometimes, he just takes the rifle and walks as far as he's able into the vast, endless vista that seems to swirl around him in shifting colors and he finds a place to sit and listen to the wind.

The desert is red, then gray, then glittering with some kind of crystal. The desert has all kinds of secrets—hidden canyons and ravines and sudden dangers—that have to be discovered, they can't be foretold. *This is freedom*, is what Haran thinks. This is what it means to be free of everything, chained up to nothing. He remembers the prophets they used to talk about in Sunday school and how they'd go into the desert to meditate and see visions and Haran thinks, *Anyone who goes into the desert without a rifle is bat-shit crazy. And take a rifle if you go into freedom, too.*

He scouts for snakes. He uses the Winchester barrel to toy with scorpions.

This is exactly what I'm after, he tells himself. This is what I need. And someday it's gonna help me screw my head on straight again and when that happens, I'll know it. For sure.

He lets the time pass.

Bobby Dane can't tell you how far into his time the real trouble starts but he knows that the first warning is Baker coming out of their cell saying, "We got company and I'm not home." The old man looks spooked, even paler than most days and his thin hair seems even more pasted down on his sweaty head.

Baker is right near the cell door and tries to push past when Bobby Dane grabs his skinny arm. It's Store Day, when the cons are allowed to hit the canteen.

"You don't want to be home, either," Baker says.

Bobby Dane nods and, in that deepest part of himself, gets set to fight. Going hand-to-hand means nothing now, Isolation Unit means nothing and most of the other inmates, even the ones made of deadness and tattooed steel, steer clear of him because he's crazy and it's not worth the scars.

Bobby Dane steps forward. He's holding his bag from the canteen. Extra toothpaste, candy bars, writing paper, small things that are easy to trade and that keep alive the civilized notion of shopping. At the cell door, he makes out a vision of three other cons lounging in his cell, one on his rack, one lolling against the wall, and one standing up waiting for him.

The man standing is Tonjay.

He's gone pure Otherworld-and-Underworld now, even worse than when he was pushing payoff money across the table to Bobby Dane. He's got a swirl of tattoo crawling down one side of his face and his features are carved from a dead man's bones, like the flesh isn't necessary. Big, too, and Bobby Dane gets a gander at the way Tonjay's muscle shifts under the prison shirt. Tonjay makes sure he sees. The other cons do the same. They're the meat the slaughterhouse couldn't kill.

Tonjay lifts a letter, opened, so that Bobby Dane can see Kira's name in the return address. Then he kisses it. And fans himself.

"Sweet," he says. "A boy and his gal."

Bobby Dane hasn't read any of Kira's letters but he hasn't been able to throw them out, either, and she keeps writing even with the divorce.

"This is how we begin," Tonjay says. "Maybe some friends will pay her a visit," and he reads out loud the return address on the envelope. "Not really payback but more like...the beginning of payback."

"You're making it very easy to say, 'Stick it up your ass,'" Bobby Dane says. He can't figure out how long it's been since that brick of money was slipped across the table. He doesn't want to know.

Tonjay's two cons stand still and let their menace, very real, spread across the cell like the whip-crack blare of a siren. Even so—Bobby Dane knows he's got one advantage. Because once, long ago, he took their money, they've got him pegged as easy.

"Give the bag over here," Tonjay says.

Bobby Dane drops his canteen bag on the floor by his feet. He's remembering the raid and how he fucked up when he took the grenade and everything that came after. That's not going to happen again.

"Why don't you come here and get it," Bobby Dane says.

One of Tonjay's cons, the one on the right, says, "That's rude and nasty and it makes Tonjay here sad. Now pick up that bag and hand that shit over." He takes a step forward. "Then, get down on your knees and apologize."

"Your wife's already all but fucked," the one on the left says. "When she comes to visit and cry about it, you don't want to be talking back to her with no teeth and a busted up, blind face."

Bobby Dane nods and mumbles as in: Y'know, you're right. He bends to pick up the canteen bag. "Who was it who said: Don't die over groceries or sneakers?"

And he hands the bag over to the big guy on his right. "Now, get on your..." the big guy's hand is out and he's in the middle of his tough guy line when suddenly the world explodes and goes up in a cascade of sparks all because someone—Bobby Dane—has come palm up and jammed stiffened fingers in his eyes and stamped into his forward knee. The other big guy is having trouble, too, because when he comes forward with the shiv, clumsily, Bobby Dane sweeps the arm to one side and hits him across the trachea, thinking all the time that it's impossible to disarm a knifer unless the guy's a complete fuckwit asshole. Tonjay doesn't move, just watches as Bobby Dane gives the dummy, the knifer, a solid kick in the side of the head.

Baker is outside the cell yelling, "MAN DOWN! MAN DOWN!"

Bobby Dane takes a quick start forward. Tonjay steps back. There's a hand on Bobby Dane's bicep, squeezing, pulling—Baker—and it's Bobby Dane who's guided away, swiftly now, a dancer, spinning, disappearing, moving like he can't be seen.

And pulled by Baker, Bobby Dane has already disappeared, heading out and blending into the swirl of inmates as COs in riot gear start into the cellblock. As they near, the inmates freeze and drop to the floor as per regulations. Bobby Dane and Baker, too. It's Tonjay who's just stepping out of the cell as the cops move in.

"Nobody else has got the guts to love you now, son," Baker's voice is a quiet rasp, as the two of them stay on their bellies on the cold concrete floor.

Then, Bobby Dane thinks he hears Baker say the name of the town: "Mortales." But he's not sure. And soon, all Bobby Dane hears is the shouting, now from the COs, "Man down! Man down! Get back to your units!" while he looks at the concrete and how the gray paint is chipped, fissured, lined with the black scars of endlessly running wheels.

Sometime later—Bobby Dane couldn't say exactly when—Baker starts talking about how "Trouble is the last thing that admin wants," and Bobby Dane can't figure what that's got to do with anything. Baker says, "Maybe it's an election year." And not long after that, Bobby Dane is marched to the Warden's office where he's asked to take a seat at the big wooden desk as the Warden—who seems genuinely saddened—breaks the news to Bobby Dane that his ex-wife Kira has been killed in a car accident. Strange circumstances around the crash, but nobody's getting pulled in.

Bobby Dane doesn't want to hear the rest of it but he can't move his mouth as the Warden keeps talking. She apparently, according to the police, lost control of her car driving at night just off the Ventura freeway. A tragic accident. We thought you should know.

"We know she's still writing to you," the Warden says. Then he says, "Hey. Hey. Are you listening? Do you hear me? Bobby Dane?"

They take Bobby Dane back to Isolation for two days. When he gets out, he doesn't speak to Baker for two more days, even though they're sharing a cell. And pretty soon, there's talk that Bobby Dane and Tonjay are heading for a good, old-time showdown, complete with sideline bets on who's gonna die.

"Don't do anything stupid," Baker says. "Even if it goes against the grain."

Bobby Dane won't answer.

"I've got ideas," Baker tells him. "Just hold out. Do it. I'm telling you."

The banner on the wall of the prison gym reads: "CDR JOBS FAIR."

Maybe there are thirty tables set up, all of them with signs that say things like "Tree Line Green Construction" or "Wallace Landscaping" or "Eco Friends Inc." The men stand in line as well behaved as if they were outside the door of the parole hearing.

Baker brings Bobby Dane to the table marked, "As Tomorrow Goes, Inc." There's a woman at the table and Bobby Dane feels his breath catch—she oughta be a dancer, he's thinking, 'cause then he'd latch his eyes onto that long dark hair as it swings, as she moves across the floor.

"This is who I told you about," Baker says to her.

The woman introduces herself as Pilar Sabato. "Mr. Baker tells us you were a police officer. With tactical and special operations experience."

"So? Here I am."

"At As Tomorrow Goes, we might have a position that could offer you something of a future," Ms. Sabato says. "When you finish your time."

"If he finishes," Baker says.

"If I live," Bobby Dane is trying to keep his eyes on her eyes.

"If you're interested, we can assist you," says Ms.

Sabato. "The safety of our people, even in here, before reporting to work, is of our utmost concern."

"What are we talking about, exactly?"

"I think that after your present circumstances, you'll find our accommodations and requirements very much to your liking," she says. "Much of the work is outside in a healthy, interesting environment. The food is good. You'll have more freedom than you can imagine, more than you've ever worked with before. And, as a self-starter, you can pretty much write your own rules. Within reason."

For a moment, Bobby Dane, Baker and Ms. Sabato sit in silence and the light echo from the gym, like they're inside a tin can, is all they hear.

"You can make something of yourself. Much more than that I'm not at liberty to say just now," she says. "But from what I've been told and from what I'm seeing here, you're exactly the man we want. But I have to warn you: it takes a certain kind of person to say yes."

"He says yes," Baker says.

Bobby Dane nods.

"An honor," Ms. Sabato shakes his hand and Bobby Dane holds it just one moment longer.

"We'll be in touch," she says. "As I'm sure Mr. Baker has cautioned: stay out of trouble. We'll do what we can."

About four days later, by Baker's count, Tonjay is shipped downstate, in shackles, so that he can be separated from Bobby Dane and maybe from his own crew. When Baker breaks the news to Bobby Dane he says, "No more trouble for a while" and then he waits for some kind of reaction and gets nothing.

"Mortales," Baker says then. "That's what she won't tell you."

After that, Bobby Dane begins thinking about the past. He lets himself think back on Kira and on Haran and for a moment and he lets himself think that someday soon he might actually get out. It could be different. He could have another life.

Then he stops. Kira's dead. And if she were alive, she wouldn't know him anyway. Haran, too. They'd pass him by on the street without recognition. How could they know him? Not with the way his face is set. Not with the heavier frame, the prison muscle, not with the tattoos that now run all down both arms and that other one: like a liquid lightning bolt that runs down one side of his face.

"Mortales," Baker says again.

Part Two

When Jessie turns off the neon sign that reads *JESSIE'S* in front of the bar, when the neon buzzing stops, it's like there's even more silence across the face of the desert, an even deeper darkness.

She walks over to where Haran is perched in a chair, crooked back so that it's tilted against the wall. His hat's down over his eyes, his boots are up on the table, his broom has fallen on the floor.

Jessie picks it up. She knocks his feet off the table. "Okay, Prince of the Desert. Sleepy time's over."

Haran comes to, shakes his head.

"And thanks for sweeping up," Jessie says. "And you look like hell."

Haran wobbles to his feet, one hand in his pocket. The keys clatter to the tabletop. "I'm a little bit tired," he says. "You drive me?"

"I'm a little tired, too. And I'm getting real short on good sense and charity."

"Jessie," Haran says. "Friends don't let drunks drive drunk."

She drives him back to his trailer.

Haran climbs down from the cab of the truck and lands like he lost his knees, he has to grab the side of the pickup to steady himself.

"I'm fine," Haran says. "I can walk."

"You can walk, maybe, but you damn well ain't fine."

Inside what she always calls *your crummy trailer* Jessie sees that it's the usual bad dream: tousled bed, clothes in a hurricane pattern, empty beer cans and scotch bottles, dirty dishes like a crumbling castle in the sink.

She curses under her breath.

"What?" Haran says. "Nothing's changed since the last time you hauled me home."

She curses again. "Bust out some beers. Sit for a while. Now I'm wide awake."

He's about to drop into his war-torn, ragged chair when Jessie stops him. She sees something, kneels down. Shoved in underneath the chair leg, holding the chair even and steady, she sees that there's a military Silver Star medal jammed tight. She looks at Haran for a long time before working it out and letting him sit down. Which makes the chair rock back and forth.

"What the hell is it with you, Ty?" she says, and holds up the medal. "I don't care if you fly the flag, but you oughta have some respect for yourself, at least."

She tosses him a can of beer.

"I'm not staying long. Not without one of those nuclear attack safety suits."

"That's why I like having you come over, Jess," Haran says. "So I can get lessons in how to be a better man. Take the truck. Pick me up tomorrow."

On a nearby counter, Jessie places the medal next to a small, carved piece of stone, the crude statue of a little man.

"Who's this?"

"That's God."

"Oh," she says. "I didn't recognize him there, for a moment."

"Some people think he's God, anyway. The man who gave Him to me, he thought so."

"Yeah? Who was he? One of the Flintsones?"

"Just a guy in the war." Haran takes a long swig of beer. "I saved his life. Or he saved mine. One or the other."

The water's already running and she's already grimacing at the grime that seems to live on the dishes. Washing them, not wanting to get too close to them, she says, "I know you don't want to hear this but damnit, someone oughta give you an earful once in a while..."

Haran's snores ripple over the sound of running water. "You're a real piece of work, mister," Jessie says.

When she finds the dishtowel and picks it up, that's when the tarantula makes itself known. It's a hairy, plump little bastard and uncovered, it begins to scuttle across the counter until Jessie, keeping to her own rhythm, takes a dish and brushes the spider to the floor, then nudges it towards the door and kicks it back out into the desert. Haran shifts in his sleep with another snore.

Jessie changes the linen and makes the bed, sweeps, cleans the place clean as a barracks. Then she finds a blanket and drapes it over Haran in his chair, walks outside and drives away in Haran's truck.

A clattering outside. Like gunshots. Like rioters throwing rocks. Like someone banging on a trailer door which is what Haran now realizes, waking up, pushing off the blanket, looking at nothing and only wondering who the fuck is rapping at his trailer door. When the morning hits him, he says, "Oh, shit!" and has to slap a hand over his eyes. After that, he sees that there's a short, old man standing outside who looks even more worn out than Haran.

"Morning," the old man says. "My name's Baker. That woman, Jessie, said I'd find you here."

"Why'd she do that?"

"Because I'm your friend Bobby Dane's prison buddy."

Inside, Baker looks around the trailer and whistles. "Damn!" he says. "This place is spotless!"

"Neat, clean and out of trouble, that's me," Haran says. There's a silence that makes them both uncomfortable so Haran starts making coffee. When they're sitting down, he says, "So, he's out. I'm glad. A long time. But between him and me? There's been nothing since they slammed the door on him and that's the way he wanted it."

"You wrote to Kira," Baker says. "I read her letters. That's how I found you."

"Haven't written for a long time."

"She's dead," Baker says. He watches for a reaction, gets none. "Car accident. Maybe. The *accident* part, anyway."

Haran just sits there. "Look," he says then. "Bobby Dane and me, we're even. Or it doesn't matter. Nobody has to repay nobody."

"When you take the rap for a guy, when you go to prison for him, that's not exactly your conclusion," Baker says.

A moment now where Haran is quiet again and Baker lets him stay that way. Or he does until he settles back, looks up at the roof of the trailer and says, "Bobby Dane's been kidnapped."

Haran takes Baker out for a walk in the desert, carrying along his Winchester and saying that he's going to kill dinner while also thinking, *And maybe you, too.*

"He went down to Mexico," Baker says. "I set him up with a job down there and they grabbed him."

"Down there you can get grabbed for bus change."

"Minute he crossed the border they took him."

"You sent him down, you go get him out."

"I am," Baker says. "By coming here to get you."

Haran takes a deep breath of the dry desert air and motions to Baker to get down behind a nice sized rock and he pushes the Winchester over the top, watching through the sight.

"They think he knows things," Baker says. "About how the cops operate."

"They're right."

"I guess. Something. They're holding him, that's all, that's what I really know."

"You have any idea where he is?"

Haran sees the rabbit, all bones this one, annoying to cook and eat. But he wants to fire the Winchester and he wants Baker to hear it.

"I know where to bring the cash," Baker says.

"How much?"

"Fifty thousand."

"And how much were you planning to pay me?"

Baker says nothing. Which is also his answer.

"Now, why would I want to make a deal like that?" Haran says.

Baker answers first by keeping his mouth shut. Then he says, "The way I figure it, you owe him."

"See, Baker," Haran says. "The trouble is, you're not used to living here with us on the outside. You're used to three-hots-and-a-cot and a bunk buddy anytime you're itchy. And all of it for the price of a walk. But not out here, old-timer. Not where you are now. There's no something-for-nothing out here in the Wonderland of the Free. "

When Baker stays quiet, Haran says, "We're quit, me and Bobby. Haven't connected with him for four years. Haven't even thought about him once, not once in all that time. Didn't like each other much anyway. He's got ideas he should have given up when he was twelve and it was only a matter of time before he got it in the neck."

Haran fires. The shot cracks the desert silence and ripples off in an echo. Tossed into a cartwheel—that's how the rabbit gets dead and drops off into the sand, with a little skid. Right after that, Baker stands up, brushes off his pants, walks back and forth, tosses a handful of sand, then tosses a small stone.

"What's the fucking problem?" he says to Haran finally. "What are you bullshitting me for? Jesus, man, you know you're gonna say yes."

They cross into Mexico.

This could almost be an ordinary crossing from the States except that Baker directs Haran to drive to one specific guard post where the inspector pulls them over, makes them get out of Haran's pickup, takes their cell phones and their wallets, their passports, takes just about anything that might help. Haran finishes his flask before that's taken. Then the guard takes their truck. Other than that, it's ordinary.

"Maybe now's a good time to tell me what you got us into," Haran says. All the way to the border, through the cheap-shack then the no-shack landscape, Haran has been thinking about Bobby Dane. He gets the prison story from Baker until he can't stand to hear any more and Baker tells him to expect a different guy when they meet. It changes people, you're never the same as you went in, it's like going through Hell—Baker is full of all the usual observations.

"But I'll tell you something," Baker says. "He talked about you like you were God."

Haran lets him sink into the silence. "I'm on this trip for me. Not anyone else," he says. "So maybe Bobby's right."

They're waiting by the inspection station to get their truck returned when a limo pulls up. The inspector tells them to get in. That means a long hesitation for Haran— Baker gets in right away. "Come on," Baker reaches out, motioning with his hand, "it's okay, part of the deal, they're not gonna kill us 'til they get their money."

The limo pulls away.

The desert in Mexico must be as sweet as the desert in Arizona, it's just that Haran and Baker can't see it because of the blacked-out windows and the partition that blocks the front seat. Maybe they've been on the road for about two hours—that's Haran's estimate.

Then he feels the limo slow down, pull over and stop. The driver opens the partition and tells them to get out.

"Head for the doorway," the driver says, nodding towards the expanse of desert.

"What doorway?"

Doesn't matter that Baker is shouting "What doorway?" and "Christ! Come back!" over and over as the limo drives off because in the vacuum quiet of the vast landscape—now that the limo kicks up sand and leaves them there—Haran and Baker stand by the road which really isn't a road—isn't paved—and they have no fucking idea of where they are or what to do. That's what Baker says, anyway.

"Like the man said, head for the doorway," Haran takes him by the shoulder, half shoves him along.

"We're gonna die out here."

"Probably," Haran says.

Haran has a feeling of almost joyful desolation. Fucking Bobby. Everything he does is goddamn trouble. Haran knows desert living. He fought his war in the desert. He's lived in the desert as a drunk. The heat is an animal on his shoulders, he's just the prey. Haran's at ease with the surefire knowledge that the land is unforgiving, offers no quarter, the land doesn't have to do anything, it just has to be there to get you to die. The desert expanse, the silence, with the mountains off in the distance and everywhere else the rolling dark surface—anyone can tell you it's as deadly as the sea.

Haran likes that. At least, he knows the score.

And then he moves around a small hill and finds the doorway.

It's a frame doorway free standing in the middle of the desert.

No door. No house. Nothing else.

"You gotta be fucking kidding," Baker says.

They walk up close and Haran motions Baker to move carefully. "May be booby trapped."

They circle it. Slowly get closer. Haran picks up a small stone and tosses it through the doorway to make sure there's no unseen surface, no wires. Then he says, "Okay. Who's gonna walk through?"

The wind comes through and only the sand moves.

Finally, Haran moves forward, his eyes on the sand, scanning for any possible hint of mines or traps. When he gets up to the doorway, he stops. He tries to think of something to say but his mouth is too dry.

Then he steps through the doorway.

Every sense is in overdrive. He's seeing, hearing, feeling like it's all turned on high and so when his boot comes down in the sand on the other side, for just a moment, he feels some kind of shift, some strange unevenness in the surface of the desert. Haran stamps down into the sand, kicks some of the sand away, stamps down harder.

"Something's here," he calls to Baker who's now by his side.

Haran's boot heel hits some kind of metal. He kicks away more sand.

"Here's the doorway," he says to Baker. "Down here, look."

Marked by the doorframe but buried in the sand, there's a kind of flat metal covering, maybe a hatch. No handle or anything else to grab onto. So Haran kicks at it, raps his knuckles on it. Scrambles for a nearby rock and raps that against the metal surface, listening to the hollow echo.

They wait.

The hatch comes open.

A head of dark hair pops out, shoulders, too, and the barrel of an AK-47. The underground man scrambles to his feet, looks around, motions them to go down into the hole.

Haran gives off just the slightest laugh. And the two of them climb down into this hole in the desert. The underground man follows. When he closes the hatch and twists the lock, everything goes black.

In a darkness so complete they can see only the fluid of their eyes, Haran and Baker descend into what seems like a well, a bunker entrance, a long, hollow cylinder expanse that drops down there in the middle of the desert, and feeling their way down the strangely cool concrete sides, they struggle to keep hold of the handrails.

Then they hit bottom. A clumsy landing, cursing, banging into one another. When the underground man drops down, they can hear him and smell his hair grease.

"I like what you've done with the place," Haran says.

There's the sound of mechanical motion—a part of the wall opens, a purple light washes the scene in a surreal stain. The underground man motions for them to move through the wall. He'll follow with the gun.

Down a dark, narrow stone hallway. There's one odd factor about this place, other than that it's deeply underground in the Mexican desert—one wall is a giant fish tank, floor to ceiling. And inside the tank, besides fish, Haran and Baker see the dead men.

Two bodies, two very dead men. They're held upright with their hands locked behind their backs, the faces slightly eaten away, hair billowing in the water.

They haven't been staring at the dead men for very long when another door opens, this one at the end of the hallway and a short, rotund man stands there in silhouette.

"Come inside," he says, "please. And wipe your feet."

Inside? An underground library, high ceiling, dark wooden shelves, perfect for cigars-and-brandy. Haran doesn't know whether to crane his neck around admiring the view or stare at the rotund little man who welcomes them: jet black hair swept back in a ponytail, goatee, black suit. And here, beneath the desert: sunglasses.

"Please pardon the dramatics, Commander Haran," he says. "The door, the strange entrance, all the rest of it. It's just there to make you believe the impossible."

Baker sits down in front of a huge wooden desk and then Haran follows his example but he can't take his eyes off the fish tank with the two dead men hanging inside. He keeps turning around, looking at them. He feels a tap on his shoulder.

When Haran turns back, a skeleton's finger is tapping him. He jumps a little. Then sees that the skeleton's boney hand is protruding from the sleeve of the man in sunglasses.

"Pay attention, please," the man says. He studies the skeleton hand, then pulls it from his sleeve and sets it on his desk like a paperweight. "A practical joke,

Commander. Unfortunately, I find these very easy to come by."

Baker is laughing. "I'm sorry, that was funny."

Haran turns to him. "Who is this clown? Is this who you've been dealing with?"

"I'm Mr. Tom," the sunglasses man says. "I sell insurance."

"Let me guess," says Haran. "You get the ransom, I get Bobby Dane."

"I wish life were that simple," Mr. Tom says.

"If it's going to come down to money, let's not waste time."

Mr. Tom caresses the fingers of the skeleton hand. "Money always means something else, doesn't it? For instance, what is it we rich men are really buying? Or, perhaps, are we using our money to direct your attention elsewhere? Like a magician. What is it we don't want you to see?"

"Come on," Haran says to Baker and gets up and strides towards the fish tank, towards the closed door of the library. Which won't open when he pulls the handle.

"If you're going to be difficult," Mr. Tom says, "I'm going to kill you."

"He's serious, Ty," Baker says. "Sit down."

Haran stands at the door. "Go ahead," he says. "Kill me."

"Jesus, Ty, don't! What the hell's wrong with you?"

"Kill him, too," Haran nods at Baker.

Mr. Tom begins to laugh. After a few moments he says, "Your friend is being held in the town of Mortales."

This slaps against Haran who now makes the return trip and sits at the desk.

"That's a jailhouse fairytale."

"No, Mortales is very real," Mr. Tom says. "And I am, let's say, its wealthiest and most influential citizen."

He offers cigars. Haran shakes his head and when Baker reaches out, Haran shoves down his hand.

"To get you there, to keep you alive in that place," Mr. Tom says, "certain conditions must be met. Those who reach Mortales, those who can afford to stay, may remain there in complete safety. With all of the delights of life. Completely protected from interference. Forever."

"If this place is real," Haran says, "you're talking about a place completely populated by assholes on the run."

"Because the citizens of Mortales are of a special breed, we have no laws, only suggestions. And some citizens choose to disregard those suggestions. That was the case of your friend unfortunately."

"Bobby Dane did his time and got out."

"I see Mr. Baker hasn't completely informed you. There were a few unhappy incidents shortly after his release. That's when he made his way across the border."

"Son of a bitch," Haran says, turning to Baker. "What the fuck are you pulling?"

"All I know is the word he got out to me," Baker says. "And you owe him, Haran."

"I think they're now holding your friend in such a manner that they only want to hear him beg and plead. Eventually he'll be killed. Or, maybe worse, they'll remove a foot or a hand and put him up for sale."

"I thought they wanted information about the police," Baker says.

"If that's what they wanted," Mr. Tom says, "I'm sure they already got it." Mr. Tom now takes the skeleton hand and gently toys with it, then begins to snap off fingers, one-by-one. "Mr. Baker has paid me to get you this far. And I will get you inside the town of Mortales."

Haran's so pissed he can't respond, just stares at Baker sitting next to him.

"I said that once you're inside Mortales, you're protected. But the arrangement is, to ensure security, no one is permitted to leave. And no one ever has," Mr. Tom says. "So, I will get you in. Getting out is your own affair."

A woman comes into the room. Pilar Sabato—Baker nods at her. Haran can't take his eyes off her. Mr. Tom clears his throat.

"Pilar will show you out," Mr. Tom says. "She'll bring you to Mortales."

At the far end of the library, they go through another door and this puts them at the head of a small, underground canal, dimly lit, the ceiling is tiled and vaulted so that their voices and the lapping water echoes. They get into a small boat. Pilar pushes it along with a pole. The trip is quiet until the walls become fish tanks. With more bodies displayed naked inside.

Pilar begins explaining who it is that hangs there.

"After a year of hospitality, Senor Galleston decided that the Mortales life was not for him," Pilar says, as the boat glides past a dead man whose long, dark hair moves with the motion of the fish tank water. "He attempted to leave. But he didn't realize he was already home."

They pass more bodies.

A man who called himself "Lucky Lad" who is heavily tattooed and who also attempted to leave Mortales, a muscular woman named Harrigan who brought some bad habits with her to the town. Another dead man, another dead woman.

"You don't have to do this," Haran says. "A simple threat will work out just fine."

They glide past a naked corpse hanging upside down, this one decapitated, the body stark white and collecting hungry fish.

"My ex-husband," Pilar says. "He had nothing to do with Mortales."

"What if Bobby Dane is dead and we get stuck in this idiot town," Haran's voice bounces softly off the tiled walls. "If that's what's up, I just might revisit Mr. Tom."

"Shut up," Baker says.

Haran doesn't say anything after that. He's busy thinking about Bobby Dane and thinking that now Bobby Dane owes him. Big time. Bobby Dane fucked up again and it's Haran who's supposed to get him out.

"I have a good feeling about you, Commander," Pilar says. "And your friend Bobby Dane has told me you've been on a hero's journey. I think you will free him. And then, after that? Probably die like a dog."

And now they see Mortales.

The underground boat journey leaves them at another upward tunnel where Pilar points skyward and motions for Haran and Baker to start making their way up rung-by-rung along the concrete well.

They come out through a door hidden in a small pile of stone ruins, either what's left of some ancient settlement or somebody's smart idea of camouflage. Pilar has told them: When you push through the door, face to where the sun is setting and in that direction you will see Mortales.

Way up there, way up on the mountain, they can see the outline of a small Western town backed by the burnt orange flash of beginning sunset. That's it. That's Mortales.

"Damn," Baker says.

They begin climbing the mountainside. Both men leaning forward. Slow footfall in the steep, desert earth. Breath coming hard now, sweat in rivulets down the dust caked the sun heated flesh. Neither Haran nor Baker ready for the climb. And when they stop, it's Haran who tries to catch his breath while surveying the mountainside, the desert flowers and small cactus and so it's Haran who sees the mine. A small, deadly metal dot in the sand.

"Where?" Baker says. "Holy shit."

Haran points down and to the left. "Bouncing Betty. Old fashioned type. Step on that and it'll kill everyone here."

"There's only us."

"You get my point," Haran says.

The first gunshot buzzes past Haran's ear and then they hear the quick crack of the shot. The second round kicks up dirt near Bakers foot. Haran shoves the old man down and shouts at him to stay low and stay still.

"They've got us caught,"—breath coming fast—"walk us into a minefield and then start shooting."

Another shot, this one overhead with that particular cutting razor *zzzzzz* that's owned total and complete by gunfire. More after that. And the steady pow-pow-pow of the shots afterwards, with Haran pressing his cheek to the dirt and Baker rattling off, "Oh shit, oh shit," in a hoarse whisper. "They're gonna kill us."

A few more shots—maybe six, maybe seven—Haran's lost count and then there's silence and after that, laughter.

Haran leans up from the dirt and he sees far away against the sun, three or four men with rifles, standing along the ridge, laughing. Pointing below and laughing.

So Haran stands up. Brushes himself off.

"Jesus!" Baker has one hand on Haran's ankle, "get down you dumb son of a bitch, they're gonna kill you!"

"If they wanted to kill us, we'd be dead already," Haran says. He walks over to where he can spot the prongs of the mine sticking slightly above the sand. And as Baker screams, Haran jams his boot down on the mine hard.

Nothing.

"Dud," Haran says. "They're fucking with us."

Baker is up quick and patting himself down in a cloud of dust. "I knew that."

"Idiots," Haran says to himself.

They start climbing again, until they get to the crest of the mountain. At the top, the three men who'd been shooting at them—and they all look deadly enough— they keep laughing but make room for Haran and Baker as the two men hit the incline and pass through. Beyond, they can see the small Western-style town of Mortales, the two rows of buildings with a single street running between, like gunfighter territory, like a film set. And coming down the middle is a big man dressed in black, difficult to discern because he's got the sun to his back. Maybe a beam catches the barrel, the surface of the rifle he's carrying. And another one hits the old style, five pointed, sheriff's tin star he's got on his chest. And even in silhouette you can tell he's hosting a bandolier of ammo strapped across his chest, and that he's a man who's dead certain, tough, chiseled, tattooed, smiling.

"Welcome to Mortales," says Bobby Dane.

Haran thinks he sees the sun flash and go out then flash again.

"Nothing to say?" Bobby Dane is up close now, different, hardly recognizable. "Well, don't get too damn angry, Ty," he says. "I learned all this from you."

Part Three

Later—after Haran's shouting, his repeated "Fuck you's" to Bobby Dane, his one moment when he spit in the dirt and pulled back his fist then decided against striking—later, Bobby Dane and Ty Haran stand on the roof of the Mortales Hotel, the only three story building in town, and look over everything along Main Street.

"Doesn't matter what you say," Haran has to keep his gaze locked out over the desert below the mountain and the range much farther in the distance. "You lie. That's what you do. Everything's a lie. You sold out the unit. Now you lie through your teeth to me."

"Would you have come down here otherwise? I don't think so."

"I'm not staying."

"Everybody stays in Mortales," Bobby Dane says. "Nobody leaves."

Finally, Haran looks at him. "Freak," he says. "Prison meat. That's what you look like. First your idiot buddy Baker tells me you're kidnapped, then you're in trouble with the law down here. And now this, which is probably horseshit anyway."

"I wish that were true."

"And what about that fucking dummy minefield with your snipers playing cute?"

"I wanted to show them what you're made of," Bobby Dane says. "And it worked."

"I think they scrambled your brains in the joint."

"They re-set those mines out there. For real. Don't start working on any stupid ideas." Bobby Dane points out the town of Mortales: "This is the hotel where almost everyone lives, that's the general store, that's the sheriff's office (my office)," he says, "there are clothing stores over there and there, that's the movie theater, that's the whorehouse, those are the saloons and they all have gambling, that's the mechanic shop..."

"I'm getting the hell out of here, Bobby," Haran says.

Bobby nods. "If I catch you trying to leave, I'll lock you up. Anyone else catches you, they'll kill you.

"And over there, way, way out there in the desert so tiny from here you can barely make it out, right over there,"—Bobby Dane points out an encampment of trailers, tents, dirt bikes, men, some kind of small, strange, makeshift, travelling town—"that's Tonjay. His people. If this town had tracks, that would be the wrong side of them."

The far off encampment is on a war footing. Every couple of minutes they hear distant small arms fire. Clouds of dust—the shifting of the dirt bikes and the jeeps. Men in groups listening to instructions. That much they can all see.

"How'd you get yourself into this?"

"I need your help, Ty," Bobby Dane says quietly. "They hired me on as sheriff to save this place. I took the job. Because they knew Tonjay was on his way."

"Bobby. What the hell do you care?"

Bobby Dane takes a very deep breath. Haran thinks he sees Bobby Dane push his chest out a little, getting ready for a speech, like he knows he's underlining his words.

"Not many people get a second chance," Bobby Dane says quietly. "We're different. Right here, in Mortales, we can make all of the past go away. We can wipe it all out. We can be remembered. We've got a chance to do something good here, Ty. We can make something out of this place, Ty. Something good. Something terrific. We could do terrific things."

"Bobby," Haran takes the time to size him up, paying intricate attention to the expression in his eyes. "Everyone here's a skell."

"You're not hearing me," Bobby Dane says. "We could make ourselves good."

"Bobby," Ty Haran says, "first you're a hostage, then you're a criminal, now you're a hero? Look. Let me tell you, I think you've had some rough times. Maybe I'm to blame for some of that." He puts a hand on Bobby Dane's shoulder. "We're both of us gonna get out of here. I'll take you out, if it comes to that. Maybe no one's ever left Mortales alive but that doesn't mean there can't be a first time."

Bobby Dane's face gets on a strange, disconnected look, like his eyes are following the movement of something in some other realm, some zone that nobody else can see. The expression isn't completely strange to Haran—he's never seen this exactly but he's seen something like it, he's heard almost that same calm faraway voice and seen something very much like that odd light in the eyes. He remembers a guy from the war. And two that he arrested long ago. And one other, the one that he killed in a gunfight on South Vermont Avenue.

"You don't have to understand me, Ty," Bobby Dane says. "But I still need your help."

And he tells Haran to follow him back to *my office*, the sheriff's office, where Baker is waiting to talk strategy.

"This must be your idea of Heaven, Bobby," Haran says. He gives Bobby Dane his back as he moves to climb down from the Mortales Hotel rooftop. As he steps away, Haran's getting a good look at that far off camp, the enemy, grabbing hold of the ledge and the rungs that lead down to the street.

Of course, when the blow falls and there's one shock of impact before everything goes dark, even Haran can tell himself that he knows that was coming.

So, Haran is now sure of it: Bobby Dane is completely, totally, out there batshit crazy. And so is this old idiot Baker, his good buddy, who's helping him along.

He's come down to Mexico on a bullshit story. And the guy who's telling it turns out to be absolutely nuts.

Haran comes in a jail cell. It's the sheriff's office. Bobby Dane must get his rocks off here because the room is in a one-story adobe structure, a little office with a jail cell in the back just like in the old movies.

Haran moans and sits up on the cot, sees Bobby Dane sitting on a small wooden stool just outside the bars. He feels the lump rising on his scalp. "Jesus, you could've killed me, you idiot."

"I had to do that and you know I had to do it."

"And a man's gotta do what a man's gotta do," Haran says. "If I get the chance before your fat friend puts me in a fish tank, Bobby, I'm gonna knock your fucking teeth out."

"No, you won't, Ty," Bobby Dane snorts, smiles. "You'll be too busy fighting right alongside me."

"You are nuts, Bobby. Maybe you always were."

"You ever been executed?" Bobby Dane says. He knows Haran's not going to answer. "On the inside, a few years ago, I was being escorted down the corridor by three COs who were supposed to take me to Isolation. Then I got that same sharp hit as you got back there and everything went black. And you know where I woke up, Ty? I woke up in the execution chamber. Strapped down to the gurney. Strapped down to where they put the needle in your arm and put you to sleep like an old dog."

Haran sits back. From his pocket, he pulls the small, stone statue of the little man, God, the one he took home from the war.

"I see you still got Him," Bobby Dane says. "Maybe you'll need Him. Yeah, so there I am, strapped down to the execution gurney and my mouth's gagged and I start struggling. Because all I can see is the ceiling and the bright light and then Tonjay's face hanging over mine.

"He says something like, *Hi there, baby. Hey, I know how you feel. But you owe me. So I have a deal for you. You come to work for me and I swear I will not tear you a new asshole. You can keep the one you have.* See, he's going down to Mexico to take over this mythical town called Mortales. Where he's gonna live like a king. For real. And forever.

"I shook my head and groaned and his people beat me up pretty bad. Threatened to cut off my nuts. The usual. And then, after I'd screamed enough, he said, *I take that as a yes, sir. So, now I have to sign the contract.* And he had me tattooed on the forearms. Signed his name. Here. Look."

Bobby Dane holds out his forearms. The inside of both arms read, "Property of Tonjay."

"How the fuck am I gonna get that off?" Bobby Dane says to himself.

"Oh, I'm sure it can be done," Haran says. "Write to me when you figure it out."

"Sure, Ty," Bobby Dane rolls down his sleeves and stands up. "I'll let you sleep on it. I mean, hell. You know you're gonna say yes."

Baker comes in later that night. Haran knows it's night because he can see the stars through his barred window and because he's alone in the lock-up. He'd probably passed out after Bobby Dane walked away.

"You oughta eat something," Baker says. He's carrying a tray and the food looks, smells good—steak, potato, beans, a shot of tequila, Mexican beer, thick bread.

Haran lets him come into the cell without any trouble and then takes the little statue of the man and sets it upright on the bed. That done, he gets on his knees on the floor in front of it and silently begins to pray with his eyes closed.

"What are you doing?" Baker says. Nothing from Haran so Baker says, "What is that you got? A little god or something?"

He puts the food tray down on the bed carefully so as not to disturb the little man's balance. "I didn't know you were religious."

Haran keeps on praying.

"I'll leave this right here but do yourself a favor and eat something. There's tequila, too, you like that."

Now, Haran's head suddenly dips forward and then he shakes like he's coming out of a trance. Startled, he turns to see Baker.

"What are you doing here?"

"I brought you dinner."

"I don't want dinner. Or breakfast, either. Or lunch. I'm on a hunger strike."

"Damn it, Ty," Baker says. "Don't be on that." He scoops some of the beans into his own mouth ignoring Haran's expression of utter disgust. "It's good, man. You don't know what you're missing. Besides, you're gonna need it for the fight."

Haran takes the little man and starts touching it lightly.

"Is that, like, a little idol or something?"

"It's Jocelito," Haran says. "My friend."

"You pray to that little guy?"

"You don't pray to Jocelito. You talk to him."

"But he's like, I don't know, a toy or something."

Haran stares at the little figure for a long time. "You're not a toy, are you, Jocelito?" he says. "No. I know you're not."

"You've been doing this a long time?"

"Since I was in the war," Haran says. "I only do it in times of trouble. Didn't Bobby ever tell you about Jocelito when you two were inside?"

"Not a word."

"Jocelito saved my life in the war. Saved both me and Bobby Dane in a couple of scrapes."

Baker reaches out towards the little figure but Haran pulls back.

"Can I just see him for a moment?"

"NO! Don't touch Jocelito. Let me ask him if he'll speak to you."

Haran has a silent conversation with the little figure. Then, finally, he hands the tiny man over to Baker and says, "Speak to him with your mind. Not your mouth."

Baker moves his lips, holds the little man up near his face.

"Jocelito can't hear you," Haran says. "Hold him close. The mind speaks quietly."

Baker moves the small statue closer.

"Now, Jocelito is listening. He's answering. Can you hear him?"

Baker shakes his head as in, "No."

"Jocelito says, it's time to go."

Haran slams Baker's hands and Baker's hands send the little man into Baker's eye. Baker shouts, jackknifes, and then collapses as Haran slams the edge of his fist down onto Baker's neck.

He handcuffs Baker to the bars and locks Baker in the cell, grabs Baker's M-4 and thinks, *I can't believe that worked.* Haran makes a run for it.

Moon and star shine.

The main street of Mortales is quiet and mostly empty except down there by the saloons and gambling parlor. That's where Haran can see the shadows look like ghosts, hear the noise and walk through the slivers of light. There's a touch of some kind of desert flower in the cool night air, Haran doesn't know which one. Two guards who want to look like cowboys with leather vests and machine guns patrol the darkness and walk right past him. Haran nods. In return, he only gets the long hairy eyeball.

Haran works his way over to the same steep incline that brought him up to Mortales. He figures he can make his way downhill, back to the secret trap door in the desert, back to Mr. Tom's underground abode. He figures that if he has to, he'll move in and kill Mr. Tom and anyone else who gets in his way. Then he'll backtrack to the desert and try to find his way to the border.

Night in the desert goes on forever. There's enough moonlight to make it down the hill but he has to watch for mines and there might not be enough moonlight for that. As he starts his way down, going very, very slowly, one foot solid, then the next, hearing his breath, eyes locked on the dirt looking for those little metal fuckers that mean oblivion, Haran makes the decision that if he dies here then dying was better than staying here. He settles that in his mind and doesn't think about it again. He's too busy trying not to die.

One step dislodges some rock. He crouches, waits. The small stones roll down but hit nothing more dangerous than other rocks. Way off in the windy distance, he gets an eyeful of Tonjay's people. Maybe a dozen, maybe twenty. Maybe more? He can't tell. They have a certain rhythm to them, like they're ready for orders, like they're ready to move. Lights on motorcycles. Laughter across the desert. Small fires. He wonders if Tonjay thinks it's smarter to attack at night.

It's the thinking-too-much that makes him lose his footing.

He realizes that in the instant his boot slips off the loose stone, just for that moment. The rest of the time, Haran lets himself relax so that he'll land soft and ready and as he hits and rolls, he makes sure to keep hold of the M-4 and to get just enough control of his downward roll. He scans himself quickly—not injured. He's on his belly but okay. And there, not more than six inches from his nose, he gets the moonlight glint off the metal prongs of the land mine.

Haran shifts carefully. Turns onto his back, draws his knees in and brings himself to a crouch. Not too far from the mine, he sees the skeleton. He sees it. Lying in the sand. It looks like it used to be a man but the flesh has all been stripped away by animals and the elements so only the bone lies clean in the night. Most of the clothing has rotted away.

For just a few seconds, Haran is overcome by an odd, comforting feeling that he's in the absolute, certain presence of his own death and all the mysteries are solved and the waiting is finally over. That passes. He goes back to an oozingly slow step-by-step pathway downhill, now seeing in the distance, near two small mounds, the shadow of the ruins where the secret door-way is hidden.

He legs it carefully towards where he remembers the door is located but can't find it on the first try. Or the second. The ruins just seem like that and nothing else—ruins and two small mounds that long ago gave up their surprises. But he knows this is where he emerged and he's certain he'll find it. That's until he hears behind him the shifting in the sand and then the two small mounds behind him suddenly rise up and show themselves to be two men in desert camo holding M16's.

They say nothing. Just keep their weapons pointed at Haran. As they stand there wordlessly, the popping sound of a motorcycle comes wafting through the desert air like smoke and Haran is not surprised to see a motorcycle and sidecar roll around the ruins and pull up on the other side.

On the bike is Tonjay. In the sidecar, a dog that looks half-wolf, half-insane.

"Hitler liked dogs, too," Haran says.

"He would have loved this one," Tonjay gets off the bike and Haran now sees that in the sidecar, it's not a dog. It's a man. Naked with his arms cut off at the elbows, legs cut off at the knees, he's covered in beads and bangles and where he's not bearded or longhaired, he's heavily tattooed. There's a bit in his mouth and the leash is in Tonjay's hand.

"If you're good," Tonjay says, "maybe I won't kill you. Maybe I'll keep you in my kennel."

The two gunmen laugh. Tonjay looks Haran over from boots to face.

"Oh, yeah. I know who you are," Tonjay says. "So. You'll figure this out. But now, it's up to your buddy. I want Bobby and anybody stupid enough to follow him, to put down their weapons." Tonjay looks off towards Mortales. "A town full of bad guys? Okay, maybe. I'll ride in there and take the town and everyone can go on just like before. Except for young Mr. Dane."

"Don't think he'll go for it. In fact, I can almost guarantee that he's gonna sorta be, I don't know, sort of an asshole about it. Know what I mean?"

"He was an asshole before. You didn't know him inside."

"You didn't know him outside. He was an asshole then, too."

"That's not gonna help you," Tonjay watches as Haran visually traces the tattoo that runs down one side of Tonjay's face. The man-dog shuffles over on all fours to the ruins and raises one leg, takes a piss on the stones. "I don't care much for you," Tonjay says. "But I could abide your staying on in town. Bobby's the only one who has to disappear. You go tell him. All he's got to do is hand over the keys to the city and give himself up. As we say. He likes to be a hero. He'll save a lot of lives. Actually, you know what? If you kill him, and bring me his head to prove it? I'll let you go home. You'll be the first dude ever to leave Mortales breathing. How would that be?"

Haran doesn't answer.

"Go think about it," Tonjay says as he scoots his man-dog back into the sidecar. "Oh. And you'll have to make your way back up that hill. Which is full of mines, as you know."

"I'll just leave from here," Haran says, looking at the ruins.

"Not gonna happen." Tonjay nods. "Go on. Go tell him. That's what you're worth to me, nothing else. You take any other direction and I'll kill you dead."

The Mortales Saloon is packed when Haran walks in. The place is an old Western gin joint with some modern touches—Haran walks past a long bar with standing room only where the drinkers every so often look up to see the strip show on stage at the end of the room. Then they watch Haran. A piano player slams out a tune for the girl who's dancing. He follows Haran's path, too. The rest of the place is circular tables with card games and drinkers and a few people eating and Bobby Dane and Baker sitting all the way in the back.

"Holy shit," says Bobby Dane when he sees Haran walk in.

Baker's face turns the color of cheap paper and he sits there with his chin edging towards his chest. Haran just stands before them.

"I want to have a word with you."

"Whatever you have to say," says Bobby Dane, "you can say right here."

So, with the piano going and all the talk noise banging off the walls, Haran flat out tells them everything. He's got an offer to kill Bobby Dane and bring in Bobby's head. Or Bobby Dane can give himself over to Tonjay and save the town. Elsewise? Tonjay and his people are going to assault the place and kill anyone who needs to be killed. And take Bobby Dane anyway.

When he's done he looks at the table next to them and says, "That oughta make its way around town pretty perfectly."

"And what?" Bobby Dane says. "You're going to kill me, Ty? Just for the money? Just to go home? That's not you."

"How about this one?" Haran says, nodding towards Baker. "He looks like he's starting to think about it. And now you'll have the rest of the town giving it some thought, too. That's my bet."

"I've known this one a long time," Bobby Dane puts a hand on Baker's shoulder. "We've been through a lot together."

"Right," Haran says. "Okay, here's my plan. Let's get the hell out of here now. This minute. Take this old fart if you want. But let's get the hell out of town and leave the rest of your amigos to fend for themselves. And let Tonjay have the fucking place."

"That's the fear speaking," says Bobby Dane. "Not you."

"No, it's me," says Haran. "The one of us who's not full on fucking crazy."

More music. Louder for some reason. Then another girl comes on stage and there's some lazy applause from the bar.

"This is my town," says Bobby Dane. "And I'm not giving it up to nobody." He leans forward so that the badge on his vest catches the saloon light and Haran wonders whether he's figured out how to do that on purpose. Haran is also looking at the edges of the "Tonjay" tattoo on his forearm where he's trying to hide it beneath a shirt. "I'll be on the up-and-up with my people. I'll be honest. I'll put out word. I'll tell them just what's happening. And then we'll get ready to fight."

He stands up. He picks up the M-16 that was leaning against the table and puts it down on the round wooden top.

"You get ready, too," Bobby Dane says. "We're going rough-and-tumble. We're going to show them what this is all about. We're going to kill these sons of bitches."

* * *

Maybe twenty, twenty-five people live in the town of Mortales and they're all hunted men, criminals on the run or men who've done time and want to get out. Then there are the whores and those residents who skipped the country before they were caught the first time. No guns allowed. There are a few fistfights now and then but most of the time they live together quietly.

Bobby Dane, standing outside in front of the jail, calls them *My people* and says, "There's honor among thieves and dignity among murderers." Hearing this, sitting in the sheriff's office, Haran just turns away and shakes his head.

A little while later Haran says, "Tell me something, Bobby. There must be another way out of here. Some way that nobody's supposed to know but that you know. Some way that's saved only for the important people. So they can escape."

Bobby Dane comes inside and gets that shit eating grin on his face.

"You're not gonna tell me, are you?" says Haran.

All around Mortales, on every building, Bobby Dane has put up posters on the walls all down the main street calling for the people of Mortales to gather in the morning in front of the sheriff's office. The posters say the town will begin to organize its defense. Weapons and ammo will be issued. Positions will be taken. Now is the time to stand up for Mortales!

That night, Haran lies awake on his bed in the Mortales Hotel and listens to the music and noise from the saloons and the gambling parlors and the whorehouse, a strange mix of sounds like the creak of a big ship at sea. The room has the odd smell of dust and cleaning fluid. Just before he drifts off to sleep, Haran hears an explosion. Not near enough to toss him out of bed, but enough of a blast to pop his eyes open. There's another after that. And then he hears the sounds of men's voices moving in the street below, speaking like they're trying not to be heard. That dies down and soon there's the weird hum from the street and then a little later, just as Haran is about to drift off again, a louder explosion that sounds like it's coming from the desert.

Then a few shouts and then the street hum again.

The morning is unusually quiet.

Haran gets up, shaves, jams his boot down on a thumb-sized roach that's crawling under the door, and then he walks out into the street.

Where the people of Mortales were supposed to be gathering but where he sees that not a single person has heeded Bobby Dane's call to arms. He listens to his footfall in the dirt as he makes his way to the sheriff's office. Haran pictures it as if the town were speaking, telling Bobby Dane...nothing. Silence. Whether Bobby Dane runs the town or Tonjay? It's all the same shit. That's what Mortales wants Bobby Dane to know.

Haran gets a look at Tonjay's encampment, busy and raising dust, but he doesn't stop to watch.

In the sheriff's office, Baker is playing solitaire and laughing to his crazy self and Bobby Dane is cleaning his M-16 and talking about the old days, meaning their time together inside.

"Nobody's in the street," Haran says.

"They'll come," says Bobby Dane.

"This is a town full of hard cases," Baker says. "They'll be up for a fight."

Haran sits down at the table. "What exploded last night?"

"Somebody tried to get out. Hit a mine," Bobby Dane says.

"Asshole got what he deserved," Baker shuffles his cards.

"Maybe he was one of your hard cases up for a fight," Haran says. "You don't want to lose too many of them."

The cleaning rod clicks against the barrel as Bobby Dane pulls it out of the rifle. "They'll be fine. Why don't you take that rifle for yourself, Ty," Bobby Dane nods towards another M-16 against the wall. "Might want to clean it up first."

"What about the other explosions?"

The snap of cards and the metallic click of the cleaning rod—that's all Haran gets for an answer.

"Hey, Bobby..."

"Speaking of assholes, there was an attack," Baker says. "They raided the armory."

Haran takes the M-16 from where it's leaning, sits back down and starts to laugh. "The town armory was attacked? Tonjay's people were here?"

"Nobody carries arms in Mortales except the sheriff," Baker says.

Haran stops cleaning his weapon. "Your own people attacked the armory? And took the weapons? And ammo?"

"Like I said," says Bobby Dane. "They're ready for a fight."

Haran's chair falls backwards, clatter cuts through the silence as he lets his rage drive him up from the table and take him outside. He stands under the deadly sun, in the rising desert heat, in front of the sheriff's office and stares down the empty street and he's sucking at the air, the anger deep inside.

Then Bobby Dane's people start coming down the street.

At first one, then a few more, almost all of them men. Rifles held by their sides or held read, automatics on their hips, knives, all them armed in some way. Maybe twelve or fifteen people. They assemble in front of the hotel, talk for a moment, and then march themselves down the street half-mob, half-military, coming to see Bobby Dane in a cloud of kicked up red sand.

"I told you they'd come," Bobby Dane has walked out of the sheriff's office and he's now standing in the sun behind Haran, the newly cleaned M-16 held in one hand.

"Bobby..." Haran begins, but he can't finish it.

"You don't know them," Bobby Dane says. "You haven't been where I've been."

Baker says something from inside but Haran can't understand him.

The crowd now reaches the sheriff's office and stands in a group in front of Haran and Bobby Dane. There's the usual mob murmur and then quiet. To Haran's eye this is a pretty down-and-dirty bunch, shitheels every one of them, gritty faces, unshaven, cut off T-shirts beneath leather vests, some bellies swelling over the pistol belt line, a bad crowd. One of them leads—a man built like a machine, maybe six-five with black leather pants and a fringed black, sleeveless, leather vest. Mean looking, too, with a graying ponytail and iron wool beard. And on his hip, tied to the thigh, a king-size revolver, maybe a magnum, Haran can't quite tell.

"Jenx," Bobby Dane nods at the big man. "I'm glad you're in command."

Jenx returns the nod. "You're gonna have to come with us, Bobby."

"What I figure," says Bobby Dane, "is that we'll set up a few rifles on the roofs all along the main drag. If the mines are all laid out, that is. Surround the place with mines and then put our rifles on the high ground with maybe one or two below. And we'll wait to see what they do then."

Jenx says to Haran, "If you just step aside there won't be any trouble."

"Mister...*Jenx* is it? Why don't you take your people back up the street and let me handle this," Haran says.

"If Tonjay don't try us in, say, three days," Bobby Dane says, "then I guess we'll have to organize a raid of some sort. Probably at night would be best. I don't like that idea, but it might be what we need to do. We'll hit them hard and finish it out there, on their own turf."

"I don't have anything against you, Bobby," Jenx says, "but a whole lot of people are gonna get hurt if you don't come with us."

"This is about the offer from Tonjay, I take it," Haran says. "I know about that offer more than anybody standing here."

Jenx says, "You and Bobby Dane got history, I realize that. And I'm not trying to put you in a bad way. But you understand what's going on, so let's just get this dirty business over and done." Nobody else says anything.

"Look. I'll talk to him, Mr. Jenx," Haran says and he turns to Bobby Dane. "Come on inside and I'll explain what's happening."

Haran turns his back to the mob and puts a hand on Bobby Dane's arm, trying to guide him to start for the door behind them.

"Nobody's going inside," Jenx says. "Bobby, now's not the time to be an asshole."

"Give me a minute with him alone," Haran says. "I don't like this any more than you."

"Can't do it, buddy," Jenx says. "Like I said, it's got nothing to do with Bobby Dane, he's been all right, been just fine. But now, well, this is what's best for everyone. So, Bobby, you either come with us. Or I'm gonna kill you."

"I'm not above saying *Please, Mr. Jenx*." Haran turns around just in time to see Jenx explode.

The rounds that cut off most of Jenx's head also seem to weave through and pepper the men standing behind him so that small arms fire cracks and echoes in the air and the vision in front of Haran becomes pocked with spattering blood and people jerking in spasms, falling or throwing themselves to the ground or here and there running, screaming. Haran reacts, only reacts. There's no thought about it. Ducking, he shoves Bobby Dane backwards and gets to the door behind, tumbling inside, getting one quick look at Baker, who is standing outside, to the side of the crowd. Opening fire.

Baker had come out a back door and then around, opening up with an M-16 fed by a banana clip, hitting the crowd from the flank. He got a few rounds in return fire but the ambush kicks hell out of their aim and Haran hears the door open and close with Baker back inside, laughing, crawling along towards them, even as what's left of the crowd starts shooting at the sheriff's office, Haran and Bobby Dane, safely on the floor, the doors and windows bolted and locked.

"Fuck 'em," Baker says. "Fuck all of 'em."

Haran wants to knock Baker's teeth down his throat but he keeps it tight. He listens to the gunfire, the rounds shocking the adobe and the wood outside and he finally lets himself look over to Bobby Dane who says nothing but lies flat on the floor with his eyes following some strange path of movement that no one else can see.

"How the fuck long are we gonna last in this dump?" Haran says. "If they don't shoot us, they'll burn us out."

Baker is still laughing. "I saved your lives, you dumb pricks! So now what are you gonna do?"

"Where's the other way out?" Haran says.

"I can talk to them," says Bobby Dane. "They'll listen. They don't know what they're doing..."

Bobby Dane shifts around to stand up as Haran hauls him back to the floor. One round ricochets off a door hinge with a metallic, grinding whistle and a few more slap into the adobe in small, dull, deadly beats.

"You know where the exit is Baker? How do we get out?"

Baker's laughing goes into the high range, the range of I'm-gonna-die-crazy. "Maybe I know. Maybe I don't want you along."

"There's another way out of this place," Haran says, "and, Bobby, you're gonna tell me where it is even if you stay here yourself and die like a goddamned dog."

Baker keeps on laughing.

"You owe me, Ty," Bobby Dane says. "For saving your hide and now you'll owe me for pulling you out of this shithole. How much does that add up to? Those are my people out there, Ty, and I'm here to…"

Bobby Dane makes another move to stand and Haran jams him down harder this time. Baker's laughter gets crazier and when Haran tries to stare him down, he gets back that wild-eyed face that screams for you to walk the other way. And the laughter can't cover the gunfire.

And then from outside they hear a voice shouting, "We got no fight with you, Haran. And even that old fuck can go, the murdering bastard. All we want is for Bobby to come out. Unless you mean to kill him yourself. That'll go down, too."

"What say ye," Baker puts his face in his folded arm, he's laughing so hard, "should we just give them ol' Bobby boy? Why not?

"Because they're gonna kill us anyway, you horse's ass," Haran says.

"Or that lunatic Tonjay. Or that fat bastard Mr. Tom, he'll kill us," Baker laughs. "Boys, we are truly fucked."

More gunfire, voices outside, too, sounding closer now.

"Okay, I'm out of questions," Haran says. "I'm gonna hold 'em off. You take Bobby Dane and go down the rabbit hole or wherever it is that's gonna save us. I'll follow."

There's banging now, shouting, they're slamming against the door, kicking it, hitting the steel doors that cover the windows. They're trying to break in.

For an old man who's spent most of his life in prison, Baker moves fast. He's up, on his feet, moving towards the door, playing with the security bar and tearing the door open almost in one movement. Men stand stunned, like scarecrows, on the other side. Faces stupid and frozen in shock. They stay that way just long enough for Baker to kill the two men at the door and fire at everyone else. The door closes. The laughter begins again. It takes a few beats before the gunfire outside begins again.

"Enough, enough," Baker says. "I hate those rotten pricks."

He kneels and puts the barrel of his M-16 into Bobby Dane's mouth.

"Jesus," Haran says, "don't..."

"You ding-wing motherfucker," he says to Bobby Dane. "You want to talk to your bros outside, don't let me get in the way. But you better tell me the secret of how to get out of this shithole. Now."

Bobby Dane looks up at him. The rifle barrel is against his teeth. Slowly, Bobby Dane reaches forward and pushes the weapon away.

"No secrets," he says. "I'd tell you if there was. There is no way out. Just down. Through the minefield."

Baker looks to Haran. "All right," he says to himself. "All right."

"Are you lying, Bobby?" Haran says.

Baker's already at the door, the door's already open, Baker's already got the M-16 leveled and he's firing wildly, screaming that anyone in his path is a son of a bitch dead bastard and the pausing for as long as it takes to pull the pin and toss a grenade.

"Holy shit," Haran says. "Come on, Bobby."

But Bobby Dane won't move. Haran curses again. And that's it. He figures he's all paid up now, he did what he could and he ducks behind the open doorway taking cover for a only three seconds, long enough to see Baker in the street walking, firing, like he's armor plated, and what's left of the mob either dead or ducking down, or firing back without aiming.

Haran gives him cover. He says once more to Bobby Dane, "Let's go, kid, we've got a chance." But Bobby Dane just stays on the floor. Haran says, "Shit," and then he's out in the street, too, Baker and Haran firing wherever they see someone stupid enough to poke their face up.

And then they both run. They head for the hill, for the minefield. They leave Bobby Dane behind.

A couple maybe three rounds kick up around them but whoever's still alive has lost interest, they've now realized that two men came out but the one they want is still inside.

When Haran and Baker reach the edge of the hill, they hit the dirt, flatten out and look back—see three men going inside the sheriff's office with rifles ready. And far off in the desert, there's Tonjay's people, who look like they're just waiting, ready—lined up on motor-cycles, in jeeps, on foot—ready and listening to the war from the hill. There must be twenty-five of them at least.

"I hope both of us make it through the minefield," Haran says. "That way it'll be us two against twenty-five of them. The odds are better."

Baker's about to answer but he stops. He motions for Haran to glance back to where they've come from. There, two men have Bobby Dane by the arms and they're half-walking him half-dragging him out with the third man in front as guard. They're leading him straight to the minefield, to where they can signal across the desert to Tonjay.

"Can you hit them from here?" Haran levels his rifle.

Baker makes a "yeah" sound and takes aim alongside him.

"Let 'em walk in just a little bit more."

They wait until the men in charge of Bobby Dane get closer, closer and even closer than that. Then they open fire. The guard in the lead goes down first along with the man on the left, both drop like their legs suddenly went invisible. The man on the right gets time enough to make one move, like he's going to grab Bobby Dane and make him a hostage, but Haran puts a round through his chest, perfect, center body mass and this last man spins away falls hard onto his face and belly.

Baker runs out and grabs Bobby Dane, hauls him over to where Haran is lying in the dirt and throws him down alongside. Dust rising up all around them and they can smell the clay, taste it, the dirt, feel the sun beating down on them. It's time to move.

"What now?" Baker says.

Bobby Dane is a ragdoll, too stunned to answer. Haran says, "You ever been through a minefield, Baker?" He waits. "I didn't think so. You've never been anywhere besides an idiot's jail cell."

Baker nods and then nods again. "Okay, tough guy," he says. "Okay."

And Baker stands.

Then Baker begins to make his way, very, very slowly, down the hill. Haran watches. Bobby Dane stares at the dirt. Baker steps like he's crossing a canyon on a paper rope. Stops, turns, "Right here," he says quietly and finds a stick to put in the ground nearby. "Step in my footprints."

He moves on down the hill. "Another one," he says, this time louder, and finds a good sized stone to put next to the prongs of the mine.

"All right, I'm coming," Haran yells to him. "I'm gonna have to bring Bobby Dane and that's not..."

The explosion that kills Baker knocks Haran backwards on top of Bobby Dane. He rolls off. Haran's eyes are fully open when the dirt cascades down from the sky. Dirt, small pieces of metal, jelly-like pieces of a man, nothing large enough to recognize except maybe the small part of an ear that Haran glimpses on the back of Bobby Dane's hand. Shrapnel sizzles through the air and falls nearby. And when Haran stands up again, he can see that Baker has been nearly cracked in half, with part of him still lying in the sand down the hill, his head still intact, the eyes staring out in eternal surprise.

For a moment, Haran can't move. He hears motors, even some shouting, watches the dust cloud that grows and wanders, wafting across the desert from Tonjay's camp.

They're getting ready to ride. He turns. Bobby Dane's face is spattered with Baker like an outbreak of tiny blood blisters. Bobby Dane just sits there staring. Haran is saying something to him but Bobby Dane can't hear, there's only a man moving his mouth and an off-on-off-on surf sound in his ears.

Bobby Dane wipes a small, uneven piece of Baker off of his lips.

Haran says, "Pull it together. We're gonna have to..."

"The other way out is through the jail," Bobby Dane says. "There's a tunnel. Back there. You go through the floor."

Not even a broken fragment of a second, that's how long it takes—Haran grabs Bobby Dane by the shoulder, raises him to his feet, shoves him. And the two of them begin to run.

They go carefully.

The main street of Mortales is empty and at the end of the dirt road, near the sheriff's office and jail, they can see the bodies lying on the ground, hear the moans, whimpering, and see the office door open. Haran and Bobby Dane duck into a doorway, wait, run a few more steps and hit the dirt, lying flat, waiting for gunfire. They get only the wind and the sounds of creaking wood, of a hinge squealing. Haran doesn't trust it. He eyeballs the rooftops, picking off each foot of roof with a definite moment to check whether there's someone positioned there or the telltale glint of a rifle barrel.

Nothing.

Haran taps Bobby Dane on the shoulder then points. Then they run. When Haran whispers, "Now!" they kneel down quickly behind the cover of a roof support or in the dirt against the building. Then, once again, they're on their feet and moving, expecting that every inch, every step forward brings the possibility of death from a weapon they cannot see.

And finally, they're ducking behind a large, concrete planter just across and to the side of the sheriff's office, where the door stands open.

"This is it," Haran says.

They run. Haran hears the tromp of their footfall in the dirt. The rush of their clothing. The creak of the swivel holding the strap of the M-16. Their gasping for breath.

The bodies lying in the dirt outside, the darkness on the sand from outpourings of blood, the flies on lips, on open eyes, the grotesque, twisted positions of the bodies—this is what they tell themselves not to look at and this is what they can't turn away from as they rush towards the open door and go into the office and jail.

Haran sees the rifle barrel first. Later, it registers that he saw a shotgun pointed at him but as he steps inside, all he notices is the dim black metal eye staring up from the floor, with the shooter lying prone and hiding behind the doorway that separates the office from the cells in back. By instinct and experience, he opens fire from the hip. Not aiming. Just pointing. Haran lets the shotgun have what's left in the M-16, hears the shotgun come back at him with a curt, sharp roar, sees the fire flash and feels a hot, whistling wind pass by his right ear.

Haran rushes forward and kicks at the barrel but the shooter doesn't mind, the shooter is dead and the face is bone fragments, the flesh splayed out by Haran's rounds. The shooter shifts as Haran kicks the barrel away but that's it. When Haran catches his breath, he sees that the shooter is Pilar, the woman who met them with Mr.

Tom, who hired Bobby Dane. He sees that in one of the jail cells behind, the door in the floor is still open.

"Don't look at her," Haran says. Then, "She came up through the tunnel."

Bobby Dane, on the floor, can only shake his head. After that, without any sound, he starts to cry, or that's what Haran sees anyway.

"Maybe there's more bad news down there," Haran says.

He pops another magazine in the M-16 and fills his pockets with more.

"Grab a piece," he says to Bobby Dane. "We're going down. We're getting the hell out of here."

Bobby Dane doesn't move. His shoulders are shaking. Haran goes over and shoves him—not all that hard but hard enough—with his boot.

"Let's go," Haran says. "Now."

Down into the tunnel.

The winding tunnel, built with care, built with an eye towards escape and secret movement, professionally, with small lights alongside to guide you to where? Haran thinks about tunnels, the tunnels he read about from Vietnam. The GIs would go down in the tunnels with a .45 and a flashlight and search for the enemy. Haran and Bobby Dane have to crouch over as they move and Haran, taking point, keeps his rifle ready. But the tunnel is built so that there are no corners, no sharp turns, no place for a man to hide. If anyone is down here, Haran will see him. And he'll see Haran.

He can feel his heart beat like a rabbit, his breath

coming like a miler's. Bobby Dane, too, panting, coughing, moving like every twitch or cough or snort might bring death down upon them. They carry their fear controlled like a tarantula locked in a box. Under wraps but scratching at the surface. Their eyes click off inches of dirt, wiring, support beams, eyes burning to discover booby traps and mines, I.E.D.s, anything that might be hidden there for the purpose of killing.

So far, nothing.

Nothing until they come to a split in the underground passageway where the tunnel becomes two diverging paths, one right and one left.

"Your choice," Haran says.

Bobby Dane can't speak. Haran gives his eyes a close look, shrugs and decides that there's no way to tell, they've lost all sense of direction, so they might as well go left.

They follow that tunnel until they find it—the steps embedded in the wall leading up to a hatch, up to the surface. A way out. Without taking a beat, Haran climbs up the steps, gripping the handrail, trying to keep the M-16 from slipping off his shoulder, and at the top, he unlocks the hatch from the inside.

He raises it slowly. No more than an inch, maybe two.

"Holy shit," Haran says.

Bang. He brings the hatch down. Locks it.

"Tonjay," he says. "And all those dumb sons-of-bitches with him. We're in the desert. With the guys we've been watching. That's where we are."

Bobby Dane says nothing.

"They're getting ready to move," Haran says.

"Probably head into Mortales to see what's left."

Bobby Dane starts to slide past Haran, grabs the handrail and takes a step up.

"Wait a minute, where the fuck are you going?"

"I'm going up there," Bobby Dane says. "I'm going to kill the bastard."

"Not today," Haran says.

Bobby Dane brushes him off. He's still got his prison muscle, when he pushes Haran back the sense of gravity, of shifting weight, is all on the side of Bobby Dane, Haran wouldn't stand a chance. Not if there were rules and a referee.

"Leave him," Haran says. "Let him have the fucking town."

"It's more than that."

"No," Haran says. "It's not. And if that's how you still think, they ought to lock you back up until you get your head on straight."

Bobby Dane makes one final move to go up to the surface and kill Tonjay but this time, Haran puts a hand on his shoulder and Haran feels the movement and the situation change, it's all there in the sinew.

"You know I'm right," Haran says. "The world is full of first-grade assholes and if they're not coming for you, let it lie."

Bobby Dane lets go of the handrail and comes down.

"I'd bet cash money that the other tunnel will take us right back to that fat Mr. Tom," Haran says. "And if you decide to break a few commandments up there, I just might help you."

They head back to the other branch of the tunnel.

When they get to the other end, right below the hatch

and ready to go up to the surface, that's where Bobby Dane changes his mind decides to go back to kill Tonjay.

"I have to do it, Ty. That's what it's been building to," Bobby Dane says and when he says it, his back is to Haran, he's walking away, retracing his steps in the tunnel.

"So long, Bobby," Haran says. "Idiot."

But Haran can't leave it there. He watches Bobby Dane walk away and Haran's thinking, *Don't let him go up there. Kill him.* He knows that if Bobby Dane goes up after Tonjay then Bobby Dane's gonna screw it and the whole, evil Tonjay world is gonna come back down after him full force and then nobody in the world—no force, no army—is gonna save Haran's life.

But Haran can't pull the trigger. Maybe it's only that he won't shoot Bobby Dane in the back. *So yell for him to turn around.* Maybe he's making a bet with himself. Maybe he wants to die.

Haran curses, grabs the handrail and starts up the steps to the top.

Twisting the lock like he's balanced a million feet in the air, Haran opens the hatch so slowly that beads of sweat pop along his forehead and drip down like little salt stingers into his eyes.

Then he's got it open.

Haran's not even thinking about Bobby Dane. Haran's thinking about the first person he sees through the slight inch-wide opening of the hatch, a solid muscle-builder-type who's on guard duty and who's standing in front of the glass of Mr. Tom's human fish tank, smoking a cigarette with his rifle relaxed in one hand.

The guard scrambles almost stupidly when he sees the

muzzle of the M-16 come up from the floor. His own weapon swings wide and he stiffens as clumsily as if he were jumping up from the toilet, suddenly alert but alert too late.

Haran kills him with the first shot. The sound cracks and echoes and the round hits the guard square in the sternum so that he goes down on his ass with a little black hole in his center and blood coming out in spurts. At the same time, the glass of the fish tank shatters and falls away and two hanging bodies, men with rotted corpse faces, dance crazily from the wires around their throats as the water and fish cascade to the floor in one giant wave, stinking, reeking of soaked dead flesh.

The wave washes over Haran and rivers down into the hatch, into the tunnel. And Haran, soaked with death, gives it all a split second of thought and then nothing else, that's it. Soaked, stinking, he clambers up through the hatch seeing the shattered tank, seeing that he's in the hallway outside of Mr. Tom's library. Seeing through the tank to Mr. Tom at his desk inside.

Haran walks through the tank. With the barrel of the rifle he shoves one of the hanging dead men out of the way, lets the body swing and sway as Mr. Tom sits in piss-pants shock and says, "Jesus Christ."

Haran wipes the dead man's water from his face, points the weapon at Mr. Tom's fat belly.

"You're already dead," Haran says quietly. "Maybe I'll bring you back to life. We'll see."

Mr. Tom's right hand makes just the slightest movement on the desk.

"Either we both leave this scene alive. Or not. Both of us. Tell me you don't believe it."

"I believe it." Mr. Tom's hand stops moving.

"That's right. If any of your people come into this room, I'll kill you. No matter what else happens. Do you hear me?"

"I hear you."

"Your friend. And my friend. Bobby Dane. He should be here in a few seconds."

Mr. Tom nods as in *Okay.*

"He had a momentary lapse of reason. He'll change his mind and..."

Bobby Dane walks into the library. He comes through the shattered fish tank and closes one eye against the vision of the hanging dead man. Bobby Dane stops, looks around, says, "Jesus Christ."

"What did I tell you?" Haran says.

Mr. Tom nods again.

"The town, Mortales. It's all yours," Haran says. "Or it belongs to our tattooed friend out there in the desert. Either way, you deal with it."

"May I speak?" Mr. Tom says.

"Sure, let him speak," Bobby Dane says.

"You're placing me in an incredibly difficult situation. If you don't mind my saying so. Let's talk about a renegotiation of terms. What if I double the payment for both of you. We forget all of this nonsense. And you go back and do the job I hired you to do."

Haran hears the bolt action of Bobby Dane's M-16. Without shifting his gaze from Mr. Tom, he reaches around and softly guides the barrel of Bobby Dane's weapon downward.

"Triple the payment?"

"You're going to get us both back over the border," Haran says.

"I'm afraid that's quite impossible."

"What I think you're saying," Haran says, "is that you still think you're going to find a way out of this."

Haran doesn't move as Bobby Dane brushes past him. For a moment, he thinks maybe it would be a good idea to step in and stop it. But even while he's thinking about some kind of move, Haran knows he's going to stand still with his weapon pointed at Mr. Tom's chest. He knows he's going to stand there and do nothing to save anyone as Bobby Dane grabs Mr. Tom's hand from the desk and in one fluid movement sweeps across with what looks like a Marine K-bar knife.

He severs maybe two fingers at second joint from Mr. Tom's left hand.

Haran can't quite tell. There's a quick splash of blood and a lot of screaming. After that, he's crouched down behind a chair, aiming his rifle, waiting to kill the next person to come into the room.

Mr. Tom's car is a decent sized limo and he's done well to pay off the border guards and after a while he begins to get some color back in his face, mostly as the car crosses into the U.S. It's then, after they get through the paid-off formalities of the crossing, that Bobby Dane goes back to holding the 9mm against Mr. Tom's right knee.

There's a small bar in the back of the limo and Haran offers Mr. Tom a drink but he won't have any. No cigar, either. The driver says nothing, just deadpan drives.

Bobby Dane keeps his gaze on Mr. Tom like any twitch—the slightest, stupidest physical action—might be a giveaway of rebellion, punishable by death. And Mr. Tom knows it—that Bobby Dane, with the prison muscles and the huge swirls of tattoo on his face and the utterly mad look in his eye, is hot for any excuse to put just one final round into this, his only body.

Before Haran and Bobby Dane finally get out of the limo and send Mr. Tom back down south, Haran says to all of them, "We've all been living in some pretty crude circles and I personally think we—all of us, you too, Mr. Tom—can do better. That's it. That's all I got to say."

Haran's not even certain why he needed to say that but at the time it sounded like good advice. And he tells himself silently: *Stop giving people good advice. See how far it got you.*

They're almost where Haran has directed them to drive. Just before they reach the stated destination, he says to Mr. Tom, "Oh, one more thing. Have that hand looked at as soon as possible. You don't want it to get infected. You don't want to lose anything else."

When Haran and Bobby Dane get out of the car, Mr. Tom isn't paying any attention, not even to the neon sign that reads *JESSIE'S* over the ugly little concrete building in the distance. When the limo pulls away, Mr. Tom doesn't twist around, doesn't watch Haran and Bobby Dane as the two of them start walking in that direction.

The air never tasted sweeter. That's what through Haran. Even the desert heat makes the day seem like the first morning of Creation and welcome like it split apart the bottomless Dark and Haran has never been so glad to be anywhere or to see anything.

Goddamnit if he ain't still alive.

They're on the roadside where *JESSIE'S* bar is still a good solid walk away. Haran stops. Bobby Dane swivels around and makes some kind of groaning sound as he takes in the whole scene.

"Well, Ty, I'll tell you," Bobby Dane says. "After all that? I'm not glad to be back here. This place is a damn dump and we were better off back there, where we could really make a stake for ourselves. Be somebody. You owe me, you son of a bitch. That's what I got to say. That's it."

"No," Haran says. "*This* is it. This is as far as we go."

Bobby Dane says nothing.

"This is how it is," Haran says. "You and me? We're all paid even. I'm going to make a call, get someone to come out here and pick you up. I'll see if I can borrow a little cash, you can have whatever I can muster. We'll consider it a gift. I won't take repayment."

Bobby Dane is silent.

"But where you go from here," Haran says, "that's up to you."

Bobby Dane is still close-mouthed. Then he smiles. Haran just stares at him.

Something strange happens then, something that Haran will think about for a long time afterwards, whenever he thinks about Bobby Dane which is a little bit every day from now on. With the desert wind loud in his ears and the heat sweeping across his face and his eyes stinging from the invisible mist of sand in the air, Haran decides that he could kill Bobby Dane. That he should kill him. He could get away with it.

He decides that the only way to wipe the slate clean, completely and forever, is for Bobby Dane to disappear. Bobby Dane is a walking reminder, a marker of bad times. Haran hates him. His asinine outlook and his crooked ass smile. And as Haran stands there and lets the killing swirl around in his imagination, it travels though his mind without guilt or sorrow or recrimination. Haran could kill this lunatic, out-of-his-mind Bobby Dane easily. His thumb finds the slick edge of the 9mm in his belt. He sees that if he drew on Bobby Dane right now or told Bobby Dane to walk on ahead, that Bobby Dane would be over and done without anyone to miss or remember him.

Haran knows that this is the only way to begin life over again. He looks into Bobby Dane's eyes and there's another wind across the desert. And the feeling passes. He decides he'll keep even the bad times.

"That's how we're gonna leave it," Haran says. "Forever. I've got nothing more to say to you. After today, if you ever see me—and I mean anywhere or at any time and I don't care what's happening—you nod hello and you'll get the same back. But that's it."

Bobby Dane nods.

"Wait here."

Haran starts walking to Jessie's bar. He's only thinking of how terrific it is to see that piece-of-shit concrete shack again, nothing else, and maybe he's wondering whether Jessie is still there or whether she's taken up with someone else and he turns back around twice to see Bobby Dane still standing alone on the side of the desert road.

Haran walks on.

After a few more steps, he thinks he hears the brakes of a truck behind him, the whoosh of air and the horse-neigh of tires slowing down and Haran stops walking. He waits. He hears a truck door open and slam shut and he hears the motor rev of a truck heading back on the road. And it's only a few moments afterwards that Haran turns back around and by then—which, of course, he knew—Bobby Dane is gone.

Haran smiles. Slowly, he walks back up to the roadside to the place where Bobby Dane had been standing and he stares off to the south and then to the north where he thinks he might still be able to see the tiny dot of the truck disappearing into the desert, unfocused in the desert sun.

Haran gets one short glimpse of the truck before the road becomes empty.

Right then, Haran has a single, piercing moment of uncertainty. About Bobby Dane. And about everything else he's ever done in his life.

It doesn't last. He takes a breath and that finishes it. But before he begins the trek back to Jessie's bar, Haran lets himself stand there alone on the roadside and, watching himself, posed there in the desert, he looks off into the distance where he believes Bobby Dane has disappeared.

"So long, amigo," Haran says, even though he knows there's nobody around to hear him.

SMOKED

TIM O'MARA

To my Missouri River Queens, Maggie and Elise.
I love you both. (Honestly.)

I'm not gonna lie to you.

It was the perfect plan. Except it didn't work.

But it should have. It really should have. Even with all the things that ended up not going the way I expected, and all the ways I had to improvise and come up with shit on the fly, and the way it seemed at times you couldn't tell the players without a scorecard, it had all the elements of a great plan. But, then, well, here I am...

Let me start at the beginning and you'll see what I mean. You'll see *exactly* what I'm talking about.

Hey, can I have another one of these before I keep going? I always talk better when—well, who'd know better than you? Thanks. That's good.

I knew she—*they*—would be out of the house and I could get in and out of there in less than five minutes. Hell, I've been doing it since I split that joint, y'know? Shit, I built the place. Okay, I didn't *build* build it, but I did most of the renovations so I knew the place like the back of my hand. Like it was my own.

And it was. My own, I mean. It was hers really, although truth be told—like I said, I'm not gonna lie to you—the place was *owned* by her parents, if you wanna get technical about who's money actually bought it and whose name it was in. They bought it for her—which then became *us*—two years before we got married. She was working. I was working. We were paying her folks about four bills a month in rent, which is a really sweet deal if you think about it. But then when we both lost our jobs—mine through no fault of my own; people just stopped adding on to their homes 'cause of the economy—the deal stopped being so sweet, y'know?

Her dad's all, like, "I can't afford two homes." And I'm, like, "Cool, sell the place, give me the money I put in for the repairs, the landscaping and my labor, and we'll move in with my dad at the river." Then the old guy felt the need to remind me that it was *his money* I used to fix the place up, so that wasn't going to happen. And since I'd been living there rent-free for all those last months, he figured that just about covered my labor costs. The guy had a green spiral notebook where he had figured all this shit out. To the penny. He even used freakin' decimal points.

And the whole idea of moving in with *my* dad—which was a really great idea because I love that house—well, that was the beginning of the end for our marriage. I swear if it weren't for the kid—her name's Brooklyn, that's her picture on my phone here—I swear we wouldn'ta lasted as long as we did.

Brooklyn. Not my choice of names, by the way. My wife's best friend from high school was from there— moved out here 'cause of her daddy's job—so we just *had* to name the kid Brooklyn. Coulda been worse, I guess. Best friend coulda been from Staten Island.

Anyways, I love that kid to death, but having a daughter made me make some decisions—my parole officer calls them "life choices"—I *never* woulda made if I were a single guy without a kid and an unemployed, soon-to-be ex-wife.

So, like I said, it was a perfect plan. You see, one of

the things I put into that house when I was doing all that fix-me-up crap, was I installed a false wall in the basement. I can't help but smile when I think of how smart I was to put that in. A false wall in *my house* where I could keep my shit and even my wife and kid didn't know about. How many guys dream of that, right?

Well, I'm not a dreamer—I'm a doer.

So, I got myself this hiding spot and at first it was where I'd hide my booze and a little bit of my bud, y'know? My wife's always had too much of a taste for the hard stuff—we don't use the word "alcoholic"—and she hated that I still smoked weed now and again, so the false wall started paying dividends about five minutes after I built it. My whiskey and weed had a home. Sounds like a Willie Nelson song, don't it?

That's one of the reasons my high school friends called me Smoke, by the way. I was the guy who could always get some decent pot. By eleventh grade I was *the guy* in high school when it came to procurement. Call me up at two in the morning, I could have some of that sweet stuff in your hand by three. I made 'em pay a little extra for the late-night service, but it was worth it.

The other reason they called me Smoke was I could throw a baseball, man. One day, Coach K borrowed one of them radar guns from the local college—kinda like the ones the cops pulled me over with that time, and I had to do the whole breathalyzer slash walk-a-straight-line slash touch-my-nose bullshit 'cause I was going, like, *three miles* over the speed limit—and Coach tells me to get out there on the mound and give it all I got. So I grab the ball and start warming up with my catcher—I think his name was Johnny or Gabe or something but we just called him Spaz 'cause he had that thing with his non-throwing arm he broke when he was a kid and the doctor screwed up the surgery.

I'm out there warming up and tell Coach I'm ready, and I let it fly, man. I was clocking in at ninety-three, ninety-five. Coach put a coupla batters up there, and I blew it right by them. I mean they were swinging at the *sound* of the pitch. So, that's another reason they called me Smoke: I could *blow* it by anyone. Anytime.

Until I blew the arm out, of course. Not in a real game, mind you. Coach said I'd have to learn to throw them over the plate with something approaching consistency before I got to pitch in a real game. I blew it out showing off too much during batting practice. Heard a pop one day and after that, I wouldn'ta made the fucking bowling team.

There went my baseball scholarship and the free ride to college, right? I didn't get any offers, mind you, but it was just a matter of time. So I had to pay for college the only other way I could: selling pot to my friends. I'm not so good with the numbers shit—not as good as my ex-father-in-law, that's for sure—but I figured out how much weed I needed to sell to get me through the first semester of community college and I sold it. Sold enough to pay for the books, too.

Never actually made it to college, though. I was working so hard at running my business, I missed the cut-off date for the fall semester, and then things got real busy during the holiday season—that's when I added a little coke to my inventory and started selling to the bankers and lawyers in this two-faced fucking town—so

I missed the application date for the spring semester, too. Funny thing is, I ended up spending lots of time on campus as it was 'cause that's where a lot of my best customers were. Students and faculty.

Anyway, it was a blessing in disguise, as my mother— the good Lord rest her soul—woulda said. She always said that when something bad happened and I was feeling crappy. Like the time I ran over my toe with the lawn mower and missed the senior trip, and it turned out that it rained the whole time the kids were up in the woods. Same thing: What the hell did I need to go to college for? Some piece of paper sayin' I could get a job that would pay me *half* what I was making selling pot and coke? I figured that shit out with a quickness.

That's how I met my wife, y'know. She was a friend of a friend of a customer, and then she became a friend of mine, and then we hooked up one night and started talking about all the things we had in common: the joys of marijuana not being the least of them. But we also liked the same music, spending Saturday and Sunday on float trips not giving a damn where we ended up.

But kids. She loved kids.

That's what she did when we met. She was a teacher's assistant at one of those private schools just out of town where some of my best customers sent their rug rats. That's irony, right? Here's all these rich folks spending money on their kids' private educations so they don't end up *like* me and then spending more of that money *on* me to help 'em forget they got kids. Shit like that makes me laugh.

Me? I just went along with it to keep gettin' laid and said I liked kids, too, but—truth be told—I hated the little fuckers. Too needy, always whining. Gimme, gimme, gimme. Shit, I got enough of that with the people I sell pot to. I don't need it from someone who can't wipe his own ass. Now that I think of it, some of my best customers struggle with that from time to time.

Anyway, back to yesterday—no, wait, the night before.

There I am, slipping through the bathroom window of *my house.* My ex always keeps it open even in the dead of winter and when the AC's on. We used to argue about that all the time. "What're ya trying to do?" I'd say. "Heat the whole neighborhood? Cool off the back-yard?" I'd have to vary the speech depending on the time of year. Waste of energy, ya ask me, but she was all about having a little fresh air in the house.

That's why I knew the window'd be open and I could get in without setting off the security system—another thing I installed. Okay, *had* installed. But I called up the company and watched as the guy put it in and run the wires and shit. And I picked the code—five, six, four, three—that she changed after I moved out. Thirty bucks a month for that alarm system. Ask her dad. It's in his notebook.

Anyway, I slip through the bathroom window smooth as a snake, and I land on my hands and tuck into a somersault that'd make a Russian gymnast proud. Even with my backpack on.

You're probably too young to remember—you look like you're about my ex-wife's age—but those Commie chicks could move. Looked like they fell off the ugly tree and hit every branch on the way down, but they had *bodies.* Unless you like breasts. They weren't big on them, but I've never been a big-boob kinda guy. I'd a like to spend some time rolling on the trampoline with them, know what I mean? Wonder if that's where the word "tramp" comes from. I love words. Hafta put a bag over their heads, but it'd be worth it.

Back to the point: I had to get at my stuff in the false wall. Had it there for a few weeks and I needed it and I wasn't too sure when *the "family"* would be getting back home, so I just wanted to get in and get out. Besides, I had a business meeting I had to be at, so...

So I'm in the bathroom and I turn my little flashlight on, and next to my kid's and ex's stuff I see all of the new guy's shit in there, y'know? Shaving cream, razor, a third toothbrush. I'm like, shit, the guy's *living* there now. Or at the very least spending enough time at *my house* to be shaving and brushing his teeth. I don't even know if he's got a job. Hate people who sponge offa others. Don't like my daughter around those types. When Brooklyn gets to be a teenager, I don't want her hanging around losers like that. My wife's got a maternal responsibility to watch what—*and who*—she exposes my daughter to. Heard from some friends she's been bringing Brooklyn by the restaurant on weekends—puts her in a booth while she works her shift—like my in-laws're too busy to watch their own grandkid.

I'd do it, but that's my busiest time of the week. My customers need me to be available twenty-four/seven from Friday after work to pretty much 'til Sunday after church. You'd be surprised how busy that time of day is, right after church. I got people driving by after dropping off their families at their big houses along the golf course and telling the loved ones they're out getting breakfast. I guess all that worshipping gets a person all riled up and my services keep them grounded.

Ha! I keep 'em grounded while getting them high.

That's another thing I was always good at—writing. Not on paper or anything like that, but coming up with clever stuff. Like that metaphor of being a snake crawling through the window. Or was that a simile? But "grounded while getting high?" That's good. An oxymoron, I think they call it. Like the drug that fat radio guy was addicted to. Don't see the connection, but... Anyway, I coulda been a *great* writer if I ever put half the shit that came out of my mouth on paper. I just always hated writing things down. Again, not like my ex-wife's dad. If he'da spent a little more time with words instead of numbers, maybe I wouldn't be in this shit now, huh?

What's that?...Yeah, that'll work. Appreciate it.

And, not only does this new guy have his shit there, I can smell his cigarette smoke. She *never* let me smoke in the house. It was always on the back porch whenever I wanted a quick one. "Not around the baby," she'd say. Like she's a health freak all the sudden. Got so embarrassing, not being able to smoke in my own house, I went out and got a dog. Called him Marlboro 'cause I was always taking him out for a drag. Get it?

I told you, I should write the stuff down. I just don't have the time.

Anyway, she and the kid fall in love with the dog, which, believe me, was *not* my intention. And when I finally left—when I was *asked* to leave—she wouldn't let me keep the damn dog. "Brooklyn's too attached," she said. Yeah, too attached to the dog, not so much to her dad.

I got her back, though. One night when she was out with the new guy and the kid was at the grandparents, I took Marlboro back. That was the first time I pulled that bathroom window thing. Took him over to a lady friend of mine I was staying with at the time on the other side of the river. That did not work out—that lady was one crazy bitch—so me and Marley were outta there in a month.

I'm good with animals—all kinds of animals—and I'd take care of them all the time. Horses, goats, rabbits, dogs. I kept them fed and clean, and she's—the one on the other side of the river—is on my ass about getting a job. "What the hell am I doing all day with those animals if it ain't a job?" I said. I think that was the *last* thing I said to her, and there went my idea about breeding rabbits to sell for Easter. Ya gotta time rabbit breeding just right, and we broke up at the wrong time. Three months later woulda been perfect, but...Again, not my fault.

So after Crazy Lady kicks me out, I gotta move back in with my dad for a while and he's allergic, so I can't bring the dog there. So the next time my wife goes out, I put the dog back in the house, through the window again. I figured I made my point and besides, Brooklyn *was* attached to the mutt, so who'm I to keep a girl from her dog?

Anyway, back to it. When I walk out of the bathroom on the way to my hidey hole, who do I run into? Our dog. Think I woke ol' Marley up 'cause he's looking all drowsy and he starts growling at me. I get down and hold my hand out for him to sniff and say, "Hey, boy, it's me. Hey, Marls. It's Daddy." Mutt starts growling louder, like my ex'd been coaching him or some shit. This is *my* dog—know what I'm saying? Wouldn't let me pass into the hallway, so I grab him by the collar and pull him into the bathroom and shut the door behind me. I mean, I wouldn'ta minded petting him a bit, but not after he's growling at me like I'm some sorta stranger or burglar, y'know?

I go over to the basement door and turn the knob, except it doesn't turn. She put a goddamned doorknob with a lock on it. Probably to keep Brooklyn from going down. She was always whining and worrying about Brooklyn falling down the stairs. But, being the penny-pinching miser her dad is, it's one of those cheap pieces of crap you could pick with a decent paper clip, *which* I happen to have on me 'cause I think ahead like that and carry lots of stuff in my backpack.

Always wanted to be on *Let's Make A Deal* and have the host ask me if I had a certain item in my pocket. I bet I would've. Anyway, I figure it'll take me about ten seconds to open the door, but before I can do that I hear this sound behind me. I think the dog got himself outta the shitter, y'know? I turn around, and it ain't my dog.

It's the new guy—at least that's who I figured it was in the dark—and he's got a gun pointed at me. *And I'm pretty sure it's my gun.* The gun I thought I'd misplaced just before I moved out. My ex musta taken it and put it somewhere "safe," and now it is being pointed at me by the guy who's banging my ex.

I think that might be irony, too. I'm not sure.

I'm looking at the gun and looking at him, and he

comes out with a line I've heard a hundred times in the movies. "You picked the wrong house, motherfucker," he says. Real original, right? So I take a few seconds and a big swallow and follow up with a movie line of my own. "This is *my* house, asshole. And, if I'm not mistaken, that's my gun you're pointing at me."

He goes into some shit about knowing *exactly* who I am and possession being nine-tenths of the law and—again—I ain't too good with the math but I think it means that just because he's holding the gun, most of it belongs to him or some shit.

Now, I gotta figure: Do I stand here and argue with this guy, or do I do what I gotta do and get the hell out of Dodge?

"I thought you were out," I say to him.

He smiles at me and says, "Got sick at the last minute. I was asleep on the couch until I heard you coming through the bathroom window. I told her to keep that thing shut."

And I'm, like, "Yeah, I know, right? Wasting all that energy. And who knows who's gonna crawl through when you're out of the house?" He nods at me, and so here I am agreeing with the guy who's holding a gun on me and I'm thinking maybe I can tell him what I'm here for and he'll just let me get on with it. So I tell him. Then he starts thinking about it and says, "How much ya got down there?"

Did I tell you I had some meth down there? Yeah. I keep the weed at my dad's place now so it's nice and handy, and I sell more of that than the meth, so I need it where I can get at it quicker and with more frequency. I'd rather stick with just the pot, little bit of coke, but with the way things are now, I gotta deal a little meth to keep me in the black. Or the red. Whatever the color is that means I don't owe anybody.

Now I'm thinking this guy wants in. He doesn't look like a dummy. But I lowball it and say about three pounds of pot. It's really closer to five pounds of meth—I broke it up into two bricks—but if this guy's gonna try and horn in on my stash, I'm not letting him know how much and what I got.

He's thinking about that for a while, still pointing the gun in my face and says he'll let me go down to the basement for a thousand bucks. Guy wants to charge me to go down into my own basement and get my own property. Like I even have that kinda green on me. And for three pounds of pot? Shows ya what he knows about the price of marijuana.

I'm like, "No way," and he says, "Fine. Get the hell outta my house before I call the cops."

My house, he says. The nerve of some people.

"How about I just go down and get it myself anyway?" I ask.

Now he's all smiles and shit and says, "How about I just shoot you right here and tell the cops you broke in?" He goes on about knowing about how I've got a record and how I'm behind in my child support payments and how he'll show the cops my stash. Says the cops won't even make him leave the house to tell that story. Then he starts in about the self-defense laws and about some shit called the "Castle Doctrine" that says he can shoot me and say that he was in fear for his life and say he used—and here's where he sounds like a lawyer—"necessary and appropriate force" to protect himself. Basically, he's telling me he can use my gun to kill me and then have a Coke with the investigating officers. Like we're in Florida or some shit.

"You'd do that?" I ask. "To Brooklyn? My baby girl? You'd leave her without a daddy?" I swear to God I started to tear up, laying it on real thick. He keeps smiling, and I wanna reach over and smack that grin off his smug face, but he's got that gun, y'know? He's one hard man, this guy. But I don't got a thousand dollars on me to give him, so I gotta come up with some other plan.

I'm good at thinking on my feet. Ya gotta be in my line of work, so I offer him a deal. Let me get my shit, do my business, and I'll come back and pay him three hundred. No way I'm going to drop a thou with this guy not *earning* shit. He thinks about it and says, "How about I go with you while you do your business, and I get my thousand?"

My thousand. You believe the balls on this guy?

"I thought you weren't feeling well," I say.

"I'll be feeling a whole lot better with a thousand dollars in my pocket," he says. And then there's that stupid-ass grin on his face again, like he's clever or some shit. The only clever he's got is the gun he's holding in his hand, and I'm starting to wonder if it's even loaded.

So I stall him. Figured I played my hand too soon, 'cause now he knows I got my product downstairs and I ain't getting it without him getting a taste. Start running the numbers in my head and all I can come up with is *something* minus a thousand's gotta be better than *nothing* minus a thousand. Don't need much math to figure that one out.

I nod my head and say, "Okay. Here's the deal. We

get the shit from the basement, you come with me to my dad's and drop off what I don't need, and then we drive over and take care of my business. I'll drop you off back here and you're up an easy five hundred for taking a ride with me."

"A thousand," he says back. Like I said, balls.

I look at my watch—my dad's watch, I borrowed it 'cause since he's retired he doesn't have much need for it and it looks really good on me—and I'm running late, so I say okay. He goes off to get the key to the basement door and when he comes back he's all, like, "Storing your product where your daughter lives, man. Shouldn't be shitting where she eats."

Thank you, Dr. Phil. *Asshole.*

So we go down to the basement, move some shit around, and I open the false wall. I can tell he's impressed, but he ain't gonna say squat to me about it. Probably kicking himself inside 'cause all this time he's been living there—I don't know exactly how long—he had no idea what I had stashed down there. And I got it all packed up in two bricks, so he can't tell that it's meth and not pot. But he ain't as dull as I originally thought 'cause he looks at what I'm pulling out and says, "That don't look like three pounds of pot, man." I shake that off and say something like, "You ain't never seen this much shit at one time so don't go all gangsta dealer on me."

We get the stuff out to my car, and I'm thinking about a way I can take him down and get the gun from him and get the hell outta there. But I just couldn't pull the trigger, y'know? No pun intended. I make sure I got the car keys and head back inside and he says, "Where you going?"

"Out the bathroom window," I say. He gives me a look like I'm batshit and I say, "It's bad luck to leave out a different door than you came in."

He reminds me I came in through a window, so the door rule doesn't count, and my luck was already going from not-so-good to *really*-not-so-good. I couldn't think of a quick one to come back with, so I just gave him the one-finger wave and went back inside and out the bathroom window the way I came in. Damn Marley was still growling at me. I could hear him barking all the way to my car. Short memory on that pooch.

Cool, thanks. Getting better the more I talk. Hope I'm not going on too much. "Too much candy for a dime," my mother would say, so don't be afraid to tell me to shut up if ya want. I appreciate that.

We drive out to my dad's house by the river, and by the time we get there the rain's really coming down. A real toad-strangler. We pull in to my dad's driveway, and I can see the light on in his room. The whole house is dark 'cept for that room of his in the back he likes to call a "den"—when all it's got is a TV, a recliner and a mini-fridge—so I know he's drinking. All the doors'll be locked, he'd've checked the gas on the stove three times and unplugged all the major appliances, except the fridge and the TV he's watching. He's got what they call OCD, I think. Obsessive Composite Disorder or something. He's never been the sharpest hook in the tackle box but he knows when he gets to drinking and when the rain starts up he's got to make sure the house is lightning proof. Growing up he wouldn't even let me take a shower during a thunderstorm 'cause he was afraid the lightning would hit the pipes and travel down and electrocute me. Never heard of that actually happening but he swore it could so...

We sat there in the driveway for a few minutes—New Guy's still got the gun in his hand—and I'm thinking what's the best place to stash the stash. That sounds funny when I say it out loud like that. I don't wanna go into the house in case Dad set the alarm, and then the beeping'll wake him up and he's gonna ask "What's in the bags, son?" He thinks I'm still working the home repair thing, so I don't want him asking too many questions.

It hits me that his boat's probably the best bet for a temporary storage solution. He's got it locked up in the garage right now on a trailer, and the garage ain't hooked up to the security system.

Why the garage? Because we don't got a dock at the moment. I blame myself for that 'cause—truth be told—I *kinda* stole the old one. I know, stealing from your own family sucks, but I needed the cash to help pay off my guy—my cooker—and that was the only thing I could get my hands on at the time. I knew a guy up the river that needed a dock, so I sold it to him. I was planning on getting a new one right after this last deal, so it wasn't like I *stole it* stole it. More like I *borrowed against it*. My ex-father-in-law used to like to tell me that it takes money to make money, so I think he woulda liked that idea. My dad's planning on going away next weekend to visit his brother in Kansas City, so I was gonna surprise him when he got back by having a new dock waiting for him. Was gonna pick him up at the airport, drive him home and do the whole blindfold thing, and surprise!

Best laid plans, right?

So I take one of the meth bricks and leave the other one with New Guy. I only gotta drop off one, and that's gonna gross me a little over ten grand. Minus what I paid the cook and now minus the thousand for this ass-hole, I'm still up close to five thou for the night. That's enough to get a new dock and play a little catch-up on the child support. I'm always behind on that, what with the economy being what it is. Lot of my customers are cutting back or buying some inferior shit. That's one thing I won't do is sell a product I'm not proud of or wouldn't do myself. Although, I gotta tell ya, I don't ever go near the meth. But if I did, I'd use the stuff I sell.

And about that child support, I don't know what the hell my ex is feeding Brooklyn that costs me five hundred a month. And it's not like I'm seeing new clothes on the kid when I do see her. I don't think I ever cost my folks five hundred bucks a month, I'll tell you that.

So I'm in the garage stashing my spare brick in Dad's toolbox, then I climb on the boat and remember that sometimes my dad gets drunk and accidentally leaves his gun on board in the engine hole. Not everybody you meet on the river these days is friendly, and my dad ain't no fool. I open up the engine hole, and there it is. I take it out and figure "Okay, Jesse James, let's see who's the clever one now."

I check the magazine—Dad's gotta a semi-automatic from his old job as a security guard; it's a nice piece of hardware, I tell you—and it's fucking empty. I look around for some ammo and come up with squat. What the hell good's an unloaded gun gonna do me, right? But then I think New Guy doesn't know it's unloaded, so I stick it behind my back and head out.

"What took ya so long?" he asks when I get back in the car, and I give him a line of crap about finding just the right place in the garage for safety reasons. "Yeah," he laughs, "You're all about safety, aren't ya?" I'm not even sure what that means, but he says it in that stuck-up tone you get when *you're the one* holding the gun. My dad used to say that your IQ goes up in direct proportion to the size of the gun you've got. There's fucking math again, but I know what he means. Except Dad's gun's a pretty good size, it's just empty. How does that figure into the equation? I wanna know.

I pull outta the driveway with the headlights off, 'cause if Dad's still conscious I don't want him to know I came and went without saying hey, 'cause then I gotta come up with a story—if and when he remembers I was there. I turn on the headlights, stop at the turn-off just before the highway, and I make like I'm scratching my back. Then with a quickness I pull out Dad's piece and stick it in New Guy's face.

"Get the fuck outta the car," I tell him. "Now." I use that voice I used when I worked with the Mexicans at my own construction company two years back. Called it Aardvark Handy Man, 'cause I figured with the two A's in the beginning of the name, it'd be the first one people saw when they looked at the phone book. One guy had triple A's in his company, but I didn't care too much about that since AArdvark was only a front in case anyone wanted to know where my cash flow was flowing in from. Anyway, New Guy looks at the gun and—Jesus, if he ain't all calm and shit—and says, "The safety's on." Like a jackass I look, and he reaches up and snatches the gun outta my hand like he's Doug Henning or something. Huh? He was a magician back in the day. Looked like a gay Kenny G. Shit. Kenny G looks like a gay Doug Henning. I half-expected New Guy to go "Shazam!" or something. How'd he know the safety was on?

Now that I think of it, maybe it wasn't. Damn it!

So now I'm thinking that's it, I'm a dead man. Or at the very least, I'm walking back to my dad's without my stash and New Guy's gonna have himself ten Gs worth of crystal he ain't gonna know what to do with. And if I don't show up at my business meeting I might be a dead man anyway, so I gotta be cool here and think fast.

"It's meth," I say, sounding like a kid who can't keep a secret, but I want him to know what he's got so he knows it'll be worth his while not to kill me or kick me out. He's not gonna have a clue where to sell product like that and, like I said, the guys who're expecting me ain't gonna take it too lightly if I don't get them what I promised.

I tell him all this—again, he's as cool as the other side of your pillow—and he says, "Drive, asshole."

So I drive. We head back over to the other side of town, not too far from where the evening started actually. We head outta town just past the soccer field named after that rich asshole whose son is now one of my best customers, over the creek and the railroad tracks, and to the old storage facility the city used to use for confiscated vehicles and snowplows. I pull in and drive around behind the building and park.

"What happens now?" New Guy asks me.

I'm about to say we hafta wait, when these headlights pull in behind us and two cars pull up, front-end first, on both sides of my car. We're practically fucking blind now, that's how these guys roll. Big entrance. We wait about a minute and then the headlights go off, and the other guys—four of them like always, two in each car—get out. One guy, I swear, he reminds me of Lurch from *The Addams Family*. That was a show I watched growing up. You're too young for that, but Google it or something and you'll see what I mean. Big tall dude, didn't speak much and scared the crap outta everyone.

"Wait here," I tell New Guy, and go to open my door. He puts his hand on my arm and says, "I'm going out there with you." I tell him these guys ain't expecting two of us, and they're not likely to appreciate any deviations from the plan. He tells me, "Too bad," and grabs the brick of meth and gets out of the car.

So we get out, and the guys in the other car get out, and they all look at me like I brought an uninvited guest with me. Which I did.

"The fuck are you?" That's the guy who calls himself Mickey, and he's the scariest of the bunch. He's short, but he's got these eyes that'll drill a hole through you if he looks at you long enough. I don't think his real name's Mickey though, 'cause he calls the other guys Raymond, Dashiell and John D., and those're all names of famous mystery writers. Dead ones. My mom read 'em all. I never told him my real name either, so he just calls me Agatha. Real funny, huh? Coulda gone with Ross or Ellery, but he's gotta call me Agatha. Long as he pays me my money, though, I'm good.

"He's my partner," I say, the words just coming out. I told you I'm good on my feet, y'know.

Mickey thinks about that and shakes his head. "You ain't got a partner," he says. Then he throws in "Agatha" for effect. And while he's talking, Lurch takes a coupla steps towards us.

New Guy smiles and says, "He does now."

Everybody's quiet for a half a minute and Lurch moves a little closer. New Guy looks at Lurch, then at Mickey and says, "If the big guy comes any closer, we're gonna have a problem."

Mickey says, "We?" Lurch takes one more step, and New Guy steps back like a field goal kicker and lets one go right into Lurch's balls.

We're all in shock about this and, as nervous as I am, I gotta stop myself from laughing, 'cause the guy who played Lurch on that TV show? He was the same guy Paul Newman kicked in the nuts in *Butch Cassidy and the Sundance Kid.* Lurch hits the ground hard and New Guy pulls out my gun and says, "You're right. Maybe not *we.* Can we talk now?" Mickey shakes his head, gives that killer grin he's got, and spreads his arms out like he's Jesus or something. "G'head. Talk."

But before he talks, New Guy goes up to the guy he just kicked in the balls and helps him up. He puts his hand on his shoulder and one on his back, but Lurch just shakes him off and says something that sounds like, "Duck poo." New Guy raises his hands like he's saying, "Just tryin' to help," and then he backs off. Lurch goes over and stands with his guys, but he ain't standing too straight, y'know?

"Me and Agatha are partners as of tonight," New

Guy says. I guess he called me Agatha to get on Mickey's good side. "Whatever deal you two had, the proportion's gonna stay the same." *More fucking math,* I'm thinking. "What that means," New Guy says like he figures we all need a little schooling here, "is that you keep paying whatever you've been paying for the pound, we make sure there's more pounds to pay for."

Mickey thinks about that and says, "Whadda we need you for? Agatha can increase the volume anytime I ask."

"How come you never asked then?" New Guy says and that shuts Mickey up. "Because," New Guy goes on, "you don't have complete faith that Agatha can deliver. You've been happy with a pound or two here and a pound there—and obviously you're a careful guy, which is why you show up with your boys and all, I can dig that—but you can't honestly tell me you don't wanna be moving more product?"

Mickey looks over at Lurch, who's still trying to stand without bending over. "I got other suppliers," he says. "I get what I need."

New Guy's about to say something, but I step in. It's my show, right? At least it's supposed to be. Not that I was looking for a show, but, hey...

"Every supplier you got," I say, "increases your risk. Reduce your risk and you reduce your overhead. Less overhead, more money for you."

I said that last part to Mickey, but now everyone's looking at me like I'm freakin' on *Fox Business News.* So, I decide to keep riding with it. "You buy more from me," I say, "and I'll cut down on your overhead." I use that word again because I can't think of the word proportion at the moment or even if it fits here so I say,

"*And* I'll throw in a nice discount 'cause you're buying more."

Even I'm impressed with the shit that's coming outta my mouth, and I'm thinking the opposite's true, too, y'know? The less people I *sell to*, the less risk *I got*, but I don't say that out loud 'cause I want Mickey thinking he's the big winner here. I'm also thinking New Guy being at my ex's house that night mighta been one of them blessings in disguise I told you my mother always talked about. I never worked with a partner before. But hey, life's all about change, right?

Again everybody gets quiet, and in a minute or so we all got happy looks on our faces. Except for Lurch who's still holding his nut sack. "Let's give it a try," Mickey says. "And just to see if you guys're as good as you think, let's say we make it ten pounds before sunrise."

"Sunrise tomorrow?" I ask.

Mickey smiles, makes a big show out of looking at his watch, and says, "Yeah. Sunrise. You two *partners* can handle that, right?"

That's when I feel like grabbing my own balls to make sure they don't head up north to my stomach. *Ten pounds before sunrise?* I wanna say I can't do that, but my grampa used to say *You wanna play with the big boys? Play with the big boys.*

New Guy talks before I can and says, "Absolutely. But not here."

Mickey says, "I like it here" and New Guy says, "Been doing it here too many times. New deal requires a new locale. Something safer."

"Like where?" Mickey says, and New Guy says, "The access point up north. You gotta boat?"

Mickey laughs and says, "You new to town, boy? We all got boats."

New Guy says, "Cool. The access point off the highway at sunrise tomorrow."

"You gonna bring ten pounds of product to the river?" Mickey says.

"We're gonna bring ten pounds of product *on* the river," New Guy says.

Well, lemme tell you. That shut everyone up. We're all thinking the same thing: Between Fish and Wildlife, Conservation, Highway Patrol and some other law enforcement officials I'm sure I don't even know about, the river ain't the best place to do this kinda business, and I'm thinking New Guy just blew the deal.

"The risk is ours," he says. That makes *me* feel a whole lot better. "You be at the access point at sunrise, you don't like what you see, you never touch the stuff. You wanna come by boat, great. You wanna drive, we're fine with that. I don't give a shit if you fly in on a helicopter. This ain't my first rodeo and, no offense, you ain't the only buyer in the county. Up to you."

I look at Mickey's face and I swear I can't tell if he's gonna pull out a piece, step forward and bite my face, or drop his pants and take a shit. It's like that for at least two minutes until he talks again.

"Okay," he says. "Sunrise, tomorrow morning." He rubbed his nose and says, "If you are one minute late, the deal's off and you're gonna have more to worry about than the cops finding a shitload of meth on your boat."

New Guy nods and looks at me so I nod, too. Partners, right. I just hope it ain't the first and last time I work with one. Mickey reaches into his pocket and pulls out an envelope. That's my ten plus, I'm thinking, but he hands it to New Guy, and New Guy hands the brick to Mickey. I don't like that part one bit, but I keep my mouth shut 'cause we're almost outta there and I wanna go home.

"Oh," Mickey says. "One more thing." He steps over to me and like a Rockette—my dad took us to see them once at Christmastime in New York at Radio City—he lets me have a shot in the balls. "That's for John D," he says. I hit my knees and he says, "I know. Your partner did it, but I don't like to kick strangers in the balls. Especially ones holding guns." Then he turns to New Guy and says, "Never did get your name."

New Guy smiles and says, "Elmore."

Well, that was clearly the funniest thing Mickey's heard in a while, 'cause he and his boys laugh all the way back into their cars and drive off. New Guy helps me up and says, "Sorry about that." I was kinda at a loss for words at the moment and wanted to get out of there, so I promised myself we'd talk about it later.

We head back to my dad's place and New Guy—*Elmore*—says he wants me to contact my supplier and tell him we'll be needing more weight for tomorrow's meeting on the river. Like it's Domino's Pizza. Well, guess what? I can't contact my cook except by phone, and I'm not even sure if he's accessible at this time of night. It's getting late now, y'know? So Elmore says we'll just drive over for a face-to-face with my cook and see what's up. "How's about that, Agatha?" he says.

"Fucking shit!" I scream. "Give it a goddamned break with the fucking Agatha, will ya?"

Elmore waits a few seconds and then smiles. "Okay," he says, "let's go with Aggie. Makes ya sound more like a man. Now act like it."

The hell he thinks I've been doing the past two hours? It's my car, my cook, my deal!

I haven't told him yet that I don't actually know where my cook lives, so driving there's not gonna be much of an option, but I need time to think.

So we're back on the road and I'm starting to get mad hungry when I notice the gas tank's almost at E. I haven't had a lot of disposable cash around lately, and I haven't been able to feed the beast, y'know? I stick my hand out and tell Elmore to give me my money. I'm expecting an argument from him, but he reaches into his pocket, pulls out the cash and hands it to me. No muss, no fuss, right? He musta seen the surprise on my face because he gives me that grin again and says, "Hey, Aggie. That's yours—minus the thousand you're gonna give me." Like I forgot about that. And I had, what with all the excitement. "But," he says, "dinner's on me. *After* we see your guy."

I don't like the tone I'm hearing, so I say, "You're gonna fill up the car first, Elmore. Then we'll see if my guy's available. Either way you're buying dinner and I'm not talking Mickey D's." I knew it was too late for Red Lobster, though. That's where my dad took us for my high school graduation and they're doing that all-you-can-eat shrimp thing again this month so I'm thinking I'm gonna make Elmore get me a little taste of that thousand back, you know what I'm saying?

Elmore starts laughing. I'm not sure why—*because he's an asshole is why*—and he says, "You're the boss,

Aggie." But he didn't mean it. He was being ironic. Damn, this story's got a lot of irony in it, now that I think of it.

Shoulda been writing it all down, but when'd I have the chance to do that? My girl could read it someday. Maybe see that her old man isn't such a loser after all. I don't know exactly what crap my ex is filling her head with about me, but I'm sure I'm not coming out looking like Father of the Year material. I could tell Brooklyn some stories about her mom, but that's not the kinda guy I am. Keep it civil, my parole officer tells me. You never know what might come back and bite you in the ass someday. Like in court proceedings.

I like my parole officer. He's got a tough job. And talk about getting paid shit. He's the one that should be in on this deal with me. God knows he could use the cash. You should see that piece of crap he drives. I think Reagan was president when Detroit let that one roll off the assembly line. Anyway, the guy's been cool to me and doesn't push me when my shit doesn't come out straight. He probably knows I'm doing something but he's got, like, twenty other parolees to deal with so...

I pull into the gas station right before the turnoff to my dad's. I pump the gas, and Elmore goes inside to pay. Then he gets back in the car and I start driving. This is the part that's a little dicey, but it is what it is, right?

"We need the boat," I say.

Elmore's face gets all scrunchy and he says, "Why?"

So I tell him, "I don't know how to meet up with my cook except by the river."

He laughs. "You never drove there?" he asks, and I tell him, "No. That's how he keeps on the down low. I dock at an access point—it rotates each time—two of his guys pick me up, we drive by car for a while—different place each time—and we complete our transaction. Easy peasy, no policey."

That cracks Elmore up. I tell ya, for an unemployed sponger who's got the balls to force his way into his girlfriend's ex's business, this guy laughs a helluva lot. More than me at the moment, anyway.

We pull into my dad's driveway and I see the light's still on, but there's no way he's still consci—still awake—so I don't worry about the headlights this time. Elmore gives me a grin and says, "Bet you wished you had that dock now, huh, Aggie?" Funny guy. Should move to the city and take that act on stage it's so funny.

I pull out my cell and call my guy, see if he's available. And whatta you know, he is. That's one of the things that make him so good at what he does. Now I'm gonna see how good he really is when I tell him about this special order I got.

"Ten pounds?" he says. Then he tells me he can do it, but with such short notice it's gonna run me an extra two-point-five. I can dig that. I used to charge extra when my clients wanted shit outside of regular business hours. And besides, with that kinda weight and the potential for future business with Mickey, this was a no-brainer.

"But we need a brand-new place," he says. "One we ain't ever used before."

And I ask, "Why?"

"'Cause one of my boys almost took a hit the other night, that's why," he tells me. "Cops musta heard from someone that something besides late-night fishing was going on over at some of the usual places, and they posted a Fish and Wildlife agent there, and my man barely got outta there with his ass."

Then my cook gives me a new access point to hook up, and I'm cool with that. The river's like a road to me, man. Tell me where to be, and I'll be there. That's one of the reasons I made plans to move to Florida one day. Oh, yeah. They got these restaurants that when you ask for directions, they say, "Which way you coming? Car or boat?" I love that.

So my cook says he can have my order in a few hours and then I gotta eat a little shit and tell him I can't have all the cash tonight, but if he'll spot me, I'll give him an extra thou tomorrow night. I can tell by his silence that he doesn't like that idea, but I've been a good steady customer, never given him any blowback or brought down any heat. And I remind him of that and let him know I've got a client who's gonna be looking for this kinda order more than just tonight and it's a win-win all around.

"Ya got any collateral?" he asks me. Everybody's a fucking banker and mathematician these days. I tell him I got ten thou on me and the only other thing I got that's worth anything is my boat, but I'm gonna need that to complete the deal.

"What about your house?" he says, and I'm like "What house? I got kicked outta my wife's dad's house and my dad's letting me live in his." He gets all quiet again and does something I don't remember him ever doing. He calls me by my first name—my *real* first name—and says he's checked up on me. Shit.

"Find out anything interesting?" I ask, trying to sound calm.

He laughs and says he found out that I had my dad's house legally put into my name last year when my dad had one of his "strokes." It was really one of his Wild Turkey Blackouts, but I told the lawyer it was a stroke so I could take charge of shit. For my dad's sake. My cook also says he knows I have power of attorney when it comes to my dad's "estate." My dad's "estate" is his house and the property. And since it's on the Redneck Riviera, its worth about ten times what he and Mom paid for it back in the seventies. Somebody buys that place, they'll knock the house down, split the land, and put up *two houses* and walk away with a killing.

Yeah, I'd been thinking about that. For what I can get for the house and that land, I could put my dad in an assisted living facility and put some serious cash into Brooklyn's college fund. Lord knows my ex ain't saving anything and her cheap-ass dad's money goes towards the country club and his twice-yearly trips to Vegas. And *I'm* the one not good with personal finances? Please.

Okay, so my guy knows more about me than I know about him. I can live with that, so I say, "Yeah, consider my dad's house as collateral." I gotta show I'm willing to take a risk, right? That's what The Donald says in his books. If you're not willing to take a risk, shut your mouth and enjoy the trailer park.

We agree to meet in two hours at the new access point. I tell him I've got a guy with me and he doesn't flinch. Just tells me I'm to bring all the cash I got. I ask him if he's just gonna trust me about the house and he says, "Yeah. I know where you live." Then he takes one of them dramatic pauses and says, "And Dorothy and your little dog, too." He's pulling the freakin' *Wizard of Oz* on me. Like he's the Wicked Witch and he's threatening Brooklyn and Marlboro.

That's when it really hit me that I better not fuck this up. He doesn't come right out and say it, but if he *does* know about Marlboro, he knows about Brooklyn, too. And right then and there, for the first time since I've been in the...recreational drug business, I want out. That's how much my little girl means to me. But somehow I don't think my guy's gonna go for that. I put it out there, he took it, and now it's his, right?

"Don't you worry," I say with a whole lot more confidence than I feel. "I'm good for this. You can count on me."

"I am," he says and then hangs up. That's when Elmore comes up to my window and taps on it. Shit, I didn't even notice he'd stepped out. He's smoking a cigarette and giving me that speed-it-up circle-in-the-air move with his other hand. I step outta the car and tell him we're set.

"Let's do it," he says. I tell him it's not gonna happen for a few hours so why doesn't he go back to town and pick up some burgers or something and I'll use my dad's truck to get the boat in the river and we can eat something on the way. He gives me a look like he doesn't know whether or not he can trust me and I'm like, "Where the fuck am I gonna go? We need this deal and we need it tonight. Just get me some burgers, fries and a shake." Damn, nobody trusts anybody any more, right?

"Gimme some cash," he says, and right there I

know—like I ever doubted it—he's a deadbeat. After paying for the gas, he ain't got enough on him to spot me a freakin' eight-dollar late-night dinner? I'm thinking I'm gonna have to talk to my ex about this guy. I give him a twenty and tell him to make it quick, and he gives me one of those snorts those types of assholes love to give to make themselves feel superior. So I know I'm the bigger man and I just ignore it.

So after he leaves, I pull my dad's truck out of the garage and back it up so I can hook up the trailer. This takes a couple of minutes 'cause I gotta be real quiet so I don't wake up my old man. I get it hooked up and, outta habit I guess, start backing it down towards the river. Which is stupid 'cause there ain't no dock there at the moment. Okay. I figure I can use my neighbor's dock. He won't mind; we share things all the time. I'd ask him, but I'm not even sure he's home. And even if he is, no use in waking him.

Now this takes some real-good maneuvering. I pull out into the road past my neighbor's driveway and make sure I got enough room to back up and ease all the way down to his dock. I'd done this once before with his boat when he was too drunk to do it, so I figure it'd be a piece of cake, right? And it woulda been, except when I'm backing the boat down, the security lights go on. He's got those ones that light up with motion detection or some shit. I'm cool with that until my neighbor comes out his back door in his boxers holding his shotgun and screaming at me to leave his boat alone. I can tell by the way he's screaming he's working on a good old drunk.

"Hey," I yelled, but in a whisper voice, which I realize is kinda stupid at this point, because if anything's gonna wake up my dad, this guy's already done it. "It's me."

He says, "I don't care who it is—Get the fuck away from my boat!"

"It's my boat," I whisper-yell at him. "Yours is still in the river." I point down to the river where his boat is and he turns his whole body, except the gun, which is still locked on me, and he sees his boat. He turns back and calls me by name.

"Yeah," I answer. "I just need to use your dock, man. Take it easy."

He lowers his gun and squints at me and says, "You going fishin'?"

"Yeah. Keep it down. You're gonna wake the neighborhood."

"Sorry," he says. And then, "Got any pot?"

Guy's drunker than a skunk and he wants to get higher. I tell him, yeah, I got some, just let me get my boat wet first and I'll give it to him. He smiles at me and goes over to the biggest tree in his yard, been there since Lincoln freed the slaves I think, and takes a leak. Guy doesn't even stop to think he's pissin' all over history. I back the boat into the river, tie it off, return my dad's car to the garage, and then head back to where my neighbor's finishing up his business and sticking his junk back into his boxers. I reach into my pocket and pull out a joint and give it to him.

"Thanks, man," he says and then pats his boxer shorts. "I'll get ya tomorrow, okay? Don't got no cash on me."

"It's on me," I tell him. "Call it even for using the dock."

"Cool," he says. "Anytime you wanna make a trade like that, it's good with me."

I give him a pat on the back and say, "That'll work," but it's not going to be too long before I get my dad's dock back. A new one, I mean. After tonight's deal, I'll be good to go and have some extra green to replace the one I borrowed from my dad.

I say goodnight to my neighbor, and the backyard gets all lit up again. This time it's headlights. Elmore with my dinner. "Fishing buddy?" my neighbor asks, and I'm, like, "Yeah. See ya in the morning."

I go over to Elmore and grab the bag of food and jog it over to the boat. Elmore stays by my car and I give him a *What the hell?* look and he waves me over. He opens the back driver's-side door and says, "Give me a hand, Aggie."

I don't know what he's talking about until I look in the back seat. He's got something back there that looks like a missile or something. Before I can even ask, he says, "It's a submersible tank."

Okay. What the fuck's a submersible tank, right?

"This is where we store the product while we're on the river." He can tell by the look on my face I'm not quite understanding him. So he talks slower. I hate that. Like I'm stupid or some shit. "We put the meth in here," he says. He leans over and holds up a chain. "We drag it behind the boat so it's underwater, and nobody sees a thing."

I think about that for a few and then smile. That's brilliant. Except for one thing.

"What if we get stopped on the river?" I ask. "Fish and Game? Conservation? Highway Patrol?"

"We're gonna be on the river, Aggie," he says. "What the hell does Highway Patrol have to do with anything?" Shows you what he knows. The Highway Patrol does the rivers, too. I tell him that and he's all surprised and I'm like, yeah, I've done this shit for a while now. I give him a look and wait for an answer.

Elmore smiles and taps the top of the submersible tank twice. He's back to being the expert now. "That's the beauty of this," he says like he's selling me some used car. "We get any unwanted attention, we let her loose—" he drops the chain "—and it sinks to the bottom of the river."

"And we're out all that product and money," I say. And, I don't say this part out loud, we gotta deal with a very unhappy Mickey.

"Nope. This is equipped with GPS, my man." Now he's really turning on the sales pitch. I'm about to ask if it comes with satellite radio when he says, "We drop our load, authorities don't catch us with anything but a cooler and a shit-eating grin, and when the coast is clear we go back and pick it up."

Okay, I think. *Now* it's brilliant. I'm starting to feel a whole lot better about this partnering up thing at this point.

Five minutes later we got the tank loaded on to the boat, and we get on our way. I pull out of the dock real slow and Elmore gives me a look.

"Gotta wait for the call," I tell him. "My guy's all about security. We'll go south for a bit, eat our food and probably hear from him before we're done."

"Probably?" Elmore says. "Who's calling the shots here, Aggie?"

"Right now, he is. Shit," I say in a big whisper and start looking around, "he might even be watching us now." I don't really think he is, but I want Elmore to lose a little of that smug attitude he's been carrying around all night, y'know? "Just eat."

We're about halfway through our meal—neither one of us could come up with anything to talk about—when his cell phone rings. He looks at the number and says to me, "I gotta take this." I shrug like I could give a crap and he walks to the back of the boat. He whispers "Hello," and starts to talk real low, but I can hear him.

"I felt better," he says. "And then a friend called and I went out for some dinner." So I know he's talking to my ex, right? She got home late with Brooklyn expecting to see lover boy on the couch or some shit and he ain't there, she gets all worried. She used to pull that with me. If she didn't know exactly where I was sometimes, she'd call and hound me with questions until I dragged my sorry ass home. She was always worried I was doing something I shouldn'ta been and she was right most of the time. Hell, she met me 'cause I was a dealer, man. Now she's all shocked and shit that I'm still wheeling and dealing and hanging out with customers. How the hell'd she think I was paying the rent and bills and shit? I tell ya, having that kid changed her more than it did me.

Anyways, I'm getting a good-sized chuckle outta watching Elmore try to explain to my ex why he ain't home sick, and of course he loves hanging out with her and Brooklyn, and he'll be home right after his late-night dinner with his buddy and they'll all go miniature golfing tomorrow. Then his voice gets lower and I hear him say, "Yeah, put her on." He turns and gives me a look, but I play it cool like I can't hear shit, but inside, I'm thinking this motherfucker's gonna be on the phone with *my daughter* right before the biggest deal of my career? Shit.

"Hey, honey," he says and he turns his back on me. *Honey?* He says a buncha other stuff I can't hear, and then I hear those words every father dreads coming from some man who ain't him. "I love you, too, Sweetie. Good night."

I love you?

My little girl is telling the guy who's fucking her mother that she loves him?

He shoves the phone into his pocket and turns around all nonchalant and shrugs. "Women," he says to me. "Told her I'd be outta pocket for the next half day or so. She shouldn't bother me anymore." I want nothing more than to take his cell phone and shove it down his goddamned throat. Instead I turn around and look up at the trees.

I love that time of night on the river. It's quiet and the bats are out doing that little dance they do as they're eatin' all those gnats and mosquitoes. They can eat their weight in one night, you know that? It's a fact. If it weren't for bats, we'd be ass-deep in those flying little insects that want nothing more than to suck all the blood outta us. Imagine that? Eating their weight in mosquitoes every night. I had some customers when I managed the all-you-can-eat place—that dumbass job lasted two days—that could do half that shit, but jeez, that's impressive.

So I'm thinking about Brooklyn and Elmore and my ex, and I musta been looking up longer than I thought 'cause something got in my eye and I start tearing up. I'm allergic to some of that shit that falls from the trees, y'know? I grab a napkin from the burger bag and wipe my eyes. Elmore steps over and asks me if I'm all right. I say, "Yeah," and blow my nose to get that snot out. Fucking allergies.

Then my phone rings. My first thought is maybe Brooklyn's calling *me* to say good night and tell me she loves me. I pull the phone out and the Caller ID reads *Unknown.*

It's my guy.

These calls always go the same way. I say *Hey* and he gives me the evening's access point and then he hangs up. Supposedly if I'm not at the access point in an hour, my cook's people hit the road. I say *supposedly* 'cause I've never been late. It's business, man. I may have my share of faults—ask my father-in-law if ya want a complete list of them, they're probably in his notebook—but tardiness is not one of them. Sometimes these points're on the river and sometimes they're on a tributary, but I pretty much know 'em all.

The access point's about forty or forty-five minutes away—and then we gotta get off the river and drive for about ten minutes—so we don't gotta go crazy, but we can't sit around enjoying the night all that much either. Elmore takes a seat and looks up at the sky. It's a pretty one, too. There's no moon out, so you could see the Milky Way and just about every other star up there. Always thought that was pretty cool: you could see the Milky Way and at the exact same time we're part of the Milky Way, y'know? Kinda puts things in perspective. Especially now.

So I'm just driving the boat and keeping my eye on the water in front of me. There's not much out here, but in the dark on a trip like this, the last thing I wanna do is run into a chunk of wood or some other river trash. Ran over part of dock two years ago and it screwed up my prop real good. Had to hobble back home. Not a good deal for that to happen anytime, but when I'm on the clock, I ain't gonna let it happen.

Every once in a while, I take my eye off the water and catch a glance of Elmore. He's got his eyes closed and enjoying the ride. I get the quick idea of making a real sharp turn and dropping him in the drink, but I figure he's more valuable on the boat than out at the moment. But that whole *I love you* shit with my daughter? I just know we're gonna conversate about that sometime soon.

"This is nice," he says to me. Like we really *are* late-night fishing buddies. He's still got his eyes closed and breathing in the nature. I feel like a goddamned tour guide. He wants to know how much more time and I tell him about thirty minutes and he does that thing with his ass people do when they're getting comfortable on a boat cushion. I half-expect him to ask me for a blanket and a cup of hot chocolate.

Little while later we start getting close to the turn-off. It's easy to see during the day—I know that from fishing—but I gotta really keep my eyes open at night. There's an old farmhouse about a hundred feet before I gotta turn and the guy's got a light he keeps lit down on his dock. I spoke to him about it one day when he was out there waterproofing the wood, and it turns out he keeps that light on every night just for folks to know the turn-off's coming up. That's real nice, right? Good ol' river hospitality. That's another reason I love living on the water. People look out for each other. I mean, this farmer: he's keeping that light on for people he doesn't even know. If that's not good people, I don't know what is.

Anyway, we come up to the light my cook told me to look for and I slow down a bit and there's just enough light out that I can see the trib coming up. I'm making better time than I figured and figure we'll be at least ten minutes early. Like I said, promptness in this business is good. Don't keep people waiting—especially heavily armed people—and you'll do fine.

I take the turn and in ten minutes we're at the new access point. There's nobody there 'cause it's late at night and my guy's guys are never early. They're always on time and ready to motor as soon as they show up. I'll bet you they ain't never been parked for more than a minute in the whole time I been working with them. I'm there, they check me out for the cash and make sure I'm not packing, and we're good to go. Smooth.

So now we're early and I cut the engine. Elmore doesn't seem to notice, so I let him just sit there with his eyes closed and toss my anchor in the water. I can really go for a beer at this point, y'know? Bobbing up and down, nice breeze blowing, and the tree frogs doing their nighttime back and forth. I love that sound. One croaks in one tree and right after that the other chimes in, and it's like they're telling each other about their day.

"Caught five flies today. Croak, croak."

"How're the kids? Croak croak."

Nice life those frogs got. Hang out on the river all day, eat as much as they want, bullshit all night in the trees. Sounds like a decent retirement plan to me.

Anyway, the headlights show up, just like they always do. The driver flashes 'em twice, and I pull up the anchor and bring the boat as close to the ramp as I can, drop the anchor again, and slip off the boat. Elmore gives me a look and I tell him he's gotta get a little wet if he wants to do business with my guy. To his credit, he keeps his mouth shut—for once that night—and gets right in and wades through the water to join me on the ramp.

The driver comes out, and his passenger gets in the back. Just like every time. The driver comes over, pats us down. "Left my gun on the boat, Amigo," Elmore says.

Now, I worry that crack's not gonna go over real well, 'cause the guy he calls Amigo is an actual, real-live Mexican. Guess he gets that a lot, though, 'cause he lets it slide. I've seen him—Amigo—a few times over the past year—they're all Mexicans, by the way. My cook never sends the same guys twice in a row for security reasons or the driver gets too friendly with the dealer, and all of a sudden they're starting to cut deals without the distributor, and all shit breaks loose.

That always makes me grin. Here's a bunch of Mexicans doing the grunt work for my cook and me, and we live in an area where the folks are always complaining about illegal immigrants taking jobs from Americans. I don't see a helluva lot of Americans lining up to drive for my guy, y'know? My guess is they work for him a few months, go back down to Acapulco or San Juan or some shit for a few, and then come back. If they ain't in the states all that long, they're harder for the cops to get a line on. My guy's smart like that, and he ain't ever told me that's what he does—why would he?—but that's my guess.

These assholes out here, the ones always screaming about illegal immigration and "Let's Keep American Jobs in America" shit? I'd like to see them at the grocery store if those farm jobs went to Americans and ya had to pay them minimum wage. Love to see the faces on the anti-illegals crowd when they gotta pay five bucks for a head of lettuce or ten dollars a pound for chicken. Who the hell do they think keeps their foods so cheap, huh? *Jesus?* They don't think about it, that's the answer. A lot of my clients would probably shit themselves if my guy paid *real* Americans to do the job this driver and the other guys are doing. Especially my politician clients. Might hafta to shell out a little extra for their daily hits. And these are the same guys voting against immigration reform and shit. Cracks me up.

So we pass the pat-down, and Amigo tells Elmore to sit in the back with the other guy, and I get in the front like usual. I like that. Me and Amigo, we kinda know each other, and he's not gonna stick me in the back seat like some rookie would. Probably not gonna kick me in the nuts, either. Exactly the kinda guy I can see doing some sideline business with, and exactly why my cook probably ain't gonna send him for the next few pickups.

Now, there's no talking on the drive to wherever we're going. There never is. We just drive and, less than ten minutes later, there we are. And tonight's no different. We drive for about eight minutes when Amigo turns onto a dirt road and we pull up to a gate at the entrance to a limestone quarry.

This is a new one for me. I mean, it's a real place of

business, not some secluded dark spot where we usually end up. But my cook, he knows what he's doing, I guess. Hiding in plain sight, I think they call it.

The guy in the back with Elmore gets out and opens the gate, and Amigo pulls in. Back-seat Guy gets back in, we drive about another minute, and pull in between a couple of big yellow trucks. I mean, the tires were bigger than the car we were in, y'know? Before I know what's going on, my cook gets out of one of the trucks. Just climbs on down like he owns the thing, and I'm thinking maybe he does.

I'm not sure if I told you, but my cook? He's really big. I mean, like, played-linebacker-in-college big. He's got a big head attached to this big body, and you can tell he works out. Watching him get outta that truck is kinda like watching an alien get outta his spaceship. I mean, I *imagine* that's what it's like—not that I ever seen an alien getting outta a spaceship, not even when I was high.

Amigo tells us to get out of the car—I never get out until I'm told—and my cook takes one look at Elmore and says, "This your partner?" I say yeah, and my cook looks at Elmore for about ten seconds and says, "I know you?"

Elmore shakes his head and says, "I don't think so. I don't get out all that much."

My cook smiles at that—not the kinda smile where you find something funny, more like the kind where you know the other guy thinks he said something funny and you're just going along with it—and says, "Yeah, me neither."

My cook turns to me and says, "So. You're stepping

up your business model a notch or two, huh?"

"I guess you can say that. Figured it's worth a shot, y'know?"

He nods and says, "No going back after a deal like this. You start playing in the majors, you're not gonna wanna go back to Triple A. It's a whole new ballgame at this level, my man."

"I know," I say, but I really didn't. I just wanted him to think I did. "Let's do it," I say, and he's all smiles. He nods to Amigo, who goes over to the other yellow truck and climbs up into the cab and comes back out with a large gym bag. He drops the bag in front of me and nods at it, telling me to take a look inside. I bend over and unzip the bag, and there's ten bricks that look just like the one I sold earlier, and I say, "Cool."

"Glad you approve," my cook says. "Your turn."

I reach into my pocket and pull out the cash and hand it to Amigo. That's when it occurred to me that I've never seen my cook actually touch any money or any of the product. It's all done by his guys, and I'm thinking again how smart my cook is and how, if he's ever caught, it ain't gonna be 'cause he left his fingerprints on some incriminating evidence.

"So here's the deal, my man," he says. "You do what you gotta do with this product and bring me the rest of my money tomorrow, right?"

I nod and then I hear Elmore behind me mumble something like he's agreeing—reminding me and my cook and Amigo and the other guy that we're partners or some shit.

"I'll call you tomorrow night," I say. "Same bat time, same bat channel." That came out sounding a lot more stupid than I thought. I was just trying to keep things light 'cause I'm real nervous.

"Whatever," my cook says. "Just understand the level of trust I'm displaying here." He points at the bag and says, "That's one helluva lotta product for me to be giving you on consignment. You come back tomorrow night one dime short of what we agreed to, you're not going back to the minors, understand?"

I did understand this time, and I tell him how much I appreciated his trust. "I don't need your appreciation," he says. "I need your cash. Or whoever's cash it's gonna be. That's appreciation enough for me, my man."

"I gotcha," I tell him.

"All right. You can go."

Just like that. My guy doesn't waste any time. I got the product, I got the general idea what happens if I don't come through, and there's nothing left to talk about. I also remember what he said about my dad's house and knowing I got a daughter. He coulda repeated that, but he didn't have to. Like I said, my cook's a man of just enough words, and those words about my dad and Brooklyn don't need repeating.

So we get back in the car and Amigo takes another route back to the access point, and just like that Elmore and I are back on the boat with more product than I've ever held before.

"How's that feel, Aggie?" Elmore says. And before I can answer, he says, "Before you met me, you were nickel-and-diming your way through this shit. Me being home sick tonight was the best thing to ever happen to your career." Then he takes big pause and, I swear to God, he bows and says, "You're welcome."

I tried to come up with a smart remark, but I couldn't—probably because he's right: it took this asshole giving me the kick in the ass I needed to show a little ambition. If I could pull this off, I *am* playing with the big boys. A couple of paydays like this and I'm that much closer to Florida, and Brooklyn's that much closer to college. I'm thinking I may have to start up the handyman thing again, at least for a while, so I have some sort of job that shows some income. That's how they got Capone, you know. Truth be told, I kinda like that handyman stuff. Building things, wrecking things. Putting in a deck—shit, putting in my dad's new dock is gonna be fun—with the music playing, working in the sun. That's good, clean work. Not like...well, you know.

Before I get too lost in my own thoughts, I hear Elmore say, "Okay, Aggie. Let's get back to work." He looks at his phone and says, "What time ya got?" I look at my wrist and tell him. "Good," he says. "Me, too. We got a few hours before sunrise. I gotta hand it to ya, you made that happen."

He's right, y'know. I did. I saw an opportunity—I guess that's the word for it when your plans don't go the way you think they're gonna go and you make the best of it—and I took it. Now I really could use a beer. I feel like celebrating and the deal ain't even done yet, but I took care of my end and nothing tastes better than a beer after a job well done.

Elmore goes over to the submersible tank he brought and opens it up. We put the product in, and it occurs to me that this thing'll hold five times the amount we just put in. I shake that thought outta my head. Here I am in the middle of the biggest transaction of my life and I'm thinking about timesing it by five? Shit, boy, I say to myself. Get a grip. How much is enough, right?

Elmore shows me the waterproof lining, closes up the tank, locks it up, and then we drop it into the river. It sinks, and then the chain gets tight. Looks just like an anchor if anyone who didn't know better looked at it.

I pull up the real anchor, turn the boat around, and head back home. Slow. I'm thinking I know there's beer in my dad's fridge, but I also know it's probably not a great idea to dull the senses until this job is complete. It's like that in baseball sometimes. You got a three-run lead going into the bottom of the ninth and you think you got the game sewed up. You walk one guy, next guy gets a bloop hit over the first baseman's head, and the next thing you know you got runners on the corners, and the tying run's coming up to the plate and it's their best hitter. Happens like that. No, the best thing to do right now is to head right over to the access point where we told Mickey we'd be at sunrise. I'm thinking we'll be early, but I wanna get that worm and shit, right? So we're off.

Back on the river, I can see the chain to the tank and the tank itself is breaking the water every once in a while. I've never done it, but it reminds me of those shows on TV where the guys are going deep-sea fishing and their catch is working the line. There I am thinking about Florida again and all the shit I'm gonna do down there when this part of my life ends. I could get one of those jobs on a fishing boat. Cutting up bait and setting the lines for those rich assholes who want a picture of themselves fishing more than they want the actual fish. Maybe even get my own boat and hire it out. The guys on TV seem to be making money hand over fist doing that kinda stuff. I mean, I'm making my living on a boat now anyways, right? Might as well be escorting those rich guys around as doing this shit. You don't see any reality shows about my line of work, do ya?

That'd be cool, though. *Keeping Up with the Tweakers. The Real Drug Dealers of the Midwest.* Let's see The Learning Channel put that shit on. Maybe The Food Channel's more like it. "Tonight we're going to show you how to cook ten pounds of crystal for that holiday meth head gathering." Shit, that'd be funny.

We get to the meeting site early, and I drop anchor and, instead of a beer, right about now I'd kill for a cup of coffee. I got some warm water on the boat, so I drink some of that and hand another bottle to Elmore. He says, "Thanks," and then, "How much longer we gotta wait, Aggie?" I tell him to enjoy the water and the quiet, 'cause it's gonna get busy around here pretty soon. He does that shruggy thing I'm really starting to not like, but he keeps his mouth shut and drinks his water.

About an hour later, the sky's starting to get a little light. I look over to the boat ramp and—there's some bushes up in there—I see the bushes start to move like there's an animal moving through. I figure it's a deer probably coming down for a quick drink, y'know. But the next thing I know, I see it's Mickey. No car, no boys, no nobody. Just him, all by his lonesome. He waves us over and gives a look around like he's making sure we're all alone. I nudge Elmore with my foot and he looks over at Mickey.

"The fuck's up with him?" he asks. Like I know. I'm about to yell over to Mickey, but then I realize we're supposed to be on the down low out here and don't wanna draw any unwanted attention from anyone who might be around. I give him a sign that we're gonna pull up, and he gives me one back that says okay. I still don't see any of his guys, but I'm more focused on pulling the boat up close to the ramp and not getting too wet getting out. I tell Elmore to leave the gun on the boat, but he says no and he sticks it in his belt behind him. I don't think that's a great idea, but he's the one with the gun.

I maneuver the boat in pretty smoothly, drop anchor, and me and Elmore get out and walk over to Mickey, who's still in the bushes. Now keep in mind, the product's still behind the boat and under water, so Mickey can't see shit. My original plan was to surprise him and show off how creative me and my new partner could be, but now I'm kinda glad he doesn't know where the stuff is, as something ain't the way it's supposed to be. I'm not sure what, but something is off. Like where the hell is Mickey's car? And Mickey's boys? And before I can even ask him, Mickey pulls out a big-ass gun and points it at me. It's a few feet from my face but I can practically feel it burning a hole between my eyes.

You know that gun Clint had in the Dirty Harry movies? This one's bigger. At least that's the way it seems up close and pointed at me. And Mickey's all like, "What the fuck, Agatha? What the fuck?"

I wanna say *What the fuck?* too, but he's the one with the gun, so I figure I better be as polite as I can be. I take a deep breath and say—very slowly—"I don't know what you're talking about, Mickey."

I was gonna add the word "honestly," but that's what people who lie do. I don't need to use the word because I *am* being honest. I'm just hoping he can hear it in my voice how honest I'm being. You know how sometimes when you're scared, you don't speak normal and it can sound like you're not telling the truth? That's not the impression I wanna give off.

But Mickey starts shaking his head and he says, "What the fuck?" again and then he looks at Elmore, who I hope is thinking about the gun he's got in his belt and how he's gonna get to it before Mickey figures it out. "Maybe it was you, huh?" Mickey says.

"Maybe *what* was me, man?" Elmore says, and he sounds a lot more comfortable with a gun in his face than I do, I'll tell you that.

Mickey starts moving the gun from me to Elmore, back and forth, back and forth. Elmore starts scratching his back and I'm thinking, this is it, he's gonna pull his— my—piece, but he doesn't. Mickey starts breathing all heavy and I'm thinking he's gonna bust an artery or something, and I only hope it happens before he pulls the trigger on that cannon he's holding. Remember that look I told you he gets in his eyes? It's different this time, more intense or something.

"My guys," he says. "They all got busted. About an hour after you two left. Pretty fucking coincidental, don't you think?"

I don't know what to think, and that's what I'm about to tell Mickey when Elmore beats me to it. "You think we called the cops on you after making the deal last night?" he says. "No offense, man, but we won't treat you like you're stupid if you don't treat us like we are."

No offense. That's what people say when they know what comes out of their mouth next may be offensive. It's like the word "honestly." I also don't think it's a great idea to use the word "stupid" to someone who's holding a gun on you. I'm pretty sure the next thing I'm gonna hear is *BANG!* but he just stares at Elmore's face, looking like he's trying to figure out how many bites he'd have to take out of it before it's all gone, y'know? And Mickey's breathing picks up again.

"Mickey," I say. "Why would we call the cops and then head out and score a shitload of product from my guy and then head back here and meet you like nothing happened?" Then another thought comes to me, and I debate about whether or not to say it out loud, then I do: "How'd *you* get away?" And right away I wish I could grab those words back and shove 'em down my throat.

Mickey gives me that look. He says, "What? You think I dropped a dime on my own boys and then headed over here so I can keep the score for myself?"

I *didn't* think that, but now that he says it, it sounds like something someone might do. I shake my head no, and say, "I didn't say that, Mickey. I was just wondering how come you didn't get popped."

Mickey gets a look on his face that I can only describe as something like he's embarrassed. "I was taking a leak," he says. I wait for him to explain—hoping he'll put the gun down, too, but he doesn't—and he takes a deep breath and says, "I was outside the trailer taking a piss. John D keeps his double-wide like a pigpen, and the bathroom's worse than a port-a-potty. So I'm in the woods killing bushes when three cop cars show up and it's like Christmas in the trailer park. So I zip up and duck down, and thirty minutes later the trailer's empty— except for one cop standing guard—and I get the hell out of there and head over here to see if you guys are gonna show up."

At this point, he looks us both in the eyes again and does lower the gun. "I didn't think you would," he says. "Show up, I mean. Figured you two got popped after you left and gave us up in exchange for not getting yourselves busted. If you two didn't show, I'da found you and killed you so hard your families woulda felt it. But," and here's where he finally tucks the gun back in his pants, "since you did show up, it obviously wasn't you guys. I'm thinking maybe it was Ross. He's been all bitchy lately and making noise about doing bigger deals and how he's got expenses and shit. The fuck he think I was doing tonight? This was a bigger deal, right?"

I say, "Right," and Elmore says, "Yeah," and now we're all in this mess together, because I'm starting to get the idea that Mickey's gonna have problems coming up with the cash he needs, which means I'm not gonna have the cash I need, and my cook's not gonna give two shits about some police bust in Trailer Park Heaven. It just goes to show you: the higher up the food chain, the bigger the problems you get.

And now I realize why the look in Mickey's eyes is different. It took me a while 'cause I never seen that look before from him. He's scared. Just like me. Maybe not as shitless, but...Here's this guy who practically makes me wanna piss my pants when he gives me The Look, and he's got fear in *his* eyes. I guess we're all afraid of something—or someone—huh? So I start wondering who Mickey's afraid of and figure it's probably the guy he takes the product to after I give it to him. I got my guy, Mickey's got his guy. And then my mind starts to wander—ever notice how close the word *wander* is to *wonder?*—who *that* guy's afraid of. And I imagine, if I thought about it long enough, it goes all the way up to God, right? Another reason I'm glad I'm not a religious guy.

Obviously I don't got time to think about that all that much and good thing I got Elmore there to remind of that, because he says, "Whatta we gonna do now, fellas? We got ten pounds of product and no place to go with it." He looks at Mickey and says, "I assume the cops got the money?" Mickey nods. Elmore says, "That sucks. It's not like we can return this shit."

Thank you, Captain Obvious. That's just what every situation that goes to shit needs: somebody pointing out that the situation's gone to shit. How about a suggestion, Elmore? Anyway, the three of us are standing there for about a minute when Elmore does come up with a suggestion.

"I know a guy," he says. "On the other side of the bridge."

Now, we've been on and off the water so much, I truly cannot remember off the top of my head which side of the bridge we're *on* at the moment, but I keep my mouth shut in the hopes that whatever comes outta Elmore's mouth next is gonna be worth listening to.

"He's got a ranch."

Yippee kay aye! "Lots of people have ranches, Elmore," I point out.

"Yeah," he says, "but this guy's ranch ain't just about

horses and cattle. He's got a fleet of delivery trucks, and he's a buttlegger."

There's a new word for me, and I almost start to giggle. "What the hell difference does it make if he's straight or gay?" I ask. "We need to move this product, or we're the ones whose butts are getting legged."

Elmore lets out a big ol' laugh. It's the same laugh he gave me before—like he knows more than I do—and I feel like somehow grabbing Mickey's cannon and shutting Elmore up for good. Which reminds me: Why the hell hasn't Elmore pulled out my gun, now that Mickey's put his away?

"He smuggles cigarettes, Aggie," he says. "Truckloads of cigarettes. And, I happen to know, he's got some trucks on his property right now that need to be driven over the state line and have their loads distributed."

I look at him and I wanna laugh too, except for the fact that we're fucked here and Elmore's thinking about cigarettes. "How the hell are a few truckloads of smokes gonna help us outta this mess, Elmore?" I ask.

He looks at me and shakes his head; I'm the dumb hillbilly again. Maybe I should just go on home and watch a rerun o*f Dukes of Hazard* or some shit. "You know what an excise tax is?" he says. I shake my head no. "It's what the state adds on to each pack of cigarettes before the seller can sell them."

More math, man, right? So I just say, "Okay."

Then he says, "You have any idea what the cigarette excise tax is in this state?" I don't even answer that, 'cause I think I already did. "Seventeen cents," he says. "You know what it is in Chicago?" He must have seen the look on my face because without pausing he says, "Six dollars and sixteen cents."

Now, I may not be the best guy in math—we've discussed that—but even I know that's a difference of six dollars. Still don't sound like much money, and I tell as much to Elmore. "So?" I say.

"*Per pack*," he says, and then goes into his college professor mode. "There's ten packs of smokes in a carton. Each of my guy's trucks are holding three hundred cases of cigarettes and each case holds six hundred packs." Here's where Elmore starts using his hands. "Three times six is eighteen, add four zeroes, and you get one hundred and eighty thousand packs. Multiply that by six dollars and you're on the plus side of a million dollars."

Mickey and I let out a deep breath at the same time. I think we both had the same idea: what the fuck were we dealing with crystal meth for when the smoke business is so much more lucrative?

"So," I say. "We drive these smokes across the state line and over to Chicago, and all of the sudden we're making a six-dollar profit?"

"First of all," Elmore says, "there ain't no *we*. There's my guy and he needs drivers, who get a cut of the profits. Second, nobody's making a *six-dollar profit*. That's what they call a Ponzi scheme, and people get in trouble for shit like that."

"Whatever," I say. "As long as we make enough from *your guy* so we can pay *my guy*." Soon as I said that, that old song went through my head. The one my mom used to play all the time. "Nothing you can do 'cause I'm stuck like glue..." She always had the oldies playing.

Elmore keeps talking. "My guy needs three drivers to get these cigarettes across the state line and just about two hours outside of Chicago."

"What's he do with them then?" I ask.

"He's a distributor," Elmore says. "He distributes them. Throughout Chicago. He sells them for a profit of...let's say two bucks a pack, and then his buyers turn around and sell them for a profit and..."

"What's he paying?" Mickey interrupted about a half-second before I could. Elmore says he doesn't know, but he can make a quick call and find out. I notice the sky's getting lighter now. He pulls out his cell phone—again, if he can do that, why not my gun?—and after about ten seconds, he starts talking.

"It's me," he says. "Yeah, I know. I gotta coupla guys here with me who could use some quick cash. Real quick." He pauses for a bit and says, "I think they might go for something closer to a buck a pack." More silence.

That's what I hate most about people talking on their cell phones, you know? It's not the volume, it's that you're only getting one side of the conversation. It's like watching a TV show and pressing the mute button every ten seconds. I'd rather be next to the loudest asshole in the world talking to the second loudest asshole in the world than have to listen to a whole cell phone conversation where I'm only getting half the story. After a while it drives you nuts trying to figure out what the other guy's saying, and I start filling in shit and I know I'm wrong. Anyway, Elmore starts talking again and says, "Yeah, they'll go for seventy-five, but it's gotta be in cash."

He's quiet again, listening, and says, "Because we got

a cash deal over here that just went south and they're in need." Pause. "If it works out, I'll let you know. But just out of curiosity, any of these guys on the other end in need of some high-quality crank?" He stops talking and then, "Because I might be able to get my hands on some. And since it looks like we're gonna be on the road anyway…"

Elmore lets that last thought hang there for a bit and gives Mickey and me the thumbs-up sign. "Okay," Elmore says. "We'll be by the ranch in under thirty minutes. Who's gonna meet us? Okay, why isn't he driving for you?" Elmore looks at me and mimes somebody steering a car and drinking; the guy who's meeting us must've had his license pulled for drunk driving. Yeah, I thought. Wouldn't wanna get pulled over with a suspended license when you're transporting a million bucks of illegal smokes across state lines. "Okay," Elmore says. "I'll call you when we're on the road." He listens for a little bit longer, and then he hangs up.

"What's the deal?" Mickey asks.

Elmore smiles and says, "First of all, you're welcome. Not only did I just save your asses, you're walking away with a profit."

"What's the deal?" I say.

"Seventy-five cents a pack," he says. "And before you give yourself a brain hernia, that's one hundred and thirty-five thousand dollars. Split three ways—which is *really* fucking generous of me since I arranged the whole thing—is forty-five thou each." He looks at me and says, "What time you gotta be back with the cash?"

"My guy likes to do business as close to midnight as

possible," I say. "Tonight—this morning—was an exception, but let's say midnight. Tonight."

"Cool," Elmore says. "That gives us plenty of time to get the trucks, drive to Illinois, make the drop and get back here without having to break the speed limit."

Mickey says, "What about the meth? Your guy want any of that?"

Now all of the sudden Mickey's talking like he wants to partner up with us, 'cause he knows we got the product he needs and *my partner* just saved his ass. Besides, as of a coupla hours ago, Mickey's apparently all out of partners for the foreseeable future. Funny how this shit turns around like that. Crazy fucking business.

"He'll let us know on the way there," Elmore says. "He's gotta make some calls and see who's out there needing. So," Elmore slaps his hands together as if this were his plan the whole time. "Seems like the only one of us who's got wheels is you, Aggie. Which means we gotta head back to your old man's place and trade the boat for the car."

Less than ten minutes later we're back on the river, and Mickey's got no freakin' clue we're dragging all that product behind us. I can see him looking around the boat, wondering where the hell the shit was and chomping at the bit, wanting to say something, but he doesn't, 'cause that wouldn't be cool. So we just cruise to my dad's, dock the boat at my neighbor's, and after we get tied off, Elmore turns to Mickey and says, "Give me your piece."

Mickey gets those eyes again—the ones that drill a hole through you—and says, "Excuse me?"

Elmore repeats himself and, without taking his eyes

off of Mickey's, he adds, "If you don't give me your gun, you don't get to see the product. And before you even think of doing anything stupid, without us you're pretty much screwed. So just gimme your piece, we'll load up the car and head over to the ranch. All goes well, our business is done in"—he looks at his watch—"eighteen hours. Then we go our separate ways."

Well, two things: Mickey clearly ain't used to being spoken to like that, and he doesn't strike me as the kind of guy who just gives his gun up. I can see his brain working this out, and I get the feeling he'd like nothing more than to blow the two of us into the river and call it a night. But he knows Elmore's right. So he pulls out the gun, hands it to Elmore, and says, "Where the fuck's the product?"

Elmore takes Mickey's gun and chucks it into the water. Then he reaches behind him, and finally pulls out my gun. He smiles and says, "It's not loaded." Then he tosses that gun into the river.

I'm about to scream and he says, "You know how your ex is with a loaded piece around the house and Brooklyn. I heard you breaking in and grabbed it before I had a chance to get to the bullets." He gives me a shit-eating grin and then moves to the back of the boat.

He bends down and pulls on the chain that's connected to the submersible, and up comes the stuff. Mickey gets this look on his face like a little kid who's just got a peak behind the magician's curtain and he's, like, "Holy mother of shit."

Elmore pulls the tank onto the boat and says, "Let's get this somewhere safe."

And I'm, like, yeah, right. "Like where?" The safest

SMOKED

place that shit's been all night was in the river, and that's
not possible at the moment. It crosses my mind for a
second that maybe we can stick it in my ex's house in the
false wall again, but, like I said, that thought only lasts
about a second. The second safest place I can think of is
on us, but I don't feel like driving round-trip to Illinois
carrying this much weight, y'know? I can see Mickey's
mind working hard on this, but there's no way this side
of Hell Elmore and me are gonna trust any idea he's got.
So I'm thinking—hell, I'm hoping—Elmore's got one
more trick up his sleeve.

"Friend of mine's got a storage shed just over the
river," Elmore tells us. He pulls a key ring outta his
pocket and jingles them. "He gave me a key, just in
case."

"Who's this friend?" I ask.

"It doesn't matter who it is," Elmore says. "What
matters is he's out of town most of the time, which is
why he gave me the key. The storage unit's about five
minutes away from my guy with the ranch and the
trucks of smokes."

Mickey scratches his head and says, "You got a lotta
fuckin' friends, Elmore." That's what I was just
thinking. He's got more friends than a dirty politician.

That made Elmore smile. "My mama always told me
if you pick your friends carefully, they'll watch your
back," Elmore says. "I doubt this is what she had in
mind, but she was one wise woman, my mother. And
unless either of you guys got a better idea, I say we go
with the storage unit. Hardly anybody goes there much,
and I've never seen a security guard there. The meth's
gonna be there such a short time it ain't gonna have time

152

to get comfortable. Best-case scenario: my buttlegger calls me back and says he found a meth buyer before we get to the storage unit, we make a change."

The three of us think about it for a bit. At least Mickey and I do; Elmore's mind is obviously already made up. After about a minute and neither of us coming up with anything else, we agree to Elmore's idea. Hell, he's been running the show for the past couple of hours anyway, why stop now?

So we load the stuff into a duffel back and put it in my car—I got this space between the back seat and the trunk where I store some bigger loads of my shit sometimes. Then we're on our way, over the river and through the woods to Elmore's friend's storage unit we go.

Elmore's driving this time, and we get off at the exit for the winery up on the hill. Took my ex there once when we were still doing that romantic stuff. It's got a nice back deck where you can take in the city and watch the boats go up and down the river. Be a nice place to celebrate when this deal is all said and done. But with who?

We get to the storage place, and I'm expecting to see a gate, but there is none. Weird, right? Anyway, Elmore drives around, and after a few minutes he parks in front of the unit I guess he's looking for. We sit in the car for a bit and, like he said, there's no security that we can see. So we all get out, and Elmore unlocks the storage door, and raises it. It makes one of those sounds like it hasn't been touched in years, and I'm thinking it's *Silence of the Lambs* time and we're gonna find an old jalopy with a headless body. Love that film. Can't believe that Clarice chick's gay.

Of course, now that it's open, I see it's nothing like the movie. There's mostly a bunch of boxes, neatly stacked along the back wall. There's also a bike and a kayak and some old exercise equipment. The kinda shit people store 'cause they tell themselves they're gonna use it again someday, but never really do. Just donate that shit, man, or sell it on Ebay or something. You stick an old treadmill in a storage unit, I got news for you: you ain't treading on it anymore.

Anyway, we get the product out of the car and split it up between the boxes along the wall. One brick per box. And, just to be safe, I get the idea to put some of the exercise shit in front of the boxes so it looks all random, you know? Not that I actually think anyone's coming into the unit except us. But the way this night's been going, who the hell knows what's gonna happen next?

That's when I start thinking, what do we need Mickey for? He was my buyer, and now he's not in a position to buy shit. Okay, he's gonna drive one of the trucks and get a third of the delivery fee, but that third that's going to him should really be going to me in exchange for the meth we just stored in the boxes. That was our deal, and I held up my end. Just 'cause he ran into some crappy luck, why does that have to affect my bottom line? I probably woulda thought of that sooner, except he had the gun before, and I wasn't thinking clear. Right now though, at this particular moment, the only thing he's bringing to the party is his driver's license, and for that he's gonna get close to forty-five thousand dollars?

I know I need to think on that some more, and I'm

still pissed that my gun was unloaded this whole time. If I'd just had, like, one more hair on my balls when me and Elmore were back at my ex's house and I'd just walked past him, I wouldn't even be in this situation right now. It's like Ray Charles said: if it wasn't for bad luck, I'd have no luck at all.

That's when I decide that sometime soon my luck is gonna hafta start changing. And this time in the positive direction. Grampa used to say you make your own luck in this world and I see what he meant.

Yeah, one more would be good. You're a good listener and I appreciate that. I'll tell you, not so long from now, *your* luck's gonna change a bit. Just wait, I'm not lying. *Honestly.* Aw, I'm just messin' with ya. But I got you covered, you'll see. I'm gonna ask a little favor or two, but it'll all work out and you'll be on the upside before the end of the evening, just be patient. Ya got my word on that.

Anyway, I start thinking, depending on how the rest of the day and night goes, and if we actually get the money that Elmore says we are gonna get, maybe I'll switch over to the buttlegging business. Hell, I already got the nickname, right? *Smoke.* Pretty good nickname for a guy who's gonna start making some cash off of the difference in...whatever that's called. Exercise taxes? I figure I'll clear my debts with this trip to Illinois, stay the hell outta the meth business from now on, and stick to products that can be rolled up in paper and smoked.

Whatever deal Elmore and Mickey wanna make with each other, that's their business. I do wanna stay on Elmore's good side, 'cause he has the connection to the guy on the ranch who's got the connections outside

Chicago, so my plan is to just keep on smiling and do what Elmore says and make my own luck. This trip goes well, I don't see a reason Elmore's guy won't ask us to do more trips, and that sits a helluva lot better with me than having to meet Mexicans up and down the river at different meeting sites all the time. I need a little stability in my life. I'll miss Amigo a bit, sure, but I'll be just fine, driving and selling pot to my usual customers. Like I was thinking, maybe I'll even start taking the home repair thing more seriously. It ain't the best job in the world, but even on my worst days doing that, I don't remember anyone pulling a gun on me.

So just as we're locking the unit up, Elmore's phone rings. It's his guy again, and judging by the side of the conversation I can hear, his guy doesn't want anything to do with our product. Can't say I blame him. Why get your feet wet in someone else's pool when yours is already filled up with cash? Elmore hangs up and says, "Let's go to the ranch, boys." And we do.

By the time we get to the ranch, the sun's pretty much all the way up and, I gotta admit, I get a little nervous about the plan. Driving three truckloads of illegal smokes across state lines in the middle of the day? I don't know. I tend to keep my nefarious doings done in the dark, but maybe this *was* a good idea. We'd blend in with the rest of the traffic between here and Illinois. Long as we spread out and keep to the speed limit, we should be pretty much invisible.

Elmore pulls up to the barn—the three trucks are parked behind it—and a guy who I'm pretty sure is his guy comes out leading this beautiful horse. I told you I'm good with animals, right? Well, this one's a winner. I can tell by the face and the thighs. Damn, I start thinking, if this is what you get with the buttlegging biz, count me in. Brooklyn loves horses, and I know they got ranches down in Florida. I swear to God I got goose bumps thinking about that. Florida and horses? Man.

We all get out of the car and Elmore introduces me and Mickey using our code names, and I'm grateful he calls me Aggie instead of Agatha. His guy's name is Robert—or at least that's what he says it is—and he seems pretty cool with the idea of three complete strangers driving his trucks and his stuff several hours away. He tells us all the gas tanks're full and then gives us each a hundred-dollar bill to fill 'em back up for the ride back. No credit cards for this guy. Smart, right?

"I expect you guys back here by mid-afternoon," he says. Then he tells us he's planning on having a barbecue and we're invited. But I don't think I'll be able to make it, 'cause I'm thinking about the rest of the night's plans and how I hafta get the money to my cook by midnight, and I don't think I can enjoy a BBQ with all that on my mind. But I'll take a rain check, I tell myself. I wanna come back here and check out Robert's operation—cigarettes and horses.

Now Robert musta seen me admiring his horse, 'cause he brings him over to me and says, "You got a good eye, Aggie. This here's my lead stud, Moe."

"You a breeder?" I ask him, and he tells me he's got someone for that but, yeah, the ranch is part recreational and part stud farm. I reach up and touch Moe's face and, man, I love it. You have any idea how much a horse like that'll go for? At least a half million. You just take him around and have him get all romantic with your mares and spread his seed all over and, before you know, you got little Moes all over the place.

I recently heard that horse rustling is making a comeback. Now, that's a lowlife if you ask me—taking another man's horse—but you can see the profit in it. Horse like Moe could bring in a coupla hundred thou year with stud fees. It's like printing money. But to steal a horse? That takes a special kinda soulless crook. They used to string up horse thieves back in the day, and maybe that's what they should do now. Steal a man's horse and you get lynched. Publicly. I bet that'd put an end to it.

Anyway, Robert wants us back before dinner, so we say our goodbyes and, before we take off in the three semis, me, Elmore and Mickey make sure we all got each other's cell phone numbers. Anything happens on the road, we'll be in touch.

Takes us about twenty minutes to get to the interstate, but once we do, we're each doing about seventy—five miles above the speed limit—and people are passing us anyway. Okay with me, just as long as we don't look like three guys illegally transporting cigarettes across state lines.

I hate the interstate, by the way. This is such a beautiful state, and all you get to see of it from the highway is fast food joints and billboards for everything from Christian ads to gun shops to sex shops. I know a rich guy from town—he's the uncle of one of my better customers—keeps taking politicians out for dinner and drinks, trying to get some laws passed to reduce the number of signs along the road or at least get them set back far enough so you can see some of the beauty of the state, y'know? He hasn't had much luck 'cause the billboard owners got their guys, too—*lobbyists*—and they're always taking the state senators out for drinks and golf and shit. It's all about the money. They don't give a shit about how pretty this state is; they just wanna make sure they get their share of how much moolah can be made. Some of them are my customers. Head over to the country club on the weekend and there's a good chance you'll smell some of my herb in the air.

Anyway, we're on the road for about an hour and a half—fifteen minutes from the state line—and Mickey calls me. Says he wants to pull over and take a leak and get some caffeine before we cross over. I call Elmore and he agrees, so we pull into the last rest area in the state and hit the facilities. We park in different areas of the lot and pretend we don't know each other then we hit the men's room.

After we shake off, we walk out to the food court to get something for the road, and I almost have a heart attack. There's three state troopers standing around talking and, well, there goes the whole coffee-and-donut idea. So the three of us head back outside to where we parked.

We're practically high-fiving each other once we get outside. Then we see there's another state cop checking out Mickey's truck.

The three of us kinda freeze for a bit, but then Elmore continues walking real normal-like back to his own truck. Mickey and I look at each other, and I motion with my head to where I parked.

That's when we see the cop's got a dog who's sniffing around Mickey's truck, and the dog is paying very close attention to the back door.

Elmore's still walking over to where he parked, and Mickey slaps me on the shoulder—hard—and just walks on by his vehicle all cool, and then he takes the long way around to meet me over by my truck.

"What's that about?" I ask when he climbs in my cabin, and he says the cop was on the radio saying that his dog had picked up a scent. "A scent of what?" I ask, and Mickey says he doesn't know and how would I like to go over to the cop and ask him. Funny guy, Mickey. I don't laugh, though. I call Elmore.

Elmore's all, like, "What the fuck is going on?" and Mickey and I wanna know the same thing. Elmore tells us to hold tight while he calls Robert. I'll tell ya, *tight* is the right word for the way I'm feeling right then, you know? I'm so damn tight I could freakin' bust. I knew this run was going too easy. My mother always said, if something seems too good to be true...

Mickey looks at me and says, "Maybe cigarettes ain't the only thing on that truck, huh, Agatha?" And I'm thinking he's a dick, but he may be right.

I watch those true-crime shows on TV a lot, and I don't remember anything about any tobacco-sniffing dogs. They're trained to smell drugs, explosives, shit like that. I highly doubt they got dogs that can smell unregulated cigarettes—but who knows, what with the technology and stuff they got these days.

So we're sitting in the truck for about five minutes, waiting on Elmore to get back to us. And it is quiet. Mickey and I don't know each other well enough to do that small-talk stuff, so we're just sitting there. Now I'm really jonesing for some coffee and something sweet.

They had one of those cinnamon bun places inside the rest stop, and I don't usually eat that crap, but right about now it's all I can think about. I guess that's what they say about fat people: they don't eat because they're hungry, but because they're stressed out or angry or some other emotions that they're pushing away with food. Kinda like the people I sell to, except without all the extra poundage.

Finally the phone rings; it's Elmore, so I put him on speaker phone. "I spoke to Robert," he says, then tells us Robert thinks there might be traces of ammonium nitrate in the truck. I know, what the fuck is ammonium nitrate, right? I musta missed that day in Chemistry class. Turns out it's the stuff they use in fertilizer, and Robert's usual drivers sometimes pick up loads of it for use on the ranch. I'm, like, what's the big deal about that, and Elmore tells us it's also the stuff that people who wanna make homemade bombs use. It's what the guy who blew up that building in Oklahoma back in the nineties used, and now they got dogs trained to sniff it out.

"So what are we supposed to do now?" I ask. "Go over and explain to the cop that we're not domestic terrorists, we're just cigarette smugglers?" Elmore actually laughs at that. Mickey doesn't. He's just sitting there getting red and breathing real hard, and I think how glad I am that Elmore threw Mickey's gun in the water, 'cause right about now Mickey looks like he wants to go postal on somebody.

Elmore says that Robert told him the good news is that the truck is untraceable back to him, so we should just cut our losses and finish up with the two trucks we got. That makes sense to me until Mickey says, "Whoa, whoa, whoa! Hold the fuck up. My fingerprints are all over that truck, so when they open it up and find the load of smokes, I'm the one they're coming after."

In other words, Mickey is not going in for this whole cutting-our-losses plan. Now, Mickey and me don't know each other all that well and I don't think we'd be buddies if we did, but he's got a point. I have no clue what to do now, but the man does have a point.

"I need that cop away from my truck for about five minutes, Aggie," Mickey says, finally using my new nickname 'cause he needs me for something. "I don't care how you do it, just do it. I'm not going down for a bunch of smokes by myself. You come up with something or it's all our asses in a sling." Then he gets out of the truck and heads back into the rest stop convenience store. I start to tell Elmore what happened, and he says he heard it all and what the hell are we gonna do about it?

Now, like I told you before, I watch my share of TV, and this is where someone on a crime show usually says, "We need a distraction." So I start thinking of what kinda distraction we can make that'll get that trooper and his dog away from Mickey's truck for five minutes.

It takes me about a minute—I told you before ya gotta be able to think on your feet in this kinda business—but I come up with something, and I tell Elmore what my plan is. He doesn't like it as first. It's gonna bring too much attention on us, and what if the other cops—don't forget the three inside—decide to check out *our* trucks, too?

I remind Elmore that Mickey's not only angry, he's a

bit unstable and doesn't strike me as the forgiving kind: he gets pinched, and he's gonna get talkative. We either do this now, or deal with his shit later. Elmore thinks about that and says, "There's Mickey now." I look over and Mickey's coming out of the rest stop with a bag and heading over to the shaded picnic table area a few yards away from where he parked—and where the cop and his dog are still waiting. He points to his wrist and shows me a peace sign with his fingers. I figure that means Elmore and I got two minutes to do what we gotta do, or else. "You in?" I ask Elmore. "Yes or no?"

And three seconds later he says into the phone, "Yeah, I'm in."

So I keep Elmore on speaker and we move our trucks to opposite sides of the lot, facing each other, trailers backed into their spaces—did I tell you I used to drive a milk truck in high school? Anyway, I look over to where Mickey is taking some shit out of his bag and putting something together on the picnic table. I have no idea what he's doing, but that's his deal. Ours is to distract the cop and his dog. I ask Elmore if he's ready and he says he is. I make sure my seat belt's on, and then we both start driving. Right at each other. Not too fast— about five miles per hour. You see where this is going, right?

Just before we hit, we both lay on the horns and then BAM! We smash into each other. The noise was incredibly loud. Imagine if we were doing more than five m.p.h. I don't know about everybody else, but the trooper and his dog get the crap shaken out of them. The dog's barking and trying to run over to where the "accident" happened. Those dogs are good, man.

They're trained to be sniffers, but they're cops all the same. They see someone who needs help, it gets their attention.

Anyway, the dog practically drags the cop over to Elmore and me, and we get out and pretend to look at the damage. I do that thing where I rub my neck, like maybe I got whiplash or a concussion or something. Elmore yells a bit about *Where the hell did I think I was going?* and *Why don't I keep my eyes on the road?*— even though we were in a parking lot. The cop, for his part, asks us both if we're okay and we say yes. In the meantime, the dog clearly wants to check out the back of my truck, but the cop is more concerned about the "accident" and whether or not he's got two medical patients on his hands and hours of paperwork to look forward to. He looks at the front of both trucks and says, "Not too much damage." Elmore and I make a big thing about checking out our vehicles, and after about half a minute more—we're giving Mickey as much time as we can here—we agree with the cop. He asks if either of us wants medical treatment and we say no thanks.

At that point, the three troopers who were inside come out and head over to where we are. Our cop—the guy with the dog—holds up his hand letting them know he's got this under control. They wave back and start laughing about something. Probably how a couple of dumbass drivers can get into a head-on collision in a parking lot, and I can't say I blame them. Based on the kinda shit they see on a daily basis, this probably is hilarious.

"Well, then," the Dog Cop says. "I can call this in and you guys can spend the next three to five hours filling out forms and talking to Highway Patrol, or you can call it even and get on your way."

Beautiful, this guy. A real King Solomon, and he's right. Elmore and I smile at each other—not like we know each other; more like two guys who are lucky things weren't worse—and we shake on it. We both thank the officer, and I reach out to pet the dog and the cop tells me not to do that. "He's on duty, sir." I raise my hands and head back to my truck. So does Elmore.

And as I'm backing away from the "accident," I see smoke coming out of Mickey's truck. *Shit*, right? Whatever Mickey did, he did it with a quickness. And as far as I can tell, he got away with it. In my rearview, I can see the cop and his dog running over to Mickey's truck with the cop on his radio, and he's not paying any attention to us. Elmore and I start heading toward the entrance to the interstate, and there's Mickey with his hand out like a hitchhiker. I let him in, and he's practically giddy.

"What the hell'd you do?" I ask him as we get back on the highway.

He laughs and tells me about the souvenir shop inside the rest area and how they sell refills for lighters. "I just bought myself some lighter fluid, one of them stupid travel cups with a lid on it, stole some paper towels from the Men's room, and I MacGyvered myself an instant fire bomb and tossed it into the front of the truck." He really starts laughing now. "Let's see them get fingerprints now, huh, Aggie!"

It takes me about five minutes of driving before my heartbeat and breathing return to somewhere close to normal. When they do, Mickey says, "Fuck it." I say,

"Fuck what?" and he starts going on about how Robert said to cut our losses. "I don't know about you, Aggie, but I ain't cutting any losses. Any losses gonna be cut they're on Robert, not us."

I say something about that may not be our call to make, and Mickey grabs my phone from between the seats, and the next thing I know he's screaming at Elmore. "You tell Robert that it ain't our fault that truck smells like Muslim dynamite. I'm still *expecting* my third of the original deal."

I start thinking this whole past twenty-four hours has been fucked on account of what all of us have been expecting. But I keep my mouth shut, hoping my new partner comes up with an idea.

He ends up coming up with half an idea and says he'll call Robert and then call us back. At this point we're almost over the river and into Illinois so Mickey says to make it quick or maybe there won't be *any* drop-off of reduced-tax cigarettes. Elmore tells him to calm down, and Mickey starts yelling again but it turns out that he's yelling into a phone that's just been hung up on him. He gets so pissed off he rolls down the window and makes like he's gonna throw my phone off the bridge and into the river, and I go, "Hey! Do that and we're screwed." He turns to me and his face is about as red as a monkey's ass in heat, but he holds on to the phone.

We pay our toll and, just like that, we're in Illinois. Doesn't feel any different. It's not like you take a deep breath and say, "Gee, smells like the cigarette tax in this state is higher," or some shit like that. It feels the same.

The phone rings and Mickey answers it in speaker mode before it can ring a second time. "Yeah?" he says, and Elmore says he's got Robert on the line and we're gonna have a conference call. Just like real businessmen, I think. Good. A conference call's good. We got a business problem, a conference call sounds like just the thing to settle it.

"Okay," Elmore says. "You're on with Aggie and Mickey, Robert."

And the first thing outta Robert's mouth is, "Who the hell told you to pull over into a rest area and take a piss?"

"Nature calls, man. Ya gotta go," Mickey says.

"Not with three truckloads of bootlegged cigarettes you don't," Robert screams. He goes on about how it woulda been better if we'd pulled over and peed in the bushes and how risky it is to pull into a rest stop with all the cops that hang around those places. Mickey yells back that he's not the pissing-in-the-bushes kinda guy—even though that's what saved his ass last night—and goes off again about the ammonium nitrate and how that ain't our fault and, even with all the cops, what're the odds one of them's got a bomb-sniffing dog?

I think to myself maybe Mickey's got some urinary issues, but I'm just staying shut, y'know. I just keep driving and figure, no matter how this plays out, I'm just moving forward, man. That's my new motto: Keep moving forward.

Mickey gets tired of yelling and takes a breath, and that's when Elmore starts in with how this could've happened to anyone and maybe we should all take a cut of what's left and call it even and how we're all still gonna walk away with a nice payday after all is said and done. *Now* he's a diplomat. Last night he's threatening to shoot me in my own house—well, my *ex's* house—with my own gun and bragging about how he can get away with it, and now he's talking like he works for the freakin' United Nations.

This goes back and forth for about fifteen minutes, and I'm just glad we're fifteen miles closer to the drop. Finally, Mickey gives in and says okay, but he wants something else outta the deal. Get this: he says he'll take his decreased cut if he can bring his nieces out to Robert's ranch and let them ride for an afternoon. Tough guy, ready to take a bite outta anybody who messes with him, and all it eventually takes for him to come around is a free afternoon of horseback riding with his nieces. It just shows to go ya, my friend: you never know about people until you smuggle illegal smokes across state lines with them.

Robert laughs on the other end and says, "Yeah, why not? We'll all have a big ol' pig roast next weekend." I thought Robert was being sarcastic, but Mickey appears to take him serious and that shuts him up. We end our call and problem solved. Love those conference calls. And let's be honest: there's not too many problems that some smoked pig can't settle, right?

So we're about an hour away from the drop, and Mickey turns on the radio and we just drive on like nothing happened.

Our exit's coming up soon and I tell Mickey to go to the GPS on my phone and see if he can find exactly where we need to go. We're hooking up with the Illinois guys on another ranch—a farm actually. He finds the place and we take the exit. I see Elmore about half a football field behind us take the exit, too.

We take a few more turns, and the Lady of the GPS leads us right to the entrance to the guy's farm, and we are just surrounded by corn. Nice place to do business like this. Unless the cops are looking for you and they got a helicopter, nobody's gonna notice mucha anything. We drive for about two more minutes when we see a van blocking the road. Mickey reaches down like he's gonna scratch his leg or something and then stops.

I stop about fifty feet in front of the van and start to open my door. "Let's be careful here, Aggie," Mickey says. "We had enough surprises today." Can't argue with that. So I wait about half a minute until I see Elmore pull up behind us. He beeps once and I wave him around, figuring he can't see the vehicle blocking our way. In my rearview I see Elmore get outta his truck and start walking towards us. That's when Mickey and I get out, and then two guys get out of the van.

The guy who got out of the driver's side waves to us, and yells, "Follow us."

Mickey yells back, "Follow you where? And who the hell are you?"

The two guys laugh and just get back in their van and back away. Fast. I mean, this guy drives better backwards than my ex drives forward. Elmore, Mickey and me look at each other and do a group shrug. We agree that there's pretty much nothing to do but to follow them, so we scramble back in our trucks and keep going.

It doesn't take long to see where they want us to bring our loads. There's this big barn—I mean, twice the size of the one Robert has—and by the time we catch up to them the two guys are out of their van again, motioning for us to pull into the barn as they swing the doors wide open. It reminds me of one of those hangars they got at the airport for small private planes.

I can tell Mickey doesn't like this one bit, and he starts to make that move again where he's about to scratch his leg, but again he stops. I figured it's a nervous habit, like me pulling my left ear when I'm talking to a pretty lady.

Anyway, this is what we came for, so we pull inside, and Elmore pulls alongside us. And I get this bad feeling that the doors to the barn are gonna shut and we're gonna be in the dark and I'll never see my little girl again.

But that doesn't happen. We get out and go back outside, and there's the two guys from the van, and one of them—the taller one—says, "Hear ya had some trouble at the rest stop, huh?"

I look over at Elmore and he says, "Something like that. But we cleared it up with Robert so...What do you say we just unload these bad boys, you guys give us the cash, and we'll be outta your way."

The taller guy looks at the shorter guy and they give each other a smile. The shorter guy goes, "Just like that, huh? Unload, get paid, and go home?"

Now it's Mickey's turn to talk and he says, "Yeah. Just like that."

They stare at each other for a bit and then the taller guy goes, "Okay. The trucks stay here." He throws me a set of keys. "You guys take the van back to Robert's."

"He doesn't want the trucks back?" I ask.

"He gets 'em back," the guy says, "when we make the return trip with another shipment."

I wanna say, *Shipment of what?* but I don't.

It occurs to me that this is a shuttle business. The trucks only make the return trip when they got something to deliver. What that is, I don't know, but I'd sure like to, and maybe there's a chance we can be those drivers, too. Before I can even think about verbalizing that thought, Mickey goes, "We're heading back today, guys. If you got a delivery to make, maybe we can do it for you."

I'm like, *Dammit.* That was my idea first and I was too—I don't know—meek to say it out loud and now Mickey's gonna take credit for it and whatever money's involved he's gonna want a bigger share because he thinks he came up with the idea first. I decide right there and then that the next time I get a good business idea, I'm gonna speak right up. What's the worse they can say? No, right? So what?

"You don't want to get involved in the return shipment, boys," the taller guy says. "We got that end covered, and it involves a helluva lot more than a few truckloads of smokes." He reaches behind him and pulls out an envelope and tosses it to me. I kinda like that. He tossed the keys and now the envelope with our payment to *me.* I guess I'm giving off some sorta in-charge vibe. Mickey? He doesn't like it. And he also doesn't seem to like that his idea was shot down so quickly by someone who called us "boys."

Mickey does that thing he does where he squints and grins at the same time and says, "Guns, right? You boys are running guns across state lines. Back to Robert's ranch, I bet, and then all points west from there."

The look on the other two guys' faces made me real

glad I didn't think of *that* first or decide to say it out loud. They both look at Mickey, and the shorter guy takes a few steps closer and says, "Who said anything about guns, friend?" He turns to his partner. "You hear anybody say anything about guns?"

His partner shakes his head and says, "Just this clown. He's the only one who said anything about guns."

Well, as much as Mickey hates being called "boy," you can imagine what being called a "clown" does to him. He gets that scrunchy face again and starts to go for his leg. His hand stops at his knee, and then he gets down on the other knee like he's gonna tie his shoe. Now, I'm standing right next to him and I can clearly see he's wearing boots, so I don't know what the hell he's thinking until he reaches under his pant leg and comes out with a gun. Before he can even raise his hand, Elmore comes outta nowhere and rams him with his shoulder.

They both go rolling, but Mickey never drops the gun. He rolls a bit further than Elmore and as Mickey tries to get to his feet, he's sticking his gun hand out like he's going to point it at the tall guy, and the next thing I hear is *BANG! BANG!* and Mickey flies back like he's been hit by a wrecking ball.

Elmore screams out, "Motherfucker!" and I don't know if he's yelling at Mickey—who's not going to hear anything anymore—or the guy who shot him. But he gets off the ground with his hands in the air, saying, "That's him, man. Not us. Not us."

He looks at me and I raise the keys and the envelope in the air, too, and say, "Not us. He was crazy, man."

At this point the shooter—the shorter guy—he's moving the gun back and forth between me and Elmore, and the other guy goes over to Mickey, touches his neck and makes sure he's dead. He is. There goes the weekend on the ranch with his nieces, I think.

The tall guy with the big mouth takes Mickey's piece off the ground and keeps it at his side. Tall Guy doesn't seem as comfortable with a gun in his hand as his partner. He's pretty rattled by the whole thing and the last thing you want in a rattled guy's hand is a gun.

So they're both checking us out, and I know what they're thinking because it's the same thing I'd be thinking. They offed one of us already and the other two are witnesses. Between that and the math involved where, if they kill me and Elmore, they get to keep our share of the take, I figure I got about sixty seconds left to do some fancy talking.

I slowly lower the keys and the envelope I've been holding in the air this whole time and say, "We just wanna go home, man. This guy,"—I point to Mickey and give him a real disgusted look—"we didn't know he had a gun, and he's the one whose truck got all the attention back at the rest stop. He's the one who wanted to stop off and take a leak. He is *not going* to be missed. And if you think we're gonna tell anyone what just happened, who are we gonna tell that ain't gonna get us in a shitload of trouble? We open our mouths and we are accessories *before, during and after* the fact." I spread my arms out and say, "We're good, man. We're *all* good."

I look over at Elmore to see if he's gonna back me up on this, and he just looks at me and nods. The shooter looks at me and smiles. He lowers his gun and says, "Shut the fuck up, man." He pulls out his cell phone, presses a button and waits. After a few seconds he says, "We got a problem. One of your rookies pulled a gun." He waits and then says, "Let's just say it's the last time he'll be doing that." He listens a bit more and says, "They're cool. For now." Then he says, "I don't know. Hold on. Which one of you two," he says, "is *not* Aggie?" Elmore raises his hand, and the shooter steps over to him and says, "Robert wants to say hi."

Elmore takes the phone and turns around. I can't make out all of what he's saying but I hear a few parts: "I swear to God." "I only met him last night." "He's Aggie's boy." Shit like that. So now I'm thinking all that fast-talking I did is gonna be undone by my new partner, and he's gonna walk away—drive away—back to *my* family and pick up all of my meth and get all of my cut from the cigarette run. That's why I'm so surprised when he turns back and looks me in the eyes and says into the phone, "No, Robert. He's cool."

He gives me one of those real-big winks, like he's got this under control now. "Neither one of us had any idea Mickey was holding, I swear," he says. "I would never put you in that position. You know me better than that." Elmore listens for a bit and says, "Okay." Then he walks back to the shooter and gives him the phone.

The shooter turns his back to us now and Elmore gives me a shrug. The other guy's still standing there, looking down at Mickey, and it's clear to me this is the first dead body he's ever seen. (It's my third, but I don't got time to tell you those stories today.) He's still got the gun he took off of Mickey pointed at the ground, but now he's slapping it against his thigh. If somebody doesn't make a decision soon, this guy is gonna blow a gasket.

I hear the shooter go, "Okay, Robert. Your call." He turns around and points the gun at Elmore. I'm thinking, fuck, we are toast. But the shooter says, "You're cool." Who's cool? I'm thinking. Elmore? Or me and Elmore? The shooter looks at me next and says, "You guys can go."

That's all I need to hear, and I turn around to start walking toward the van. "Hold on there, Aggie," the shooter says, and I stop. "You can go," he says, "but you gotta take out the trash on the way home." He points with the gun at Mickey and smiles. "That's the price of egress," he says. *Egress.*

Now I'm thinking we gotta drive outta here with a dead body in the van, and these guys got all this land out here where Mickey can easily be disposed—hell, he could fertilize the corn, right?—but I don't say that because I don't want anybody changing their minds about letting us go.

I go to the back of the van, open the hatch, and motion for Elmore to help me load up Mickey's body. After I check the envelope to make sure there really is cash in it—there is—I stash it in the wheel well, under the spare. I ask the shooter if he's got a blanket or something we can use to cover the body. He goes into the barn and comes back out with the dirtiest, dustiest piece of plastic I'd ever seen. "Try not to make too big of a mess," he says. "Maybe you can stop off at a rest area on the way home and get a full cleaning job on the van." Then he adds, "For Robert. It's the least you can do, since he's the only reason the two of you are going home." And then, just to show how funny he is—and because he's the one with the gun—he says, "You can keep the tarp."

"We'll take care of it," Elmore says and then slams the back door. "Let's go, Aggie," he says, and I'm in no mood to argue.

We're about halfway out of the cornfield when I turn to him and say, "Now what?"

"Now," he says, "we find a place to ditch your friend before we hit the highway."

My friend. I like that shit. Twenty-four hours ago I was scared shitless of Mickey, then we become partners and road trip buddies, and now I'm in charge of his burial plans. Funny shit, right?

Anyway, I remember a spot, before we made the right into the cornfield, where I think we can get rid of him. There was this dirt road with a chain in front of it that led into a heavily wooded area. I highly doubt the van has a shovel in it, but I remember one time on a camping trip I had to dig a shithole in the woods with a tire iron, so I'm hoping there's one in the back. Hell, what's a grave anyway except a big shithole, right?

We get to the road with the chain and, sure enough, it isn't locked. We drive up about a half-mile and park. Judging by the vegetation growing on the road, it doesn't look like anyone's been back this way since before the spring. Seems like a safe enough place to bury Mickey, but we don't have another option either way.

We unload his body from the back, and I check the wheel well in the back for a tire iron and find one. There's one piece of luck, right? So I start into the woods to start digging and Elmore's, like, "Hold up." He takes the tire iron from me and pops off one of the back hubcaps. "This'll go faster if we both dig," he says. So we do.

Between him with the tire iron and me using the hubcap as a scoop, we get a decent-size hole dug in about fifteen minutes. We go back to get Mickey, take the tarp off, drag him over to the hole, and just roll him in. It reminds me of the time my dad and I buried his favorite hunting dog in the woods. Except I liked the dog.

We throw the tarp on top, put the dirt back, and throw some leaves and branches on top. Elmore stomps the ground until it looks pretty normal again, and says, "You wanna say any parting words?"

"Yeah," I say. "Let's get the fuck outta here." And we do.

All the way back home I'm thinking what a helluva way to make money this is. I'm still digging the whole idea of the buttlegging business and wanna see if I can get in Robert's operation, but I truly hope this is the last dead body I see, ever. Elmore and I don't talk much on the trip back, and neither one of us says anything about pulling over and taking a leak or getting something to eat. We just wanna get home, give Robert his van, and go our separate ways. We also got the meth to think about and paying off my cook with the cig money.

I'm also thinking I could go for a few cold beers when I get home and maybe hang out with Brooklyn now that I got some disposable income. There's a water park she's been wanting me to take her and some of her friends to over by the university. I hope my ex'll let me take her on such short notice.

We're about a half hour away from Robert's place and I guess I get itchy when it's quiet for too long, because the next thing I know I'm asking Elmore about his relationship with my daughter.

"Whatta ya mean?" he asks.

"On the boat I heard you tell her you love her," I say. "What's that about?"

"I do," he says. "And your ex, too. I love 'em both. They're the two best things that've happened to me in a long time." Damn if I don't hear a country song coming on.

"You gonna tell her about our arrangement?" I ask.

He laughs and says we don't *have* an arrangement, and he doesn't think my ex would wanna hear about it even if we did. "And," he says, "I definitely am not telling her about all this other shit that happened today. The sooner we forget about this, the better."

I hear that. So I ask him what his plans are with my ex and Brooklyn, and he says he doesn't know yet. "Gonna take things as they come," he says. I ask him if he's got a real job and he smiles. "I do okay, Aggie. I take care of them." Implying, of course, that I don't, like that's any fault of mine. So now I'm not in the mood to talk again. I just keep driving, and we get off the highway and take the road to Robert's ranch and we pull up, but the gate's shut. It had been open when we pulled up the last time and when we left, so that's kinda strange, y'know?

Anyway, I guess Elmore's in a hurry, so before I can say anything, he gets out and checks out the gate. He turns back to me and says it's locked. I'm about to tell him to call Robert when I hear another vehicle come up behind us. I look in my rearview and I see a truck pull up behind us. My cook's truck, I think, because I see yellow on the hood and I'm ready to crap my pants. *What the hell is he doing here?* I think. And any reason I can come up with ain't good.

Elmore sees it too and comes back to the van with a scared look on his face and I'm thinking, finally, something scares this guy. He leans through the window and says, "We gotta get the hell outta here, Aggie."

Before I can answer I see another truck coming toward us, up the dirt road on the other side of the locked gate. "What the fuck?" I say.

Elmore gets back in the truck and gives me this look. "I'm working for the cops, man," he tells me. "I'm a CI."

Holy shit! My daughter's been living with a snitch? I look back in the rearview and no one's coming out of the truck yet. Ahead of us, the other truck pulls up twenty feet from the gate and waits there. I turn to Elmore and say, "What the fuck? A fucking informant?"

"The feds got me bad, Aggie," he says. "The last run I did for Robert, they busted me with enough illegal smokes to put me away for a long time. And there were some guns I didn't know about in the shipment. I cut a deal to bring in Robert, and then all this shit happened with your people—I made the call that got Mickey's crew busted—and then they made me a better deal."

I'm, like, when the fuck did this go down and he says he was on the phone with them when we were driving to Illinois. "You made a deal with the feds while transporting illegal cigarettes over state lines?" I ask. "That takes some balls."

He says they offered him a move to Florida, a new name, new job and all that Witness Protection shit you hear about on TV. They even said they'd take my ex and Brooklyn. Tells me five minutes ago he and my ex are going to play it by ear, three hours ago he figures out how to enter the Witness Protection Program during a five-hour drive to Illinois?

And now, just like on TV, someone somewhere must've ratted out the rat and here we were.

I look out the back window and then look out the front, and I'm wondering why nobody's coming out to get us. I notice that I got a few yards where I can turn this van around and make a run for it. I also notice the light on the dashboard, telling me that Elmore didn't shut his door completely when he got back in the van.

Acting quick worked once tonight, when I talked our way out of the jam after Mickey got shot. So I follow my gut again and put the car back in drive and kick Elmore the fuck out. Literally. I take my right foot and kick his ass out of the van while I step on the gas with my left and peel the hell out of there, turning the steering wheel as far as it'll go and running over some poor sucker's front bushes and lawn until I clear the truck that was boxing me in from behind.

I get my right foot back on the gas and peel the hell out of there, and the passenger door is flying open-and-shut like crazy and I'm bouncing up and down on that dirt road with one thing on my mind: last night my cook basically told me he knows where my daughter lives, so I'm heading right there and not looking back. I'll worry about my dad later, I think. I gotta get Brooklyn the hell away from that house.

Ten minutes later, I'm pounding on my ex's door and she's not too happy to see me. Big surprise, neither is Marley. Neither of them will even let me in. Shoulda gone through the bathroom window again.

I tell her to pack up as much shit as she can in five minutes 'cause we gotta get going. She finally opens the door and tells me she's not going anywhere with me, and do I know where her boyfriend is. I take a step into the house and take her—gently—by the shoulders and tell her I'll explain everything after she gets her stuff together and we get outta there.

"This is about you and your drug buddies, isn't it?" she says. Like everything's always about me and my drug business. I wonder if she knows what her boyfriend's been doing outside the house and the kind of people *he's* hanging with that require the feds to step in. Now, I don't say any of that 'cause I don't want to make the argument bigger.

That's when Brooklyn comes into the room in her pajamas, and my heart stops. She's so damned cute, and she gives me a look before she comes up and hugs me. That look? It was like she was expecting Elmore, not me, and my heart breaks a little more.

I look up at my ex and say, "Please. Just do what I'm asking and I'll tell you everything, but we really got to get out of here." She starts in again about her boyfriend and I tell her I'll take her—them—to him, but it's gotta happen *now*. I guess she saw something in my eyes because she stops talking—can't remember that ever happening—and tells Brooklyn to go get her Little Kitty bag, and then she tells me to stay where I am while she packs. Any other time, I swear...

Less than ten minutes later, we're all in the van and she gives me a look like, "Where'd you steal this from?" I tell her it's a friend's and that's where we're going now. She asks if her boyfriend is gonna be there and I say, yeah, of course. He ain't, obviously. I'm taking them to the closest thing I have to one of those safe houses the cops use to hide witnesses. One of my customers, his parents got a place just outside of town and they're away for the week. I know that because I made a delivery there the other night. They always keep the back door open, so I know I got somewhere to stash the girls until I can give the present situation some more thought.

We get to the house and my ex and Brooklyn walk in expecting to see the boyfriend. I act surprised that he's not there and pretend to call him. I get off the phone and tell them he's on his way. My ex takes Brooklyn to the bedroom and turns the TV on, then comes back and lays into me about the shit sandwich I just handed her. I'm about to tell her everything when my phone rings.

It's my cook and he doesn't sound pissed. Which scares the crap outta me. He tells me to hold on, and then Robert gets on the phone. Another conference call. They explain to me that they got Elmore and if I wanna see him breathing again, I better hightail it over to Robert's ranch and give them their money.

You may not believe this, but I completely forgot about the money with all the drama I've just been through. "So," I ask, "all I gotta do is give you the money and this ends?"

You shoulda heard them laughing. When they were

done, my guy explains that somebody's gotta pay for the recent problems to their operation. He then explains that he's had a deal with Robert for about a year now. He also tells me that he's had a deal with Mickey for quite some time, and he figures it was either me or Elmore that dropped that dime to the feds, and one of us is gonna pay for that "overhead," I think he calls it.

"A three-way deal?" I ask.

"Synergy," he calls it.

Like I said, these guys are smart. Don't get me wrong. They're bad guys, but they're good businessmen. He goes on to explain that when something—or someone—causes harm to the business, that person's gotta be dealt with. I step a few feet away from my ex at this point and say, "Okay, you got Elmore. Make him deal with it." And my guy's like, "Not without the cash. You deliver the money, you get the walk."

Before I can even think to ask what happens if I don't bring the money, he laughs again and says, "I still know where your father lives. And your daughter? You want her growing up looking over her shoulder her whole life? Because once we visit dear old Dad, we'll find the rest of your family."

And now it hits me that all the shit I've gone through the past day or so comes down to this: I'm out any cash I was hoping to get, and my ex and Brooklyn are gonna be without the boyfriend. You could say I got the better end of that deal.

So I ask him, "How do we do this?" and he tells me to get back on my boat and he'll call. Just like a regular meet. I tell him okay and he hangs up on me. That's when my ex starts in again and asks if that was about the boyfriend. I tell her yeah, I gotta go pick him up.

"You're going to bring him back here, right?" she asks.

I nod and then Brooklyn comes back into the room and tells me how much she misses him and can we all have ice cream when he comes back. I pick her up and say, "Sure, honey. That sounds like a real good idea."

She gives me a big hug and says, "Thank you, Daddy."

That's when it hits me that all I'm doing to these two is lying and that's about all I've ever done. All they want is Elmore back, and I'm lying my ass off to protect myself and I'm the only one who knows he's not coming back. Ever. It's either him or me, and that's a no-brainer from where I'm sitting. Anyway, I tell them I'll be right back and I get into the van and drive toward my dad's.

I don't know what the hell happened, but halfway there I start bawling like a baby. It's like a storm that comes outta nowhere. It's so bad I gotta pull over and get myself under control. I mean, what the fuck, right? I'm sitting there behind the wheel, crying and shaking, and I remember one time I had a panic attack after smoking some bad shit and this is like that, except it ain't chemical. I know what it is, and as soon as I get myself halfway calmed down I call my cook again and tell him there's been a change in plans.

He doesn't like that one bit and I'm, like, "I don't give a shit." I guess there's something in my voice now because, instead of him threatening me, he wants to know what the change is and I tell him.

"You sure about this?" he asks. I mean, there's real concern in his voice, and I tell him, "Yeah, I'm sure." He says okay, if that's the way I want it. *It's not*, I wanna say. It's not the way I want it at all, but it's the way it has to be. I keep thinking about Brooklyn's face when I told her we'd all have ice cream and how happy she was when I told her I'd have Elmore back soon. I think back to Elmore telling me how he felt about my ex and Brooklyn and how he had it all set up to go to Florida and how the feds said they'd let him take the girls, too.

It's either him or me, right? This is what my mother meant when she told me sometimes I'm more trouble than I'm worth.

So, that's why I'm here, buddy. I'm just waiting for the text, and here's where I need you to do me a couple of favors.

These—let me get them out—are the keys to the van. I parked out back. In a few minutes, this guy's gonna come in—that's gonna be Elmore; he's tall, good-looking—and he's gonna be with a Mexican I bet. And when Elmore walks in, I'm gonna walk out with that other guy. Me and the Mexican are gonna have ourselves a chat on the road, too, about another extended vacation he might consider making.

After I leave the bar, you give Elmore these keys and tell him there's a slip of paper in the glove compartment with an address on it. That's where the girls are. Tell him to call his fed guys and have them meet him and the girls there. He can give it up about the ten bricks of meth in the storage unit and everything else to earn his Witness Protection for him and girls, I figure. And tell him to hurry. I don't completely trust the guys dropping him off, so he's gotta be quick about all this in case they decide to finish him off anyway. I don't think they will, but I've been wrong about a lot of stuff recently.

Are you getting all this?

This-here envelope is for my dad. It's got his watch in there and a note—well, a suicide note—telling him I'm sorry I stole his dock and mooched off him all these years, so I took off in my car to a place they'd never find me and shot myself with his gun. The note says not to miss me, but I doubt he will after he reads this. It's all in there: putting his deed in my name; the meth in his toolbox; where to find his boat; to move in with his brother for good next week before he really does have a stroke someday. And I tell Dad I found out the hard way that Mom and him really was right: always leave by the same door—or window—you come in through.

Here's a couple of hundred for the drinks and your trouble. See? I told you I'd take care of you...Yeah, maybe one more beer for the road. Thanks.

Shit, that's my phone. That's him. He's outside.

Looks like I'll have to make it a quick one.

TWIST OF FATE

CHARLES SALZBERG

Acknowledgments

I'd like to thank Brian Mori without whom this story would not have taken shape, and Eric Campbell, without whom this story might not have seen the light of day, and Jeff Weber, who got me off my ass and actually inspired me to write this tale.

Chapter 1

It was cold. Cold enough for layers. Cold enough for me to wear the bright red wool overcoat I bought so I would stand out in a crowd. But I was wearing none of that. Instead, I was freezing my ass off wearing just a black wool skirt, black tights, knee-high black boots and a heavy orange wool turtleneck sweater. Vanity. After all, I had to look good and impervious to the elements in front of the camera. This is the image I needed to project. An image of invincibility. An image that said, when duty calls there is no time to dress appropriately. When the news breaks, I am there. Anything for a story. Anything to keep the public informed.

I was standing in front of the Little Roma Social Club, a plain brick building in downtown Syracuse. Syracuse, the fifth most populous city in the state, the home of the New York State Fair, a city roughly a five-hour drive northwest of New York City. So near, yet so far. This was where I worked. This was where I'd worked for the past three and a half years. This was where I desperately wanted to get away from. But not yet. At least not before this or another story I dug up went national.

"Are you ready?" my cameraman Mark asked.

"How's the shot?"

"Don't worry about the shot, okay. That's my job."

"Okay, okay."

"You ready?"

"Hold on." I ran my tongue across the inside my

mouth, then bared my teeth to Mark, who was looking at me through the camera lens.

"Anything on my teeth?"

"Your teeth look fine. You look fine. Will you hurry it up already? I'm freezing my ass off here."

"And you think I'm not?"

"Who told you to take off your damn coat?"

"Vanity, thy name is woman."

"Enough of this bullshit. Let's get this done and get the hell out of here."

"What's the matter, Mark, scared?"

"Yes. I'm a chickenshit. Let's just get this over with."

"All right, all right, all right..."

"Rolling," said Mark, as I cleared my throat and threw my best fake smile at the camera.

"This is Trish Sullivan and I'm standing in front of the Little Roma Social Club, hangout of Fat Tony Alcante, reputed head of the Conigliaro crime family. Fat Tony was recently installed after a brief but bloody power struggle, following the shotgun slaying of Carmine Salvatore. Damnit! Where's the damn teleprompter?"

"You said you didn't need it. Remember?"

"Why do you listen to anything I say? You know I'm crazy."

"Yeah, the commitment papers are on my desk."

I looked down at my script, silently moving my lips, fixing it in my memory, then looked back up at the camera.

"We'll fix this in editing."

"Yeah."

"Okay..." I went back to my on-camera voice and

picked up right before I fucked up. "After a brief but bloody power struggle, following the shotgun slaying of Carmine Salvatore. It's here, behind this brick façade, that Fat Tony meets with other wiseguys to discuss such weighty matters as loan-sharking, arson, prostitution and murder. How long Fat Tony's reign lasts largely depends on the loyalty of the people around him. For Fat Tony's sake, let's hope they'll be more loyal to him than he was to his old friend, Carmine. Trish Sullivan, the I-Team, News 9."

I put down the mike. "How was that?"

"You hit it out of the park, baby."

"Very funny."

Mark might be cute, if he weren't such an asshole. Unlike me, he was dressed for the weather, wearing a heavy-duty blue parka and black watch cap. He's in his mid-thirties, and he's one of those guys who perpetually looks as if he hasn't shaved in two days. I wonder, how do guys pull that off? Do they shave, then hibernate for two days before showing their face? Anyway, he's not bad looking and he's in pretty good shape, but after a few more years at this job, that'll change. Devouring hoagies and beer and Big Macs will eventually find their way to his belly, like every other guy I've worked with through the years.

"Can we go now?" he asked, as he dropped the camera from his shoulder.

"Yes, Mark, we can go now," I said in my most condescending Mama Bear tone, as I retrieved my coat and muffler and put them on before I got ready to get into the truck.

Just as I was about to step inside I heard the door of

the social club open. I spun around to see a bunch of wiseguys tumble out. I recognized Sonny Palma, Fat Tony's muscular young bodyguard, followed by none other than Fat Tony himself. He was in his mid-fifties, five-five on his best day, even with his shoes on, and probably close to three hundred and fifty pounds of pure blubber. I was sure the only exercise he got was pushing himself away from the table and he didn't do that any too often.

I threw off my coat and turned to Mark. "My God, it's him. Start filming!"

"Are you kidding?"

"Mark! Do what I say. Turn on the damn camera and start filming."

I grabbed my mike and ran back across the street. I heard the truck door slam shut and felt Mark right behind me. I rushed up to Fat Tony, but before I could reach him Sonny darted in front of him with his hand jerking inside his jacket pocket. I knew what was there and he knew I knew what was there. But it wasn't going to stop me. What were they going to do, shoot me there in the street, with Mark filming the whole thing? Now that would have gone viral and gotten me national. If I survived my career would be on fast forward and yes, I would be out of Syracuse faster than you could say lake effect snow.

But no one was shooting anyone today, except for Mark.

"Mr. Alcante," I said, half out of breath, as I snaked my arm around Sonny and stuck the microphone in his face. "Trish Sullivan, Channel 9 News. Is it true you've recently been named boss of the Conigliaro crime family?"

"I don't know what the fuck you're talking about. I'm a businessman. Plumbing supplies. Wanna see my fuckin' pay stub? And the only family I got is driving me the fuck crazy. You wanna talk to my wife."

He looked at the others and laughed. He was smart. Smart enough to know not to say anything to a live camera. Smart enough to know the more he cursed the less would make it onscreen.

"Then maybe you can explain why someone selling plumbing supplies needs a bodyguard."

"Ever had your toilet backed up, doll? You call a plumber and he don't come, you wanna kill him, right? Sonny here, he's my toilet plunger." He laughed and poked Sonny in the ribs. Sonny did not seem amused.

I followed them as they headed toward a Lincoln Town Car, with Mark, his mouth wide open, always filming, following me.

"What if I were to tell you I'm in possession of certain information that suggests someone within your organization has a contract out on you?"

We reached the car. Sonny opened the back door and helped squeeze the Fat Man into the back seat.

Tony stuck his head out the door. "And who might that be?"

"Maybe if you'd agree to have an on camera sit-down interview with me I can..."

"Do I look fucking stupid? C'mon, Sonny, get inna car and let's get the fuck outta here."

With the Fat Man securely tucked in the car, Sonny slammed the door shut and jogged over to the driver's side and got in. As the car started to drive away I grabbed Mark by the arm and started pulling him toward the news van.

"Come on," I yelled.

"Where are we going?"

"Just get in and...follow that car!"

Mark got in and stashed the camera between us as I got into the passenger's seat.

"You're gonna get us both killed," he said, as he started up the engine.

"Consider this a Master Class in journalism, Mark. It'll make a great shot for the news tonight—us tailing Fat Tony and his bodyguard." I picked up the camera, turned it on, and aimed it out the front window.

"Hey, what the hell are you doing?" Mark screamed.

I turned to him, said, "You think you can shoot and drive at the same time?"

"Do you know what the fuck you're doing?"

"I've used one of these before. Now just drive, will ya?"

"What the hell was that about a hit on him? You know something?"

"Of course not. I just wanted to see if I could get a rise out of him," I said, as I filmed the traffic in front of us as Mark surprised me by keeping them in sight.

"Is that part of the Master Class—lying to get a story?"

"I'm sure someone has a contract out on him, I just don't know who it is. But I might find out by talking to him."

Sonny knew we were following him and he'd picked up speed, trying to lose us. That was fine with me. The tougher it was for us to follow the more dramatic it was on tape.

"Can you push this thing a little faster, Grandma?" I said.

"You may want to get yourself killed but I've got a hot date tonight I'd like to keep."

We were approaching the train tracks and just as the Town Car began to fly through the intersection bells started clanging and the wooden bar dropped. Mark slammed on the brakes.

"Damn, that was close," he said as he dropped his head to the steering wheel.

"It's okay," I said. "I got the shot."

Chapter 2

When I got back to the office my assistant, Jackie, was waiting for me. Jackie had been with me for six months and she was working out pretty well. A journalism graduate of Newhouse, part of Syracuse University, she was bright and ambitious, but not too ambitious. Those are the ones who don't last long because they bore easily. I try to give them meaningful jobs to keep them busy and actually teach them something, but sometimes it is a matter of just keeping the crew and me in coffee. I don't know if Jackie minds, but if she does she doesn't show it, and that's what's important. Even more important, she's the kind of kid who's learned how to keep a secret, an essential asset in a business that thrives on blowing the lid off secrets.

"How'd it go?" she asked as she took my coat.

"Not bad. Got Fat Tony on tape and, surprise, surprise, the big ape speaks."

"Sam wants a word with you when you get a chance."

"About?"

"He didn't say."

"Okay. Anything new and interesting come in?" I asked, as I started rifling through a stack of papers on my desk. Sometimes days can go by without my doing this, so I count on Jackie to go through them every so often just to make sure I'm not missing anything important.

"Well, there is one thing that might, might, might have potential." I hadn't yet broken Jackie of her habit of repeating words several times to give them emphasis, but it was still early and I don't give up easily. I love a challenge. "It's a letter from someone at a prison down-state."

"Don't tell me, the devil made him do it."

"It's a she, not a he."

"Okay, what's she in for?"

"She murdered her husband and two kids."

"America's sweetheart. Swears she didn't do it, right?"

"Right. I read her letter and I looked up the case." Initiative. Another plus for Jackie. "Her name is Meg Montgomery. But you know what, what if she really is like innocent?" *Like* innocent? Another bad habit I will break Jackie of. "You can't tell me it wouldn't make a great story if she really is innocent." She lowered her voice almost to a whisper, not that anyone was listening. The newsroom was half empty and those who were there were much too busy on the phone or doing a crossword puzzle, playing video games or on chat lines. "I know you want out of here…"

I raised my finger to my lips.

She lowered her voice even more. "I thought everyone knew."

"Everyone might think it, at least if they have half a brain, but not everyone *knows* it."

"Sorry."

"No problem. Put it aside and I'll take a look after I finish with Sam."

Sam Garber, who was in his mid-fifties, wore red

suspenders and had his sleeves rolled up above his elbows no matter what the temperature or season, had the only actual office. It was small, but it was separate from the rest of us, who worked from a series of small cubicles with no privacy. That was the way Sam wanted it. He wanted to be able to stick his head out of his office, like a turtle, and see everyone at the same time, to see what they were doing or not doing, then stick his head back in. And if you didn't look busy, he'd make a big show of it by yelling at you to come into his office where his line never changed. "You looking for something to do?" After a while, you realized it was all for show, that he couldn't care less what you were doing so long as the work got done, the show got on the air. That was Sam. All about show. He must have seen countless movies and TV shows about journalists and took on every single attribute to the point where he was even beyond caricature. Still, he was a good guy and unlike other managing editors I've worked for over the years he actually likes the on-air talent.

I knocked on the door, which was half open, and stuck my head in. Sam was sitting at his desk, his feet propped up, talking on the phone. He waved me in then motioned for me to sit in the chair in front of his desk.

He finished his conversation, hung up and ruffled some papers. I knew it was all just an act the objective of which was to make me anxious enough to get me to do whatever he wanted me to do. It worked on some, not me. But that didn't stop him from continuing the act and it didn't stop me from admiring him for trying.

"What's up?"

"I got a call this afternoon from Bill Hodge at our

New York affiliate. He told me you sent him your resume along with an audition tape. He wanted to know my thoughts."

"What did you tell him?"

"That you're an excellent reporter and that I'd hate like hell to lose you. He said it was obvious you were talented, but they're looking for someone with a little more...uh...seasoning."

"He actually called it seasoning?"

"I believe he did."

"I'm not looking to work a cooking show."

"Look, Trish, I don't mind you sending out your resume, I just wish you'd have the courtesy to let me know beforehand."

"I didn't realize I needed permission."

"There's that attitude again. You don't need permission. It's just common courtesy."

"I'm sorry, Sam, but I'm not getting any younger and as much as I enjoy working with you I don't particularly relish being stuck here in Syracuse the rest of my life. Is that all?"

"Not quite. You've done some great work on Alcante but, with sweeps coming up, I think it's time you moved on to something else. You got anything in the cooker?"

The cooker? Where the hell did that come from? I didn't. But I didn't want to admit it, so I said the first thing that popped into my mind. "You remember a murder case here a few years ago? A woman named Montgomery?"

"Yeah. Sure. Meg Montgomery. Shot her husband and their twin girls. A very sick lady. The tabloids had a field day with it. Made the wire services for about a minute and a half. Why?"

"I don't want to jump the gun, but I may have something."

"Listen, Trish, I don't want you going off on some half-cocked stale murder case. Make sure you've got something solid before you decide to run with it."

"Then I can check it out?"

"If I said no, would it stop you?"

"Of course not."

"Then yeah. Sure. Just let go of the Alcante thing for a while, will ya. The mob just ain't what it used to be in terms of ratings."

"Don't worry, Sam, I've been in the business long enough to know what I'm doing."

As I left his office I thought I heard him mutter something to the contrary, but frankly, I didn't care. Before long, I was going to be out of Syracuse one way or another.

Chapter 3

I didn't read Meg's letter until I got home, fed the cat and changed into something comfortable. Only then, after I started a fire which I needed because the temperature had dropped another eight degrees by dark and the damn heating system never seems to be able to keep up. It was a rental about fifteen minutes outside the city proper and the owners, an elderly couple who lived out of state, never seemed to be available when I needed something repaired.

It read:

Dear Ms. Sullivan,

My name is Meg Montgomery. I am an inmate at Bedford Hills Prison for Women in Westchester, New York. Nearly four years ago I was convicted of the murder of my husband, Jeffrey, and my daughters, Kimberly and Rebecca. I am now serving three consecutive life sentences without the possibility of parole. Nearly everyone in prison professes innocence, so I am sure you will immediately assume I'm guilty. But as God is my witness I truly am innocent. Only a monster could be capable of such a horrible crime. And I am not a monster, no matter how the media portrayed me.

Having occasionally watched you on the news over the last couple years, I have been impressed with your honesty, sincerity, and desire to seek out the truth. Since my arrest, I have become numbed by my experience and resigned to my fate. But I feel I owe it to both myself and to my mother, in particular, to make one last attempt to remove this stigma from my name and end my terrible nightmare. All I ask is for a few hours of your time to visit me. If after meeting me you still believe in my guilt, fine. Otherwise, I hope you will please help me.

I've been in prisons before. No one, and I mean no one, is guilty. It's amazing how many miscarriages of justice there are. But then, all it takes is one...

I went online and Googled the case. There were photos of a young, blonde, extremely attractive, well-dressed woman, led away in handcuffs. No wonder the press had a field day. Nothing catches the public's attention more than a beautiful woman accused of a heinous crime. By the time I finished reading everything I could find I was intrigued. There was no glaring indication that she hadn't done it but still the idea that a woman could kill her entire family was almost impossible to believe. A husband, sure. I'd been married and there were plenty of times I would have gladly ended the bastard's life. And if there had been a weapon handy and I thought I could get away with it, well, I might have been the story instead of reporting it.

Killing your kids, though, that was another thing. And such sweet looking children they were. I decided it was worth looking into and so the next day when I got I had Jackie get me the trial transcript. Then I made a few calls and received permission to visit Meg at the end of the week.

We sat across from each in a small, cold, cinder-block, windowless room. Although almost four years

behind bars had taken their toll, Meg surprisingly still
resembled the glamorous photos I'd seen on the Internet.
Her blonde hair was now a mousey brown, with a few
gray strands sprinkled throughout, but her youthful
figure was still intact. We were about the same size, five-
foot-five, about a hundred and ten pounds. The more I
looked at her the more I thought she resembled a
somewhat weathered Meg Ryan, before the terrifying
results that came with playing around with her face.

Her voice was soft and soothing, almost emotionless.
"I'm not going to sit here and tell you Jeffrey and I
didn't have our share of problems, or that I approved of
his sleeping around—because he was and I knew it—but
I loved him and he loved me. In many ways, he was a
wonderful husband. And a good father. Are you
married, Miss Sullivan? Do you have any children?"

"I was, but I'm not anymore. No children."

"Then you can't know what it's like to lose a child. I
lost two. But they weren't the only ones to die that day."
She paused. I could see tears starting to well up. "For a
mother to be accused let alone convicted of murdering
her own children." She choked up a moment, swallowed
then picked up. "I can't tell you what that feels like.
They were such sweet, beautiful girls. They meant the
world to me. What reason in the world would I have to
hurt them?" Her head sank. "Sometimes, I don't think
it's worth living without them."

Either she was a world-class actor or maybe she was
telling the truth. I couldn't tell which it was but I was
intrigued.

"One of the most damning pieces of evidence against
you was the witness who claimed you offered him

twenty-five thousand dollars to kill your husband."

"He lied."

"Why would he lie?"

"If I knew why it would go a long way to explain a lot of things. Somebody had to have put him up to it. I swear to you, Miss Sullivan, I never laid eyes on that man before the trial."

"Give me one good reason why I should believe you, why I should put my career on the line to help you."

"Because I'm innocent."

"Saying it and proving it are two different things."

"I know. That's why I wrote you. I can't do anything in here but you have access. You *can* do something. If you want to, that is."

This was tempting. Perhaps too tempting to pass up. But I also knew it was fraught with danger. I needed something to push me over the edge.

"Did you ever take a polygraph?"

"Yes. My attorney had me take one."

"What were the results?"

"I was told it was inconclusive, whatever that means. But my lawyer said it could have been because of the...state I was in. To be honest, it's all a blur now. I remember so little of what happened."

"Would you be willing to take a polygraph now?"

"Yes. Of course. Does this mean you'll help me?"

I stared into her eyes. They were soft and inviting, as if she were inviting me inside her head to see that she was telling the truth. I've had enough experience with liars to know one when I see one. Some are so good, so convincing, that they can lead you along for a while. But in the end there's something about the eyes, something that cannot sustain a lie for too long. I didn't know if that was the case with Meg, but it might be.

"It means I'll think about it. But, Meg, if you flunk it, I'm outta here."

"I won't flunk because I'm telling the truth. What if I pass?"

"First things first. I'll make the arrangements."

She rose. The tears that were welling were suddenly released. "Thank you, Miss Sullivan." She reached out for my hand. I took it. It was warm. And soft. There was something about the connection that felt right. "Thank you so much."

"There's nothing to thank me for yet. And let's get something straight. We're not friends. We never would have been friends. This is purely business. "

"I understand," she said, reluctant to let go of my hand, as if by holding on I would lead her out of the prison and into the light. "Really, I do."

Chapter 4

It wasn't easy to get all the parts in place, but a week later I was back with permission from the prison higher-ups and a polygraph expert in tow. We set up in one of the prison offices. I sat several feet away, behind and out of eyesight of Meg as my expert, James Shipley, scribbled check marks on a page. Meg had been allowed to wear civilian clothes, at my request. I didn't want her to feel like an inmate, giving her the stink of guilt whether she was or not. I brought her a simple white blouse and black slacks, which I brought from my own wardrobe.

"We'll start with some simple questions to establish a baseline," Shipley explained. "First, is your name Meg Montgomery?"

"Yes."

"Are you thirty-seven years old?"

"Yes."

"Were you born in Syracuse, New York?"

"Yes."

"Were you married to Jeffrey Montgomery?"

"Yes."

"Did you have anything to do with the murder of your husband and two daughters?"

"Definitely not."

"Please, just answer yes or no."

"No."

This went on for another twenty minutes, Shipley asking innocuous questions and specific ones dealing with the murder, Meg giving simple yes or no answers. When it was over, Meg looked relieved and so was I. I thought she did pretty well. Her answers were definitive and had the unmistakable ring of truth. The rest was up to the test itself.

A day later, I met with Shipley in his office.

"So, what do you think?"

"Bottom line?"

"Yes, bottom line."

"She passed."

"Really? How accurate are these things?"

"Pretty accurate."

"But not perfect."

"Nothing's perfect."

"Could she beat it?"

"It's an instrument, a tool. There's no truth serum involved. The machine isn't infallible. But I would say that in my experience it's highly unlikely. Did she ever take one before?"

"She took one for her attorney shortly after the murders. The results were inconclusive."

"Not surprising. She might have been nervous, overwrought. It could have been the examiner. Now, she's had almost five years to get over it."

"She definitely hasn't gotten over it, that much I can guarantee you."

When I told Sam about the findings he was not enthusiastic.

"It's old news, Trish," he said, hardly looking up from the papers he was shuffling around his desk.

"It could be new news now."

He shook his head. "I don't see how. Do you know

how many innocent people there are in prison?"

"And do you know how many guilty ones there are out of prison."

"So what's your point?"

"My point is, I think this is worth pursuing. If she is innocent, Sam, it could be big news."

"And if she isn't?"

"Then it's no news at all. But what harm would it be for me to follow up on it? I've gone this far."

"You could be working on other things."

"You took me off Alcante. What do you want me to do, report on traffic accidents?"

"People like hearing about traffic accidents. They can relate."

"Oh, sure, and we've got to give people what they want."

"Yes, Trish, that's exactly what we're here to do. We're here to bring them the news that affects them, the news they're interested in. Traffic reports. Weather. Crime."

"Bingo."

"Crime that affects them. Personally."

"Can you imagine the national coverage we'd get if it turns out she is innocent?"

"That's what this is all about, isn't it? About you getting her out of prison so you can get the hell out of here."

"So what if it is? It's only going to reflect well on you, Sam, and on the station."

He thought for a moment. I knew I had him. So long as you can point out to people how they can benefit from something, they're likely to go along with it. Sam was no different from me. We all want to get to some-where and away from somewhere else.

"I'll give you a week to see what you can come up with. But if there's no progress..."

"Then I'll be out there on the highway looking for the latest traffic fatalities, Sam. I promise."

A few days later, I returned to the prison to get Meg's side of the story, which she told as we sat across from each other in the same room where we first met.

"I got up around six-thirty that morning, same as usual, to get the girls ready for school. After they left, I went downstairs to do some laundry. Then I straight-ened up around the house. Around eleven-thirty, I left for the mall to have lunch with my friend, Susan."

"Where was Jeff during all this time?"

"Asleep. He didn't get home till late the night before. If you're going to ask me where he was, the answer is I have no idea. He said it was business and frankly, don't ask me what kind."

"Your husband's autopsy revealed traces of cocaine and pot in his system."

"It was one of the things we used to fight about. I begged him to get help, but he didn't think he had a problem. He said it was purely recreational, to take the edge off. I made sure he never did it in front of the girls."

"What time did you meet Susan?"

"Around twelve-fifteen. Before we had lunch we popped into one of the stores there, I think it was Bloomingdale's, because she had to pick up a sweater. I wound up buying matching dresses for the girls and a sweater for Jeff. They found the packages at the house after..." she started to tear up again and I jumped in to get her back on track.

"Then lunch."

"Yes. While we were having lunch I noticed the time—it was after two—and I told Susan I wanted to be sure to get home before the girls because I needed to take them to their dance class at three-thirty and I wasn't sure Jeff would be in any shape to do that."

"The school bus driver testified he saw your car parked on a side street a few blocks from your house when he dropped off your children."

"It wasn't me. He admitted he didn't get a good look at the license plate number. Besides, I couldn't have been home when he dropped off the girls because I was still with Susan."

"On cross-examination Susan admitted she wasn't wearing a watch—that she never wears a watch and you knew that—and the only way she knew it was after two o'clock was because that's what you told her."

Meg's face hardened. "Why would I lie when there were any number of ways she could find out the time without my telling her?"

"Go on," I said, taking notes furiously now, trying to punch any hole in her or the prosecution's story I could manage.

"The first thing I saw when I walked into the house was Rebecca's lunch box lying in the stairs. I was puzzled. They weren't supposed to be home yet. I thought...I'm not quite sure what I thought. I thought maybe something might have happened to them at school and Jeffrey had to go pick them up. I found out later they were let out early because of some kind of teacher's conference. I called out to them, but no one answered. I went upstairs. When I got to their bedroom..."

She stopped, dropped her head into her hands and began to sob. My instinct was to reach over to comfort her, but I didn't. I don't know why. Maybe because I wasn't there to be her friend and certainly not to comfort her. I was there to get her story. That's all.

"They were there. My babies," she managed in a voice choked with tears. "I...I can't go on right now. You know the rest."

"Yes," I said. "I know the rest."

Meg's attorney was Eric Santini and I found him the next day sitting on a bench in front of one of the courtrooms. He had wavy black hair, a big nose that dominated his youthful face. Dressed in a faded blue suit, white shirt and rep tie, he was reading through papers in a manila folder. He looked like a kid doing his homework right before class.

Cut off from her husband's family money, Meg was deemed indigent, so she qualified for a court-appointed attorney. At the time, Santini was only a few years out of law school but he had a reputation as a bulldog and from the transcript I could see, though he was green, he'd done a relatively good job. Now, almost five years later, he was still a defense attorney, a lone practitioner specializing in criminal cases.

I started to introduce myself but he recognized me first. He stood up and I was surprised to find that he was just an inch or two taller than me.

"That's great stuff you've been doing on the mob. Hope you check under your hood every morning."

"I take public transportation when I can."

"You looking for me or directions?"

"You."

"If it's about the mob, I try to steer clear of those cases," he said.

"I'm doing a follow-up on the Montgomery murders. I was hoping you could give me some inside information."

He looked at his watch. "Mind walking with me? I've already been late twice this week and if I'm late again Judge Langley's gonna have my ass."

"Sure."

He collected his papers and we began down the corridor.

"I can tell you it was all circumstantial. No smoking gun. But the D.A. created a strong enough chain to convince the jury. Course, you guys didn't help any. She was crucified in the press even before she got to trial. I got it, though. Great looking chick, looked like she couldn't crush a fly. Husband's wealthy family. Drugs. Promiscuity. Yadda. Yadda. Yadda. This town's hungry for anything that doesn't have to do with college sports, so a juicy domestic murder case...well, we didn't have a chance in hell."

"Given all the publicity, why didn't you ask for a change of venue?"

"I thought I'd have a better chance here. You know,

family, friends, ties to the community. But I'll tell you, she didn't make it easy for me."

We stopped at a water fountain so he could get a drink. I used the time to scribble down a few notes.

"How so?" I asked, as soon as his head popped up.

"Well, in cases like that one strategy is to use the shotgun approach. You know, throw suspicion wherever you can. But there were certain areas she wouldn't let me get into."

"Like what?"

"The drug angle, for one. I couldn't show that her husband was dealing on the side and was killed as the result of some payback or double-cross."

"He didn't need the money."

"Actually, he did. His family had threatened to cut him off. At least that was the word I got. And then there was the jealous lover thing. He liked to fool around with the ladies."

"Why do you think she wouldn't let you push those angles?"

"She never came right out and said it, but as unbelievable as it sounds, I don't think she wanted to expose her in-laws to a possible scandal involving their golden boy. Which was a laugh because they all but deserted her for that very reason."

We came to a stop in front of one of the courtroom. Santini glanced at his watch. "I've got to..."

"One last question. Do you think she did it?"

He hesitated a moment. "Personally, I really liked her. She was...I know this sounds funny, but she was kind of charismatic. You've met her, right?"

I nodded.

"So you know what I mean. She's smart, she's sweet, and she had the looks of an angel. I'm sorry I wasn't able to get her off. I tried my best. Maybe if I'd had more experience. But that's Monday morning quarterbacking. I've learned in this business you roll the dice and whatever number comes up, that's the one you have to play.

"What about appeals?"

He shook his head. "I tried, but I couldn't find anything to base an appeal on. You got something new?"

"Not yet. Got any ideas?"

"Wish I did. I hate to see someone in prison for something they didn't do. And something like that..." he shook his head. "Well, to know that people think you did something as awful as that, well, I can't imagine what that's like."

"Neither can I," I said.

Chapter 5

I'm not a ghoul, or at least I don't think I am. But I needed to see where the murders took place. There was something about this case that was keeping me arm's distance. I couldn't quite figure out what it was, but I had to "feel" it more, "taste" it more. I had to become part of it. And so I decided to do what criminals are said to do and journalists must do: visit the scene of the crime.

We found that the Montgomery home was on the market so I made an appointment with the real estate agent, Ruth Dwyer. We met at the red brick Colonial house a few miles outside of Syracuse proper. The grounds were spacious, the hedges needed trimming and there was a For Sale sign on the front lawn.

Ten minutes late, a car pulled into the driveway and a short, middle-aged woman stumbled out of the car, a clipboard in hand, and walked quickly toward me.

"I'm so sorry I'm late. I got caught in traffic."

"No problem," I said, as she lifted the welcome mat, pulled out a key, and unlocked the door.

"How long has this been on the market?" I asked, as we trudged up the stairs, toward the room where Meg found her murdered children.

"For about a year. The Montgomerys bought it for them as a wedding present, but it was put in their son's name and so after her conviction ownership reverted to them. They couldn't bring themselves to deal with selling it, so it just sat here. I've been on them for years to do something and finally my perseverance paid off and they let me put it on the market. But as you can imagine, it's a tough sell. I keep cutting the price—they're not really interested in the money—but so far no takers. Between you and me, this place gives me the creeps. You wouldn't happen to be in the market for a house, would you?"

"I'm fine where I am."

"Can't blame me for trying," she said, as she led me up the stairs toward the bedrooms. "I assume you just want to see where the murders took place."

"For now."

We turned right as soon as the stairway ended and approached a room. Ruth opened the door.

"This was the girls' bedroom. Poor things. Who could imagine a mother doing such a thing to her own children?"

I stepped inside. There were no signs that anything the least bit murderous had taken place there. In fact, it looked as if the Montgomerys had gone to great lengths to recreate a room where two girls might be running into at that very moment. It was only creepy if you knew the history. Otherwise, it looked rather sweet, right down to the stuffed animals propped up against each girls' pillow. I wondered if Dwyer had staged it, perhaps even using old photographs of the room.

Ruth stepped to the dresser and swept a finger across the top. "I should get someone in here to dust up a little."

"When was the last time you showed it?"

"Oh, my, it has to be at least a month or so. I was so

excited when you called...until you told me why you wanted to see it."

Ruth closed the door behind us and we continued down the hall toward the master bedroom.

"Here it is. This is where Jeffrey Montgomery was killed," she said, as if she were giving the murder tour.

Like the girls' room, it was fixed up so innocently that there was not a hint of the tragic, murderous spree that took place in this house four years earlier.

I had seen crime scene photos, blood spattered walls, the rooms in disarray, but only now, seeing the house recreated so innocently, as if nothing bad had ever happened there, could I get the real sense of what I was up against. The dichotomy was too stark, too disturbing, the ghosts practically palpable. There was Meg, a sweet, loving mother, patient, caring wife. And there was Meg, vicious murderer of her husband and her two little girls. Which was the real house? Which was the real woman? What was the real story?

This is what I needed to know. This is what drove me to continue investigating. At least that's what I told myself as Ruth Dwyer and I left the house.

"If there's anything else you need, please let me know," she said, as I saw her to her car. "Oh, and if you should happen to know anyone in the market..." she thought better of finishing her sentence.

"Can I get you something?" asked Detective John Knightly, as leaned back in his chair. Knightly was the lead investigator on the case and he looked the part. Big belly, two or three days' worth of stubble, red puffy cheeks that made it look as if he'd just come in from the cold, and a swollen, slightly discolored nose that prominently staked claim to his face.

"I'm fine, thank you."

"You sure. Cuppa joe? A soda? It's on me."

I didn't want anything but I didn't want to hurt his feelings, either, so I gave in. "Maybe a Diet Coke, if you have it?"

"We got everything. Hey, Joey, bring over two Cokes, will ya. One diet, one regular for the fat man," he called over to a younger, leaner uniformed cop who was sitting in a chair near the door, reading a newspaper.

"Gotta keep these guys busy or else they fall asleep. It don't look good people come into a cop office and see guys nodding off or working the crossword puzzle, not that any of these guys would be capable of anything quite so...intellectual. So, what can I do you for?"

"You were the investigating officer on the Montgomery case."

"That I was."

"From what I read I understand you initially believed the murders were committed by one or more intruders."

"That's what she wanted us to think."

"Meaning Meg."

"One and the same."

"But isn't it true the evidence you had against her was, at best, circumstantial."

"It was enough to convince the jury."

"That doesn't really answer my question."

"I wasn't aware there was one."

I didn't like this guy. He was cocky and dismissive. He didn't want to talk to me and he wasn't going to make it easy for me. I knew he was in an untenable position. He was the investigator. Was he about to suddenly claim the whole thing was a mistake, that they'd prosecuted an innocent woman? No way. But that wasn't why I didn't like him. I didn't like him because he was a dick. I was about to answer him, but he didn't let me.

"Look, honey, I don't know what your spin is or what kind of bullshit angle you're trying to push, but if you wanna go around playing Nancy Drew why don't you just do another one of them mob exposes you've been trying to peddle. 'Cause otherwise you're wasting my time here. Is that clear enough for you?"

Joey appeared and plopped down two cans of soda, one diet the other not. Knightly popped open his and took a deep slug. I stared at mine a moment. I wasn't going to open it because I wasn't going to drink it. Not because he called me honey. Not because he wasn't going to help me. But because he was a dick. Screw him and his phony hospitality.

"It's perfectly clear, actually."

"Good. Now that we've got that settled..."

"It's not settled. Nothing's settled. You thought she was guilty..."

"I *know* she is guilty."

"So you can't help me?"

"I won't help you because I can't help you. You want to prove she's innocent so you can have a great story on the news. So everybody will pat you on the back and say, 'That Trish Sullivan, what a helluva reporter she is. Trish Sullivan rights wrongs. Trish Sullivan is a savior.' Ain't gonna happen, lady."

I felt like opening that Diet Coke and when I did, I'd take it and pour it over his fat Irish head. But, of course, I did not do that. Instead, I just thanked him for his time and left him sitting there, a big fat grin on his big fat face.

Chapter 6

I found Marie Cunningham residing in a small, one-bedroom apartment not far from downtown Syracuse. It was furnished like any mother's apartment would be, with plenty of photos of her family placed on just about anything that had a surface and furniture that looked like it was one step away from the Goodwill truck.

The apartment, smelling from a mixture of chicken soup and Lemon Pledge, was immaculate. We sat in the living room, next to each other on a faded, flower print, surprisingly comfortable couch that had certainly seen better days.

Marie was a small, frail woman with white hair, but you could see where Meg got her looks because her face, remarkably unlined—I wanted to ask her for her beauty secrets—with prominent cheekbones and a small, perfect nose, was an older model of her daughter's.

"Here she is blowing out her birthday candles," Marie said, reading glasses slid down to the tip of her nose, as she proudly showed me photos from a thick album she cradled in her lap.

"...that's when we lived over near park, behind the University."

"How old was she?"

"Oh, she must have been about five or six, I suppose."

She removed the photo from the album, turned it over and there was the date, 10/4/81. "Yes. Six years old."

She turned the photo back over and stared at it a moment before she replaced it in the album. She turned the page and there was another photo of Meg, this one when she was a little older, sitting on a porch swing, reading a book.

"She loved to read. Always had a book in her hand. Straight As from the first grade on."

She turned several pages until she reached a photo of her daughter smiling, wearing a blue and gold sweater with the capital C on it.

"I was so proud of her when she was given the scholarship to Columbia Prep. At first, some of the kids used to tease her about how poor she was, calling her a 'charity case,' and whatnot. You know how cruel kids can be. She'd come home in tears and say, 'I'm never going back there again!' But the next morning, bright and early, there'd she be, ready for school. She always managed to pick herself up, no matter what the circumstances were. That's what makes it so hard for me every time I go to visit—and I'm afraid I can't make it as often as I'd like. It's harder and harder for me to walk. It's the arthritis. Terrible. Terrible. Anyway, lately she seems more and more despondent and there's nothing I can say or do to cheer her up. Her writing you was a big step for her. She hates asking for help. But I'm so glad she did. And I'm so glad you're helping her..."

I wanted to tamp down her expectations. I didn't know if I could help. I wasn't even sure I wanted to help, though meeting Marie was pretty close to reaching the point of no return.

She turned the page.

"She was valedictorian and prom queen her senior

year. Everybody loved her. She had so many friends. And then, one by one, they deserted her, and now I'm the only visitor she sees. Even my son, her brother, refuses to visit. He thinks she's guilty and wants nothing to do with her."

I was tempted to ask Marie what she thought, but what did I think she would answer? I almost couldn't help it. It's like those stupid questions we're taught to ask. Like to a husband and wife after their house has burned down. "How do you feel about this?" What the hell do we expect them to say? Or when there's a tragic automobile accident and two teenagers die a fiery death. "How do you feel?" How do we think they feel? It's as if we have lost all sense of empathy. As if we can't make ourselves imagine how it feels. Just once, when asking a question like that, I'd love to hear someone respond, "How do you think I feel, asshole?" But they don't. They want to please us. They want to be respectful. And people like us, why do we keep asking the questions? Because that's what we're supposed to do. Plumb the human soul for feeling, for experience, perhaps because we're not capable of doing it for ourselves.

She turned the page and there was Meg standing next to Jeffrey Montgomery, a handsome, clean-cut young man smiling, wearing a tuxedo.

"Everyone thought they were the perfect couple. Jeff so rich and handsome and Meg so smart and beautiful. Jeff's parents were skeptical at first. They thought the only reason Meg was interested in him was for his money. But nothing could have been further from the truth. After they were married Jeff's mother offered to pay for a housekeeper to come in and help out, but she insisted on doing all the cooking and housecleaning herself. Of course, after they realized how wrong they were about her, they grew to love her. Especially Mrs. Montgomery."

"How do they feel about her now?" I asked.

"Neither one of them have spoken a word to us since the trial."

"What was Jeff like?"

She paused and bit her lip. "He was a bit, you know, on the wild side. He always had to have his own way. I don't think he ever quite grew up. After a couple years of college he up and quit, living off his family trust fund. By then, they'd gotten married and when Meg was pregnant with the twins he forced her to drop out of school as well. It was her senior year and she was on Dean's list..."

Her voice lowered. She turned the page again. I spotted a photograph of Jeff with his arms around two biker type guys, with long hair and leather jackets. She tried to turn the page quickly, but I stopped her.

"Who are these people?"

"Friends of Jeff's. I can't say I cared for them. I know Meg felt pretty much the same way."

"Why's that?"

"Well, just look at them and you can see for yourself."

"Do you remember their names?"

"The one without the beard is Tommy Leary. I don't know the name of the other one."

"Would you mind taking the photo out? Maybe there's some information on the back."

"Of course," she said, as she lifted the cellophane

covering and removed the photo. I turned it over and saw the names Tommy Leary, Jeff and George Raimy scribbled in ink. I copied them down in my notebook.

"Would you mind if I held onto this one?"

"No. Of course not."

On the next page there was a photo of Meg and the identical twin girls, who looked like they were three or four years old. She pointed to one girl, then the other.

"This was Kimberly, this one Rebecca. They looked alike but their personalities were so different. Kimberly was always happy and smiling. Rebecca, well she never seemed happy. She cried a lot as an infant and she was always getting into trouble. Nothing big, you under-stand. But it was a little troubling. It was almost as if she didn't know wrong from right. Meg just thought she did it to get attention and although she loved both girls equally, I think she bonded a little bit more with Rebecca. It's so ridiculous to think she ever could have done what they say she did to them. Ridiculous. Hold on," she said, slowly getting up from the couch, using one arm to propel her forward. She went over to the bookcase and picked up a framed studio portrait of Meg, Jeffrey, Kimberly and Rebecca.

"This was taken less than a month before the murders," she said, handing it to me, her eyes filling with tears, "whatever problems my daughter and son-in-law may have had there's no way in the world she would have harmed her children. Never."

Chapter 7

I had Jackie try to hunt down numbers for Tommy Leary and George Raimy. When I called the one for Raimy, a woman answered. I said I was looking for Raimy.

"Who ain't?" she responded.

"Do you know where I can find him?"

"Who's this?"

"My name's Trish Sullivan."

"That don't mean nothin' to me. Why you want George?"

"I want to talk to him about something."

"I ain't his answering service."

"I don't mean to bother you but it is kind of important."

"You know where Greenhaven is?"

"I do."

"Then that's where you're gonna have to go you want to talk to him. And while you're there, remind him he owes six months back child support and I don't care how the hell he gets it. I want it."

"What's he in for?"

"How much time you got?"

I got the point.

The drive to Greenhaven in winter, especially when a light snow had begun to fall, wasn't a pleasure trip. And while I was on the road it occurred to me that I was spending more time in prisons than I was in the makeup chair.

Raimy's rap sheet was long, but this time he was in for attempted murder. It was only attempted because his victim, who was beaten to within an inch of his life, happened to pull through, though not without enough brain damage so he would be the responsibility of the State of New York for the rest of his life. This gave him something in common with Raimy, who do to the three-strike law, now had a permanent address.

I sat across from him, a pane of thick glass keeping us apart.

He was a large man, barrel-chested, with more tats than I had colors of nail polish. He was bushy-haired with a graying goatee and was dressed in prison garb that seemed at least a couple sizes too small. Nevertheless, I recognized him immediately as the man in that photograph.

He picked up the phone and motioned for me to do the same.

"Thanks for agreeing to see me," I said.

"What else I gotta do with my time?"

"I'm doing a follow-up piece on the Montgomery case."

"What's that gotta do with me?"

"You and Jeff Montgomery were friends."

"I wouldn't say we was friends."

"What would you say you were?"

"Business associates." He laughed. "Yeah. I like the sound of that."

"What kind of business."

He smiled, baring yellow teeth, one of which was gold.

"I forget."

"You're serving time for attempted murder but you've been in before, for drug trafficking. Was that it?"

"Possession with intent."

"Ten kilos of coke. That's an awful lot of intent."

"You done your homework, girl. Good for you. Maybe you should know I was framed."

"Don't you hate it when that happens? So tell me about you and Jeff Montgomery."

"Nothing to tell."

"That's not what I heard."

"What'd you hear?"

"I heard you and he were pretty tight."

"Look, you want to know about Jeff Montgomery you're talkin' to the wrong guy."

"Who should I be talking to?"

"Tommy. He and Jeff were partners."

"Tommy Leary?"

"That's right. Scumbag motherfucker. He's the reason I'm here."

"How's that?"

"Whoa, I'm not so sure I should be talking to you."

"I don't give a damn about you, George. I don't care what you've done or why you're here. I only care about the Montgomery case."

He was silent a moment. "What's in it for me I talk to you?"

"What would you like me to do for you?"

"Get me outta here then we'll figure out the rest."

"That's not gonna happen. But you know, I'm a journalist. There are things I can do."

"Like what?"

"Use your imagination."

He thought a moment. "I was doing some...collection work for Tommy. It didn't go so smooth. That's what landed me here. Tommy beat it 'cause he cut a deal to save his damn ass. I found out later some cop's got his claws into him and he sings every time he gets his balls squeezed. I guess it pays to have connections, huh?"

"Who's the cop?"

"I help you out, maybe I've got a connection, is that what you're saying?"

"Let's keep working this, George, and see where it takes us. What's the cop's name?"

"I don't remember."

"Sure you do."

He shook his head. "We'll come back to that. What was the relationship between Jeff and Tommy?"

"They was like partners. He was Tommy's bank sometimes."

"You're sure about that?"

"Yeah. That's something his old man managed to keep outta the press. At some point, though, right before he was murdered, Tommy and him had some kind of falling out."

"Over what?"

"I ain't sure, but knowing Tommy I wouldn't be surprised if he burned him on a deal. Course the thing you gotta remember about Jeff was it wasn't so much the money, he got off on the pure bang of it."

"Was Jeff's wife aware he was involved in drug dealing?"

He shrugged and shifted the phone to his other ear. "May have, for all I know, but I doubt it. She always seemed pretty straight to me. Then again, it just goes to show you can never know nothin' about nobody. I still can't believe she killed them kids, man. They was beautiful kids, y'know?"

"How do you know?"

"I seen pictures."

"She claims she's innocent."

"Maybe she is. Course I'm innocent, too. Whyn't you do a story on me?"

"Think you'd be able to pass a polygraph?"

"She passed?"

"Yeah. If she didn't do it could Leary have been involved?"

He considered it a moment. "Alone? Uh-uh. He wouldn't have the stomach for it. Or the balls."

"What if he had help?"

He put the phone down and ran his hand through his hair, as if that would help him think. He picked the phone back up. "Maybe. Could be. Yeah, maybe."

"Where can I find him?"

"What makes you think I'd want to help you? You think it's safe for me in here, babe? You think I bunk with a bunch of choirboys?"

"This could be a way to get back at him for what he did to you."

He put the phone down again and closed his eyes, as if he were deep in thought. He picked the phone back up. "Aw, what the hell...He used to hang out at this club, The Carnivore."

"And that cop's name?"

"Knightly. John Knightly."

That night, I found myself all dressed up as if I were going clubbing, which I was in a way. I put on a pair of black tights and over them I wore a red miniskirt and a low-cut black silk blouse. I pulled out the stops by adding a pair of "fuck-me" black stiletto heels and a small, sequined purse that held, at best, my car keys, a small wallet, a tube of lip gloss, a compact and that photo of Jeff, Raimy and Leary. I piled on the make-up, hoping I'd pass for twenty-eight instead of a chick pushing forty, grabbed my short, black leather jacket and white silk scarf and headed out the door.

I had no trouble getting through the red velvet rope and the large, well-muscled dude who manned the door at the Carnivore Club. I don't know if it was because he recognized me or because of the way I was dressed—women seemed to have an easier time getting in than men, who comprised most of the line that snaked halfway around the block.

Inside, it was dark and cavernous, the music ear-splitting and pulsating, as hundreds of people converged on the dance floor. I found the bar, ordered a drink, which some nerd next to me insisted on buying, and stared out onto the dance floor, which was illuminated by a coordinated series of strobe lights which were headache inducing. Suddenly, I felt old and it only magnified my sense of lost time. Could I see myself doing the same thing, in the same place, in the same way, five years from now? Unfortunately, I could, which only made me feel that much more desperate.

After I shooed away my nerdy admirer—I told him I was a lesbian—It was not my proudest moment and I don't think he believed me, but it worked—I made eye contact with the bartender and indicated that I wanted him to come over when he had a chance.

A moment later, this handsome, young dude, early twenties, maybe, wearing tight black jeans and a tight white T-shirt with Carnivore Club printed on the front was standing in front of me. "Hey, don't I recognize you?"

"I don't know. Do you?"

"Yeah. You're the chick from the news, right? What are you doing here?"

I leaned forward so he could hear me over the pulsating din. "I'm looking for a guy. I hear he's a regular. Tommy Leary. You know him?"

"He used to come in here pretty often. Haven't seen him in a while. I know why you're looking for him, lady, but he's trouble."

"So I've heard. Do you know where I can find him?"

I noticed a lanky, young Latino standing almost directly opposite me at the bar. He was checking me out. Damn, I thought, maybe I should have dressed down. This is getting in the way.

He shook his head, no.

"Are any of his friends here, you know, anyone he usually hangs out with?"

"Huh?"

"Is there anyone here he usually hangs out with?"

He nodded toward the Latino who was checking me out.

"Who's that?"

"Name's Calvin. He might be able to help you."

"Thanks," I said, as I picked up my drink and tried to break through the mob of people who stood between us.

Finally, I reached him, but only after spilling half my drink. He was smiling. "Something I can do for you, *chica*?"

"I'm looking for Tommy Leary?"

"Tommy who?"

"Leary."

"I don't know no Tommy what's his name, but if you're looking to score some coke, speed or X, I'm your man."

"Not tonight, thanks."

"Well, if you change your mind, you just ask for Calvin. That's me, *chica*."

Not much chance of that, dude, I thought. I was almost out of options, but I figured as long as I was there I might as well stick around a while longer. I climbed the stairs to the second floor and stood at the railing, looking down at the sea of dancers. I pulled out the photo and stared at it, while sipping my drink. I put the photo back in my purse and stared back down at the dance floor. A female dancer, shoulder-length blonde hair, wearing a short skirt and loose sequined top caught my attention. There was something about her. Something familiar. It took a moment, but then I realized what it was. She was a dead ringer for Meg.

A moment later, she was gone, obscured by a large man wearing a black leather jacket and blue jeans. He positioned himself in front of the Meg lookalike, looking around, as if trying to find someone he'd lost. Finally, he looked up and when he saw me he smiled. He put his hand up as if to say, "don't move," and started toward the stairs.

The smell of a mixture of sweet cologne and scotch preceded him. I could tell he was a little drunk, because he wobbled slightly as he stood in front of me.

"I hear you're looking for Tommy Leary?"

"How did you know that?"

He jerked his head the dance floor. "Calvin."

"Who are you?"

"Leo Ames, but that ain't important 'cause you ain't looking for me."

"Do you know where I can find Tommy?"

He cupped his hand to his ear. "Can't hear you. Speak up."

"Maybe we should go someplace else to talk."

He nodded his head and I followed him out of the club.

We wound up at sleazy pool hall a block or so away. Leo insisted we play, which I didn't mind. I was a little rusty, but I could still hold my own. I learned to play with my brothers—we had a pool table in the basement—and at one time I was good enough to occasionally kick their asses, which didn't go over too well with them but was fine with me. I've always liked competition and winning is a lot better than losing.

"Where'd you learn to shoot pool like that?" Leo asked, as I leaned across the table lining up a shot. I don't think he was looking at the table as much as he was checking out my legs as I raised one a little off the ground, while probably also hoping my boobs would somehow magically be released from my bra.

"Misspent youth," I said.

I pulled back the cue then gently tapped the 6-ball so that it caressed the 8, which then slowly rolled toward the corner pocket.

"Damn, girl, you're good," he said, as he reached into his pocket, pulled out a crumpled twenty and tossed it on the table.

"My dad always said I should ease up, you know, let the boys win every once in a while, so they'd like me better," I said, as I reached over to pick up the bill.

"Did you?"

I smiled. "When I play, I play to win."

"Double or nothing?"

"It's getting a little late, Leo, and we didn't come here to shoot pool."

"Come on..."

"How about you talk about Leary?"

He grabbed the rack under the table and began tossing balls back on the table.

"Tommy could either be your best friend or your worst nightmare, depending. You never know what's gonna set him off."

"Hot temper, huh?"

He made a sizzling sound.

"A few years back, I was with Tommy, this buddy of mine, Richie, and this chick Richie was banging. I forget her name. Anyway, we were all pretty wasted and Tommy starts hitting on the chick. Well, Richie, y'know, he doesn't like it, so he starts telling Tommy where he can go. Well, Tommy, he's like, 'you better not fuck with me, man.' And Richie's, you know, 'I'll fuck with you if I wanna fuck with you, asshole.' That kinda shit. Well, Tommy, just kind of up and lifts his shirt a little so we can see he's carrying and he goes, 'You wanna try, motherfucker?' And Richie's like, 'Yeah, right, you're full of it.' And Tommy goes, 'Remember that family that got whacked—the Montgomerys? Jeffie didn't believe me either, and look what happened to them. So you better not fuck with me if you know what's good for you.'"

He positioned the balls in the rack then gently lifted it. "Your break, girl."

I couldn't believe what I was hearing and I wanted to ask him to repeat it but I thought that would scare him off, so I used my TV demeanor—nothing shocks me, nothing affects me. I just read the news I don't make it. I chalked the cue.

"Uh, Leo, you wouldn't happen to know where I can find this Richie, would you?"

"I ain't seen him in a couple years. I think maybe he left town, moved down south or something. And the girl, you know, she was just some random chick. They come and go, y'know. Listen, you gonna play or you gonna talk."

We played. And this time I let him win. It was worth it. Now I had a lead and a name that might help me find out what actually happened at the Montgomery house that afternoon. I knew it might have just been some macho bragging bullshit meant to impress his buddies, but maybe, just maybe, Meg really was innocent.

Chapter 8

When I pulled up to the police precinct, Knightly was standing outside, leaning up against the building, shooting the breeze with a couple other cops, both of whom were smoking. I parked the car in a spot meant for police vehicles. I pulled my Press sign out of the glove compartment and stuck it in front of the window on the passenger side.

"You boys know that'll kill you?" I said, as I approached the three of them.

Knightly looked up and smiled. "You know you're in a No Parking zone? Get out the pads, boys, I think we got a live one here."

"I'm press," I said, as the two other cops gawked at me. I knew what they were thinking. But I didn't care. I'm not afraid to use what advantage being an attractive woman might have. Or, for that matter a press pass.

"What can I do for you, honey?" Knightly asked, as the two other cops stubbed out what was left of their butts on the side of the building. "Don't litter, boys," I said but they didn't crack a smile.

"I'd like you to help me tie up a few loose ends."

"Why don't you boys go inside and let me talk to the lady," Knightly said to his pals.

"Sure thing, Johnny," said one of them, as he and the other one headed back into the building.

"This gonna take long?"

"It depends."

"It's cold out here."

"We can go inside."

"I'm tired of staring at those four walls. Let's grab a cuppa joe across the street. On you."

"Sure thing," I said, realizing it was probably better to get him off his turf where he might let down his guard a little.

We sat in a booth in the nearly empty coffee shop. It was mid-afternoon and most of the cops who frequented the joint were either on duty or back in the station house. We both had a cup of coffee in front of us, only Knightly's had company—a cherry Danish.

"So, how do you think she did it...if she did."

Knightly smiled, broke off a hunk of his Danish, popped it in his mouth then washed it down with a slug of coffee.

"Oh, she did it all right."

"Can you tell me the details?"

"You're a smart woman. You did your homework. What do you need me to rehash it for you?"

"I like to hear the sound of your voice."

He snorted derisively. "First off, she tried to hire a hit man. When that didn't work out, she decided to do it herself. Simple as that."

"But why? What reason did she have to kill him?"

"Money. Revenge. She didn't like he was playing around. He probably even knocked her around a couple times, when he was high. Take your pick. We had plenty of motives to choose from. When the hit man didn't work out, she got desperate and decided to do it herself."

"You don't really believe that, do you?"

He stared at me so hard I thought my face would break. "You think I make a habit of railroading innocent people?"

"I didn't say that."

"Sounds that way to me."

"I just want to know how you think she did it."

"On the day of the murders she arranges to have lunch with her friend so she can establish an alibi. But before she leaves she slips Jeff a little something so he'll be zonked when she comes back. He was a pill popper, a coke head, there was cocaine and barbiturates found in his bloodstream, so she's not worried about anything showing up on an autopsy."

"Go on."

"She comes back, parks a few blocks away from the house. She gets into the house, goes into the bedroom, but not before slipping on a pair of surgical gloves."

"Where'd she get the gloves?"

"She bought 'em. We were able to track down the drugstore where she got them."

"As I recall, she said she used them to clean the toilets—that they were better than the regular clunky ones."

"Yeah. I'm sure that's why she got 'em. Anyway, she goes upstairs, finds Jeff still in bed, asleep, just like she planned. She ties his wrists to the bed with nylon cord, to make it look like some kind of ritual murder. He starts to get up, starts to squirm. That's when she sticks a gun in his mouth and pulls the trigger.

"Just then she hears something downstairs. The one thing she didn't count on. The girls were let out of school early. The kids come running up the stairs. They go into the room and see what dear old mom has done. She panics. First, she kills Kimberly, shoots her in the head. Rebecca runs. She makes it downstairs and goes into the hall closet, to hide. Her mother finds her. She puts the barrel up to Rebecca's head." He cocked his hand like a gun. "Pow! She's dead. Then she hops in the shower, puts the gun, her bloody clothes and the gloves into a plastic garbage bag. She changes clothes, leaves by the back door so no one sees her, drives around fifteen, twenty minutes, dumps the plastic bag into a dumpster somewhere, along with the gun, then drives back to the house, where she pretends to find the bodies before calling nine-one-one."

"That's a whole lot of planning. But you never found the clothes or the gun, no real evidence other than your theory."

"What about the bloody palm print we found on the side of the sink, the one she forgot to wipe off?"

"It was only natural she would have blood on her hands—I'm sure she touched her children's bodies, to see if they were still alive. Maybe even Jeff's."

"Then why only one bloody print?"

"She admitted she'd washed her hands."

"Listen, honey, you can debate it all you want but the fact remains, she was convicted and there's not a damn thing you can do to change that. So why not let sleeping bitches lie?"

I would have nailed him on that bitch line, but I needed his help, so I ignored it. Besides, was I going to change his chauvinistic piggy behavior? I don't think so. "Did you know Jeff was involved in drug dealing?"

"Yeah. But we investigated and determined that's not what got him killed."

"Have you ever heard of a friend of his named Tommy Leary?"

"Can't say as I have." He looked at his watch. "Listen, I gotta go. We can sit here all afternoon and debate this, but the fact is she did it, she's paying for it, and that's it. Maybe you ought to find yourself another story."

"If I'm not mistaken, Detective Knightly, you got your gold shield because of your work on the Montgomery case."

"I hope you're not insinuating something shady, Ms. Sullivan. Because if you are..."

"Look, I'm no different from you. We're both trying to get ahead in the world. Although it certainly would be a shame if after all these years it turns out you were wrong and the result is that an innocent woman is in prison."

"I wasn't wrong. But if you want to waste your time trying to prove I was, that's fine with me. Goodbye, Ms. Sullivan," he said curtly, as he rose from the table. "And I believe this one is on you."

Chapter 9

In the office the next morning, as I was sifting through the emails that had piled up, most of them suggesting ridiculous story ideas, Jackie stopped by and informed me that Sam wanted to see me.

"I'm beginning to think two-thirds of your job here, Jackie, is telling me the boss wants to see me."

"Sometimes it feels that way," she said, smiling as she headed off to the studio to do whatever else she did.

"How's the story coming?" Sam asked as he sat at his desk, his glasses perched on the top of his head. He had a worried look on his face.

"It's coming. Something wrong?"

"Same old same old. Budget cuts."

"We're not going to lose staff, are we?"

"Not if I can help it. But we've got to be more productive. I can't have my people spending too much time on stories that don't pan out."

"You're referring to me, of course."

"Am I?"

"I'm making progress."

"How so?"

"Well, after she passed the polygraph..."

"My psycho ex-wife would have passed any lie detector test ever invented. Tell me something, honestly, do you believe her because you think it will make a great story if she's innocent or do you believe her because she really is innocent?"

"Why does it matter what I believe. It's either a story or it's not a story. That's what I'm trying to find out."

"So what have you found out so far?"

"I've got a lead that there may have been someone else who did it."

"Is this pie-in-the-sky bullshit, Trish, or something solid?"

"I'll know soon enough. I've set up an on-camera interview with Meg."

"You're kidding."

"It wasn't easy. But I pulled some strings. Just in time for sweeps, because that's the way I roll."

"This could backfire and when I fire you, and believe me, I will fire you because I'll have to, you'll be lucky if you find another job in Podunk, Iowa."

I smiled not because I didn't believe him but because I knew it was true. "At least," I said, as I headed out the door, "I won't be in Syracuse anymore."

We set up in a large, empty room with a fold-up chair for Meg and one for me, facing her. Mark set up the lights and camera, while two female guards stood watch. I had spirited our make-up woman, Eve, out of the office and she was applying the last bits and pieces to Meg's still almost perfect complexion. I wondered how she managed that in prison when I woke up every morning looking like the Wicked Witch of the West.

"Just relax, look at me and try not to think about the camera," I instructed, as Mark did some last minute fiddling with the lighting. "And, Mark, don't make it look too good. I don't want viewers to think we're at Club Med."

"No chance of that," Mark replied.

"I can't tell you how much I appreciate all you've done for me, Trish. Even if..."

"Let's just get through this, okay?"

I had her tell her side of the story, how she felt, what it was like spending time in prison for something she didn't do, yadda, yadda, yadda. There was nothing new. I just wanted to viewers to be able to see her and decide for themselves whether or not she was telling the truth. She cried in all the right places at all the right times. She was, all in all, very effective, though not for everyone.

Meg had been taken away and I was helping Mark pack up the equipment.

"What'd you think?" I asked.

"You really want to know?"

"Yeah. I do."

"I think I'd be crying, too, if I had to spend the rest of my life in the can."

"That's a pretty shitty thing to say."

"You asked me what I thought."

"You think she's guilty?"

"I don't know and frankly, I don't give a shit. This is your story, not mine. What about you?"

"I've got an open mind but..."

"But you think she's innocent."

"Yeah. I do."

The next night, we aired the report. From the studio, sitting at the anchor desk, I began.

"I began this story with a great deal of skepticism, but what I discovered about the Meg Montgomery murder case might surprise you."

While I continued the voice-over, we showed file footage of the Montgomery house, the bodies being wheeled out to the coroner's wagon, Knightly stepping over a taped barricade to confer with other detectives, and a distraught Meg comforted at the funeral.

"On a cool spring day in March, 2008, police received a frantic call from Meg Montgomery from the home she shared with her husband, Jeffrey, and her twin daughters, Kimberly and Rebecca. When police arrived, they made a grisly discovery. Jeffrey Montgomery and both children were found shot to death."

We cut to a shot of Knightly placing Meg Montgomery into the backseat of a squad car.

"Two weeks later, Meg Montgomery was arrested for their murder.

"After a three-week trial, plus six days for the jury to deliberate, Meg Montgomery was found guilty on three counts of first degree murder. For the past seven years, Mrs. Montgomery has resided in Bedford Hills Prison for Women, where she will spend the rest of her life."

Tight shot on me.

"But is she, in fact, guilty as charged? No physical evidence other than one bloody palm print was ever found to link Mrs. Montgomery to the murders. Furthermore, she had an alibi, an alibi that has never been fully contradicted."

The screen filled with an establishing shot of me walking down the prison corridor, toward the camera.

"I recently visited with Mrs. Montgomery at Bedford

Hills Prison for Women where she has been a model prisoner since her conviction four years ago."

There was a close-up of Meg.

"I saw Kimberly lying in the doorway, leading to the bedroom. I screamed. And then I noticed Jeffrey, on the bed. His hands and feet were tied. He was covered in blood. I never saw so much blood..."

Tears welled up in her eyes. Her voice broke. The shot was frozen. Good work, Mark.

Back to me in the studio. "What was the primary evidence against her? A school bus driver claimed to have seen Mrs. Montgomery's car parked on a side street a few blocks from her house when he dropped off the twins from school. If true, that would mean she was in the house when they arrived home. And there was the testimony of a man who said two weeks prior to the murders Mrs. Montgomery had approached him at a bar with an offer of twenty-five thousand dollars to kill her husband. But let's examine that evidence. The bus driver never noted the license number of the car. Mrs. Montgomery had an eyewitness who placed her across town having lunch at the time of the murders. As for the testimony of the man who claimed she tried to hire him to murder her husband, well he has an extensive criminal record, dating back to the early nineties. And no one else at the bar remembered seeing her that night.

"It was election year politics as usual as Herman Daley, the District Attorney, was only weeks before swept into office on a get-tough-on-crime platform. And there was the press who virtually made it difficult for her to have received a fair trial.

"Tomorrow evening, we will present a further report

on the Montgomery murders, including an interview with a new witness who claims to have heard the real killer confess to the crime."

The next morning I was lying in wait in front of Knightly's apartment, sitting next to Mark in the news van.

"You're sure this is a good idea, Trish?"

"Yeah, I'm sure."

Mark pulled out a cigarette and started to light up.

"Excuse me," I said.

"What?"

"Must you?"

"I've been waiting here half an hour, what do you expect me to do?"

"If you have to smoke take it outside, please."

"It's fuckin' freezing out there."

"Then don't smoke."

He shot me a look and, like a petulant child, put the butt back into its package. Even though he turned his head away I could see he silently mouthed the word, "bitch." I smiled. What did I care? Soon, if things went according to plan, he'd be a not so fond memory.

A few minutes later I spotted a grey SUV drive down the street. It was Knightly. I elbowed Mark in the ribs and hissed, "He's here. Let's go!"

Knightly, carrying a bag of groceries, didn't know what hit him. I was only a few feet away when he realized I was closing in him, with Mark only steps behind me, his camera filming.

"Detective Knightly," I said, slightly out of breath,

"you told me the other day you never heard of Tommy Leary, but we've learned that he's been your primary witness in at least six separate cases. Would you care to comment, Detective..."

He said nothing. He didn't have to. If looks could kill, I would have been dead and buried. Instead, he simply turned his back on me and walked slowly toward his house. Just as he got to the front door he turned and said, loud enough for me to hear but not loud enough for Mark to pick up, "You're gonna get someone else killed."

That was fine. I'd gotten what I'd come for.

The next afternoon, I was at my desk having a working lunch with Jackie. We were going over a list of possible stories to do.

"I think Channel Four already did a story on that," I said as Jackie pointed to the list in front of us.

"I'll check. By the way, did you get a look at the overnights? They're through the roof."

"Murder sells."

Suddenly, there was an unfamiliar hush in the ever buzzing newsroom. I looked up and there, striding toward me, was none other than Detective John Knightly.

"Good afternoon, Ms. Sullivan," he said, as Jackie swept up her sandwich and Diet Coke and started to move away.

"Good afternoon, Detective Knightly. And Jackie, you don't have to leave."

"I...I think I'll go check on that tape for tonight," she said, as she backed away awkwardly.

"I just wanted to thank you in person for that little

ambush you pulled you yesterday. Great TV."

"You could have stuck around to answer my questions. I was simply offering you the opportunity to respond on camera."

"Bullshit." He looked down at the photos I had of Meg spread out on my desk.

"Quite a looker, isn't she? You're not getting a little sweet on her, are you, Ms. Sullivan?"

"Is that the best you can do, Detective?"

"No. I can do better. Here," he said, going into his coat pocket, pulling out a manila envelope and then emptying its contents on my desk. They were color photographs of each of the murder victims. "Maybe you can show these on TV tonight. And maybe you can fill in the rest of the story. How she shot her husband in the mouth, Kimberly in the head, then searched through the house looking for Rebecca. It couldn't have taken long to find her. All she had to do was breathe in and she could have smelled her. Poor kid, hiding in the closet, how do you think she felt knowing her mother was stalking her?"

"You never found the gun."

"That's because she ditched it when she got rid of her clothes."

"I'm sorry, but there is absolutely no way a mother, this mother at least, could be capable of committing such a heinous crime against her kids. A husband, sure. What woman hasn't at least imagined killing her husband at one point or another. But not this."

"Honey, I've been around a long time and I've seen a lot of things, things that would turn your stomach, things that you couldn't imagine possible. You'd be surprised what a person is capable of. And I'm almost gonna feel sorry for you once you realize you're wrong. I just hope you're not able to do any more damage than you've already done."

He turned to leave. He was finished. But I wasn't.

"Leary was your snitch, wasn't he?"

"He was my C.I. And if you put that on the air, he's a dead man. How'd you like that on your conscience?" He paused. "Look, I'm not saying he's not dirty. But if you think I'd go out of my way to protect a murderer, you're crazy."

"How about telling me where I can find him. He seems to have disappeared."

He smiled. "That's not happening."

"I will find him, Detective. And when I do, you'll have a lot of explaining to do."

It was early the next evening when I stood outside the door of the Little Roma Social Club. I didn't know the secret code, if there was one, so I just knocked a few times and stepped back. A moment later the door opened a crack.

"Whatchoo want? You lost or somethin'?"

"I'm looking to speak to Mr. Alcante."

"First of all, no ladies allowed in here, second of all, he ain't here."

"So who's that sitting at the table feeding his fat face?"

"Who is it, Sonny," boomed Alcante.

"It's that chick from the TV."

"She got some nerve," said another wise guy sitting next to him.

"Has she got any them camera guys with her?"

Sonny looked past me. "Nah. She's alone."

"What does she want?" asked Fat Tony.

"What do you want?"

I pushed my way in. "Instead of playing this ridiculous game of telephone, why don't you just ask me why I'm here?"

Sonny pushed back, but Fat Tony waved at me. "Let the broad in."

I approached his table.

"You want some pasta?" he asked.

"No, thanks."

"Then what do you want? You're not gonna tell me more ridiculous rumors about there being a contract out on me, me an innocent plumbing supply salesman," he smiled, playing to the several wise guys in the room, who laughed obligingly. "You ain't wearin' no wire, are you?"

"No."

"How do I know you're telling me the truth?"

"You want to pat me down, Tony."

He smiled. "I'm a gentleman...I'd have someone else do it."

"Be my guest."

He shook his head, smiling. "Okay, okay, sit down and tell me what the hell you want. But remember, I'm eating and I get indigestion very easy. So what's so important you have to interrupt my dinner?"

"I need you to help me find someone."

"You need me to help you find someone," he repeated.

"That's right."

"So you need a favor from me?"

"That's right."

"What makes you think I'm gonna do you a favor?"

"I don't know that you will, but I'm asking you anyway."

"Why me?"

"Because I'm told he associates with other...'plumbers.'"

Fat Tony smiled. So did the others.

"What's his name?"

"Tommy Leary.

"Never heard of him," he said, returning to his plate of pasta.

"Then I guess I've wasted my time," I got up.

Fat Tony spread out his arms. "Not so fast, honey. Sit down. We're negotiating here. You know what negotiating means, don't you? Just 'cause I say I never heard a him don't mean I can't help you find him. Maybe he's in the, you know, the plumber's union."

Laughter from his cronies.

"But I do this for you, you gotta do something for me. That's how favors work."

He made a washing gesture with his hands.

"Like what?"

"Let's see." He looked around at his guys. "Like for starters I don't ever wanna hear you call me Fat Tony on the air again. My name is Anthony Alcante. Not Fat Tony or Fat Anthony or Fat Fuck or Fat Anything. Understand?"

"I could do that."

"And I want you to stop bugging me. Find someone else to investigate."

"I'll consider it."

He shook his head. "This, as they say, is non-negotiable."

"All right. You help me find him, I'll find other stories."

"This Tommy Leary you're looking for, is it personal or business."

"Business."

"Must be pretty important business, huh? Go stand over there by the bar for a minute."

I got up and moved to the bar as Fat Tony motioned Sonny over. He spoke to him in a whisper that was loud enough for me to hear.

"You know that Mick that ripped us off a while back? That was Leary, right?"

"Yeah."

"I want you should find him..."

He motioned me back. "Sonny's on it. We'll get back to you."

"Thanks," I said. "And maybe you ought to consider going on a diet if you don't like people calling you fat."

"Honey, this is my diet."

He laughed.

His guys laughed.

I had to laugh, too.

Chapter 10

It was the restaurant in Syracuse where the wealthy women of leisure, the women who busied themselves with their charitable impulses, the women who had time for such things, chose to lunch. I was told that was where I might find Jeff Montgomery's mother and it was. She was dining with two other well-dressed, well-heeled older women, at a corner table. I asked for and got a table not far from them and when she got up to use the restroom, I followed her in.

I approached her at the sinks.

"Excuse me, Mrs. Montgomery."

She looked at me, puzzled.

"Yes," she said tentatively.

"I'm sorry to approach you this way but my name is..."

"I know who you are."

"Then you probably know why I want to talk to you."

"I do."

"Do you have a few minutes for me?"

"I'm with friends."

"I know. I thought maybe when you were finished..."

"I don't..."

"It'll just take a few minutes. I promise."

"I don't approve of what you're doing, Ms. Sullivan."

"I understand, but I'm sure you want the real killer of your son..."

"I believe the real killer is in prison, Ms. Sullivan."

"I'm not so sure..."

She hesitated a moment. "All right. I noticed you at your table—I'm not blind, you know—so I'll stop by when we're finished."

"Thank you."

Ten minutes later, as I was finishing the only thing I ordered (a cup of coffee), Mrs. Montgomery sat down opposite me.

"I almost changed my mind," she said.

"I'm glad you didn't. First, I wanted to tell you that Meg speaks very highly of you. She wanted me to give you her regards, if I was able to see you."

"It seems you are."

"I'll just ask you one question, Mrs. Montgomery. Do you believe Meg killed your son and grandchildren?"

She dropped her head. I knew she didn't want me to see her tear up. I understood that, but it was a question I had to ask. I felt like reaching over and taking her hand, but I did not.

Finally, she looked up. "I did not want to believe it, Ms. Sullivan. Because if I did I would have to acknowledge that there was a monster among us."

"I'm sorry, Mrs. Montgomery, but that doesn't really answer my question. Did you believe it?"

She hesitated again, as if carefully weighing the result of her answer.

"At first, no, I did not."

"Why not?"

"I just couldn't believe the sweet, loving woman I knew and came to love would be capable of such a... terrible, terrible thing."

"Then why didn't you stand up for her at the trial?"

"My husband, well he wouldn't hear of it. He is a man who sees the world in black and white, good and evil, right and wrong. He believed if she was arrested, that if the police believed she was guilty, she must have done it. He believed that the authorities wouldn't have arrested her unless she had. But I know my son was no angel. I know that quite well. It was my fault, I suppose, for spoiling him. He was my only child and perhaps that's why I considered Meg to be more like a daughter than a daughter-in-law."

"I'm going to stretch my one question into one more, Mrs. Montgomery. If Meg didn't do it, who did?"

"I wish I knew, Ms. Sullivan. I wish I knew."

"So you believe your daughter-in-law is innocent?"

She hesitated again. She cocked her head back slightly, her jaw was set firm. It looked like she was about to say something, but she did not. For some reason, she could not bring herself to say the words, the words that might crack the case wide open, the words she wanted to say but could not. "I do not believe Meg did it." Those were the words I wanted to hear and those, I believed, were the words she wanted to say.

But she did not.

Chapter 11

It was a fine day to visit the park. The January thaw had finally kicked in and the temperature was flirting with the low fifties. I parked the car and headed toward the sound of calliope music in the distance, which was soon joined by the sounds of children playing.

The carousel was just beginning to move as a handful of parents watched their kids holding on to the pole stuck through the middle of the wooden horse's mane and waved gleefully. I couldn't help but think of Meg's kids and then to the fact that I'd probably never have any of my own. It wasn't that I didn't want them, it's just that the time never seemed to be right and if it were the right guy didn't seem to be on hand. During the three years I was married, to a print journalist who couldn't seem to stay in one place too long, we broached the subject a few times but somehow the conversation seemed to morph into an argument. I don't even remember what we argued about but at the time each one seemed to be important and each one led me to the conclusion that this was not the man I wanted to be the father of my children. And now, with that horrible clichéd clock running out of ticks, even the idea of having a child seemed absurd. But to have them and then lose them, as Meg did, in such a horrible, unthinkable way, well, it immersed me in a sadness that was nearly overwhelming. And when something overwhelms me the best way to deal with it is to not deal with it, to shove back into the recesses of my mind, to replace it with something else, something more immediate.

Today, that something was finding Sam Roche whom I was told ran the park carousel ride. Heavyset and swarthy, bundled up in a ski jacket and heavy woolen scarf, as if the temperature was twenty degrees not fifty, he appeared visibly annoyed by the children's screams of pleasure.

When I was within a few steps he looked up.

"I was wondering when you were gonna get around to me," he said, never taking his hand off the controls. He looked away and yelled, "Hey, what'd I tell you kids about holding on? Keep your hands on the reins!"

"Crazy about kids, aren't you?"

"It's a job, lady. I don't gotta like 'em, I just gotta make sure no one gets hurt. So, let's get this over with."

"Fine with me. You testified Meg Montgomery tried to hire you to kill her husband."

"Yeah."

"Why did you wait so long to go to the police? Why didn't you tell them right away instead of waiting till the murders occurred?"

"I had my reasons."

"Which were?"

"I don't gotta talk to you."

"I know."

He hesitated a moment. "But you ain't gonna leave me alone till I do."

"That's right."

"I had some run-ins with the law. I didn't think they'd believe me. Besides, I don't like to get involved.'"

"Were you telling the truth?"

"What do you think?"

"It doesn't matter what I think. I just want to know if you were telling the truth."

"You wired?"

"No."

"How can I be sure?"

"I guess you can't be unless I strip down and that isn't going to happen."

"I don't think you're wired. Look, I said what I said 'cause I had to. Enough said."

"Would you be willing to say that on camera?"

"Ever hear of something called perjury?"

"So you were lying?"

"I got work to do." He moved the controls slightly and the carousel began to slow down.

"You can just say you were mistaken. That it was someone else. You'll be a hero. Will you do it?"

"You think I'm the hero type?" He shook his head. "You think being a hero means shit to me? You got the wrong guy, lady."

"How about just doing the right thing?"

He laughed, a laugh mixed with phlegm and derision. "I look like the kind of guy worries much about doing the right thing?" He paused. "What's in it for me?"

"You don't think I'm going to pay you, do you?"

"Then it looks like me and you got nothing more to talk about."

I wanted to walk away, but I couldn't.

"Way I see it, you need me a hell of a lot more than I need you."

"How much?"

"I got a certain figure in mind."

"Which is?"

"A grand."

"You've gotta be kidding?"

"Five hundred."

"I don't have that kind of money on me."

"I don't take checks."

"You'd keep your mouth shut about this, wouldn't you?"

"What have I got to gain by shooting my mouth off about getting paid to change my testimony?"

"I don't want you to change your testimony. I just want you to tell the truth."

"The truth is, it never happened."

I did not like the idea of paying for a story. Not only was it unethical and illegal and immoral, but any story I got would be fatally tainted. But in this case I justified it to myself, albeit in pure Machiavellian terms. I could tell Roche was now telling the truth. Meg hadn't offered to pay him to kill her husband and if the only way I could get him to admit that on camera was to pay him, well then, that was what I had to do. Not to get the story but to free an innocent woman. And maybe put the real killer where he belonged.

I called Mark on his cell and told him to get over to the park, pronto. In the meantime, I headed to the nearest ATM and withdrew three hundred dollars from my account, having the rest of the money already on me.

Twenty minutes later Mark arrived, his camera slung over his shoulder, to find me seated on a bench, my iPod plugged into my ears so I didn't have to listen to any more of that insipid calliope music which had started to seep into my brain. I'd already handed the money over to Roche once again, swearing him to secrecy knowing full well that since I wasn't dealing with a Boy Scout he might try to take another bite out of the apple. But that's where paying him in cash would work to my favor.

"What's up, babe?" Mark asked.

"Since when do you refer to me as 'babe?'"

He put his hand up. "Hey, no offense. Don't you know a term of endearment when you hear it?"

"No, actually. It's been a long time."

"Too long," he muttered under his breath. I could have slapped him but I restrained myself, at least until after he got it all on tape. My favorite line, completely unrehearsed, came when I asked Roche why he was now coming forward: "Hey, I gotta do what I feel in my heart is right."

During the next week, I was on air practically every evening, reporting some aspect of the case. By then, a line of picketers had begun to form in front of the courthouse, chanting for Meg's outright release or at the very least a new trial. Ratings were sky high, which made Sam and the bosses happy.

Over a month had passed since I first met with Meg but I could already feel the groundswell. Local politicians were being interviewed urging a new trial. And every story written, locally and nationally, mentioned me. I was on a roll, a roll that could only take me out of Syracuse and onto the national stage. National news organizations had picked up the story and were running with it to the point where I had to elbow my way through broadcast and print reporters to get around

Syracuse. Suddenly, I had become part of the story. It was not what I wanted but I also knew it would serve me well in terms of furthering my career and getting me the hell out of Syracuse. The truth is, I was as caught up in the excitement of it as everyone else. Even Mark and Sam had climbed on the bandwagon.

The dominoes began to tumble, one by one. And when I found and interviewed a reed-thin crackhead named Luis Alvarez about his beating by Detective Knightly, and threats against him unless he delivered the name of his supplier, and Knightly's subsequent one-month suspension for the use of excessive force, this only added fuel to the fire, which bolstered the claim by Sam Roche that his testimony was coerced by Knightly.

A few days after my weeklong blitz of stories, as I was driving toward the office I heard a siren behind me. I looked into the rearview and saw a police car gaining on me. When I pulled over the squad car pulled up right behind me and Knightly got out of the driver's side while someone I didn't recognized remained in the passenger's seat.

As Knightly approached, I rolled down the window. He stuck his head in, so that his face was no more than six inches from mine, so close I could smell his cheap after-shave.

"You can't be serious," I said. "This is harassment."

"They're lying, you know."

"Who?"

"All of them. Alvarez. Roche."

"It's on the record, Detective."

"I don't care what the fuck is on the record. They're lying. You're supposed to be an investigative reporter, why the hell don't you investigate that?"

"I know a story when I see one, that's why. And that's no story."

He pulled back a little. "Nice earrings," he said, commenting on the pair of half-moons I'd chosen to wear that morning. I'd received plenty of compliments on them and lately I'd taken to wearing them on air, kind of a good luck charm. I knew by complimenting them he was trying to throw me off, but it wasn't going to work.

"You'd better watch yourself, if you know what's good for you," he added.

"Are you threatening me?"

"I'm just saying that if I were you I'd be careful. You're not playing with choir boys."

"Am I free to go, Detective?"

"You were always free, Ms. Sullivan," he said, "but there's someone who shouldn't be."

I was shaking when he left and just sat there in the car, making no move to leave as the squad car pulled slowly past me, Knightly staring harshly at me through his window.

I sat there several minutes, trying to compose myself. I hadn't meant to go after Knightly but if Meg was innocent that meant that he wasn't, that he'd manipulated evidence to get the conviction. And it didn't matter if he believed she was guilty, he still had no right subverting the truth. As Meg's star rose, Knightly's fell. Why wouldn't he fight back? Why wouldn't he want me to back off? His reputation was on the line. But that couldn't and wouldn't deter me. An innocent woman was in prison for life. It was up to me to fix that.

I hadn't been in the office for more than ten minutes when my phone rang. An unfamiliar, raspy voice was on the other end.

"I hear you been looking for me."

"Who is this?"

"You know who it is. You want me meet me at the bus station. In an hour."

"Tommy? Tommy Leary?"

He hung up.

When I arrived at the bus station, there were several squad cars parked in front and a crowd had formed across the street. I went around the block, parked the car, flipping up my press sign, then headed to the front of the bus station. A uniformed cop tried to stop me from getting too close.

"Press," I said, flashing my badge. "What's going on?"

"Some guy got hit by a car."

My heart sank.

"Know his name?"

"Some lowlife named Leary."

"My God," I gasped. "I have to get through.

He lifted the tape and I headed toward the ambulance, which was just pulling away. As it did, I spotted Knightly and a couple other cops I recognized from the precinct house.

I went straight up to Knightly. "Leary?" I said.

"You got it."

"What happened?"

"Seems he was checking his phone, maybe texting, stepped out onto the street without looking both ways and bam!"

"Where's the driver?"

"Beats me."

"You mean it was a hit and run?"

He nodded.

"Do you have a description of the car?"

"Yeah."

"What is it?"

"Blue Infiniti."

"You think this is a coincidence?"

"You mean do I think it has anything to do with the Montgomery case?"

"That's exactly what I mean."

"Leary was scum. There are a thousand reasons he's dead. The only mystery is why it took so long."

"Freud said there are no such things as coincidence."

"Freud said a lot of things and very few of them had to do with Tommy Leary."

"What now?"

"Is that an existential question or are you really interested in what I'm going to do next?"

"Both."

What he was doing next was going to Leary's apartment to see what he could find. I didn't ask to tag along, I just did, following a respectful three car lengths behind him and his partner.

They wouldn't let me go in with them, so I waited outside, leaning against my car, surfing the web on my phone to see if any details of the case would pop up.

When they finally emerged, they were carrying a large cardboard box. Their faces were grim. Something was up.

"Detective," I said, approaching him so that I was only a few feet away. "Did you find something in there?"

He said nothing, as he brushed by me.

They got to the squad car, opened up the back seat, and shoved the box in. Knightly got in the passenger seat, his partner in the driver's seat. I leaned into the open passenger window, while trying to get a look into the backseat to see what was in the box.

"Detective, what did you find?"

His face belying any emotion, he rolled up the window, motioned to his partner to drive, and they were off. I jumped back into my car and followed them to the precinct. Something was up. Something important.

Chapter 12

Since I was persona non grata in the eyes of the Syracuse police department, I had to get information about what was in Leary's apartment from one of my colleagues. Evidently, when Knightly and his partner searched Leary's apartment they found a cardboard box in the back of the closet. In that box they found a 22-caliber revolver and a bloodstained towel monogrammed with the letter *M*. If this were true and it matched up against the bullets that killed Jeff and the girls and the blood on the towel matched any of the victims, then that was all the evidence necessary to get Meg a new trial.

Several weeks later, after being bombarded by the media and as a result of a very high-powered attorney named John Deal offering to represent her, the D.A. finally folded under pressure acquiesced to giving Meg a new trial, set for that June. With this new evidence at hand it seemed like a slam-dunk for the defense.

The trial itself was pretty anticlimactic. The D.A. went through the motions but it was obvious his heart wasn't in it. And up against someone as experienced and charismatic as Deal, he didn't stand a chance. The trial lasted a mere four days and the jury was only out a few hours before they came back with a not-guilty verdict.

It wasn't long before I received the dividend I was looking for. In fact, it came a day after the verdict came in. Jackie was the one who delivered the news.

"Congratulations, Trish," she said, as she held a

cupcake with a lit candle sticking out of it.

"For?"

"I just got a call from MSNBC. They want you to go down to the city to meet with some of the executives."

I wanted to jump up and pump the air or dance around an imaginary end zone, but instead, I just smiled, blew out the candle, and gave Jackie a hug. I wasn't ready to pack my bags just yet, but I was close, mentally ticking off all the details I'd have to take care of before I left Syracuse. For good.

"Oh, and there's one more thing. Meg called. Her in-laws are having a little party to celebrate her release and she insists that you be there."

"I don't know, Jackie. It doesn't seem very professsional."

"I told her I wasn't sure you could make it, but she was very insistent. I think you should go, Trish. You earned it and she really wants to thank you."

"When is it?"

"Next weekend."

"I'll see..."

The next day, I received a call from Meg. I could detect the joy in her voice. And why not? For the first time in seven years she was free to do anything she wanted to do, to go anywhere she wanted to go.

"Trish, I really want you to stop by my mother's place this evening, even if it's only for a few minutes. I have so much to thank you for."

"It's a pretty busy time for me, Meg..."

"I know. But it's important to me that I thank you in person. And besides, I've got some exciting news to share with you. Your assistant told you about the party at the Montgomery's, right?"

"Yes, she did. But..."

"I look forward to seeing you there, too. But I'll see you tonight first, right?"

"All right. But I really can't stay for long. And as for the party, I just don't want it to look as if this was personal, because it wasn't."

"I know that, Trish. I really do."

I didn't know what to expect when Marie Montgomery answered the door and ushered me into her apartment. I don't even know why I said yes when I really meant to say no. But we do that all the time, we women, I mean, and as much as I say I'm not going to be one of those women, I can't help myself. It's like it's hard-wired into our brains to say yes, even when we mean no. And God forbid we should hurt someone's feelings...

As soon as I came in the door, Meg, dressed in tight blue jeans and a pink tank-top, rushed over to hug me.

"I'm so glad you made it, Trish. Wait, please let me get you some champagne. Rick," she called out, "can you bring me a glass of champagne for Trish."

A moment later a guy in his late thirties, early forties, handsome in a rugged Marlboro cowboy kind of way, wearing a denim work shirt, jeans and beige work boots, sporting a couple days' stubble, appeared with two glasses of champagne, one of which he gave to me, the other to Meg.

"Trish, this is Rick Mathis. Rick, you know who this is, of course."

He stuck out his hand and I caught it. His grip was firm and he held my hand in his just a little too long.

"Nice to meet you. Finally. Thanks for all you did for Meg," he said, his arm suddenly around her waist.

She blushed. "Rick used to visit his sister at the prison, which is how we met. I don't know what I would've done if it wasn't for his visits."

"He visited you?"

"Well, kind of. His sister introduced us and then she got out and he was so sweet to keep coming back to see me. That's really why I wanted you to come tonight. To meet Rick and, of course, to say thank you again in person and not in front of the whole world."

"I think you've said it enough, Meg. I was just doing my job."

"Oh, I know that," she said, a funny little smile crossing her face. "And isn't that why I got in touch with you in the first place?"

I was getting a funny feeling. I don't know why, I just was. There was this strange vibe I couldn't quite identify. I wanted to get out of there as quickly as possible. The truth was, I was finished with Meg Montgomery and now I just wanted to get on with the rest of my life and let her get on with hers.

"I'd better be going."

"Oh, I understand. But I'll see you next Saturday, right? At the Montgomerys. I really need you to be there. To support me. It's probably the last time we'll see each other."

That sounded kind of ominous, but I let it pass because it was probably true.

"I'll make an appearance."

"Great. I really need you to be there. You know, there are still some people who think I'm guilty. And for them, it'll never be any different. But I can't help that, can I? I just have to get on with the rest of my life. Which reminds me, that thing I had to tell you."

"The good news?"

"Yes. The good news. Now that I've been exonerated the Montgomerys have insisted on giving me back our home. You know, it was on the market, but they couldn't sell it?"

"I do know that."

"Well, they've decided I should have it. I'll be moving back in tomorrow."

I didn't know what to say. She seemed so thrilled but to me it seemed downright ghoulish. How could she ever set foot in that house again much less live there? What was she thinking when she said yes?

"You think it's kind of weird, don't you?" she added.

"A little."

"Well, maybe it is, but the truth is I have such good memories of living there. And it's an opportunity for me to be closer to my babies. Oh, and if it doesn't work out, I can always sell it."

"I suppose," I agreed, though I thought that was a little flip, a little cold. But who was I to judge? Everyone mourns in his or her own way and who was I to judge Meg's decisions after all she'd been through?

"Nice meeting you," I nodded to Rick, who flashed me one of those unctuous smiles you get from guys trying too hard to pick you up in bars.

That, I thought, was kind of icky. I'm no prude, but the fact that she'd just gotten out of prison and already had someone drooling only added to this funny feeling in the pit of my stomach. Jeez, it was hard enough to find someone outside of prison much less in and here she is out for five minutes and she's already got someone hanging all over her.

As I headed back to my car, I noticed a shiny black Infiniti parked right outside the building. This was a lower middle-class neighborhood and this car seemed totally out of place. I walked over for a closer look. It was a two- or three-year-old model, but it had obviously been freshly painted within the last few months. I checked the front of the car and it looked to me like this was not the original bumper and grill. I pulled out my notebook and jotted down the plate number—ZFS 398. There was just something about this that didn't seem right. I looked over my shoulder to make sure no one was watching, then pulled out a nail clipper and scraped at the paint. There were tiny particles of blue amid the black.

Before I got in to my car I glanced up at Marie Cunningham's apartment window and there was Rick, staring down at me. Was it his car? Had he seen what I'd done?

After driving a few blocks I pulled over and dialed had a contact I had at Motor Vehicles, Harry Crouse. I asked him to run the plate for me. At first, he said no.

"Please, Harry. Just this last time. It's important."

"I could get in trouble for this, Trish."

"How's anyone going to find out?"

"Things have a way of getting out."

"You can trust me, Harry. Have I ever broken a confidence?"

"Okay. But this is the last time."

"Z as in Zebra, F as in Frank, S as in Sam, three-nine-eight. Call me as soon as you find out. I love you, Harry."

"You say that, but you never call unless you want something."

As I pulled into the station parking lot, Harry called back.

"It's a 2011 Infiniti registered to a Karen Ann Farrelli." He gave me the address.

"Does it say what the color is?"

"Blue."

I didn't bother to park, instead heading for the address Harry gave me. It was an apartment complex on the other side of town.

I buzzed Farrelli, 3B, and a woman answered.

"Who is it?"

"Trish Sullivan. I'm a reporter for Channel 9 News. I'd like to ask you a few questions."

"What about?"

"Rick Mathis."

There was a pause.

"He doesn't live here no more."

"I'd still like to ask you a few questions, if you don't mind."

A moment passed. "Elevator's busted. Take the stairs." She buzzed me in.

Karen Farrelli, wearing faded blue jeans and a brown turtleneck sweater, met me at the door. She was slim, maybe five-three, and looked to be in her early forties, though she could have been younger. She had the look of someone who'd been pretty once, but now age and life had caught up to her and it showed up on her delicate face, which was punctuated with freckles and rutted with deep lines running from her high cheekbones down to her prominent chin. She bore more than a passing resemblance to Karen Allen but with all the cute wrung out.

"I'd ask you in but the place is a mess," she said. Over her shoulder I could see that the apartment was small, cluttered, and over-heated and it smelled of cabbage. "So, you wouldn't be missing nothing if we talked out here."

"That's fine."

"Like I said, you're wasting your time. I have no idea where the sonuvabitch is."

"He was your boyfriend?"

"That would be a matter of opinion. Maybe you should ask him."

"When did he leave?"

"You mean when did I throw him out. That would be about a month ago."

"Mind my asking why?"

"Maybe you should come in. This sounds like it's gonna take longer than I thought." She moved to the side and I breezed past her into the living room which now seemed to double as a bedroom, as the couch, a sleeper, was out. Sheets, blankets and pillows were scattered over it and the floor. It was the kind of apartment you'd expect to see inhabited by a herd of cats, but if it was I couldn't see them.

Farrelli moved ahead of me and with one motion, swept the sleeper clean, the linens landing on the floor. Then, she lifted the extended portion in order to put it back in place.

"Need help with that?" I asked.

"I'm fine," she said, and a moment later it looked like a couch again.

"You sit here. I'll drag a chair in from the kitchen."

When she got back, she had a couple beers in her hand.

"Here," she said, handing me one without asking me if I wanted it.

She sat down, crossed her legs, popped the tab and took a swig.

"So you want to know why I tossed his ass outta here?"

"Yes," I said, still holding the unopened beer. I hoped she wouldn't make an issue of it. But she didn't seem to care much, so I just held onto it.

"He was sleeping with half the population of Syracuse, but I was the one he came home to until I got sick of him sponging off me. Besides, he got hooked up with this other chick..."

"Who?"

She took another swig. "Bitch."

"Which bitch would that be?"

"The chick that murdered her family."

"You mean Meg Montgomery."

She laughed. "Yeah, that's the bitch. He really hit pay dirt with that one. Them in-laws of hers are loaded. And according to Rick she's gonna make a bundle when she sues the State."

"She's suing the State?"

"That's what I hear."

"You know a lot about this, huh?"

"You gonna drink that or what?"

"Sure," I said, popping the tab. But I just held it in front of me.

"Yeah. He couldn't keep his mouth shut if you duct taped it."

"When did you first hear about her?"

"I knew about her from the get-go. When it happened, and it was all over the papers, I remembered seeing her before 'cause at the time Rick was working construction and his company was putting a new family room in her place. That was right before it happened."

"Did he work on that job?"

"It's possible. But he didn't have that gig long. Got fired for stealing building materials and reselling them. Real smart guy, Rick is. Can't even do that without getting nabbed." She looked at her watch. "I gotta get ready for work. You mind if I go change?"

"Of course not."

"I can hear you from the other room. It's the bedroom, but my kid sleeps there and I sleep out here. He's in school now. My sister keeps him while I work," she said as she headed into the other room.

As soon as she disappeared, I got up and started nosing around.

"So, it must be a kick seeing yourself on TV all the time, huh?" she called out.

"It's not as glamorous as it looks."

"Yeah, well, that's easy for you to say. I bet you make tons of dough."

I laughed, as I spotted a small desk in the corner of the room. "This is Syracuse. The real money's national."

"So whyn't you go national instead of sticking 'round this shithole?"

"I'm working on it," I said, as I flipped through a desk calendar.

"Yeah, well no matter what you get I'm sure it beats waitressing. You know, back in high school, like a hundred years ago, I was into drama and stuff. Maybe if I'd stuck with it..."

On the page with three days ago's date on it there were two words: Greyhound Sta.

I pulled out my phone and took a quick picture of the page.

"Did Rick know someone named Tommy Leary?"

"Leary?" Her voice got closer. I stepped away from the desk just as she came back into the room, now dressed in a white tank top and black jeans. "Yeah. He knows Tommy. They were into God knows what together. I could never keep track of half the shit he was into. Funny you should bring him up, since he got himself killed the other day. Hit and run. Still looking for the driver, I think. Hey, you get here by car?"

"I did."

"Would you mind giving me a lift to work? Sonuvabitch got my car stolen right before I kicked him out. My guess is he went out and sold it behind my back or lent it to one of his scumbag buddies. I wouldn't put it past him. Scams like that come natural to Rick. It's amazing he's never been in the slammer, but the asshole lives a charmed life. So until I get the insurance dough I have to take the bus. So, how about it?"

"It wouldn't happen to be a blue Infiniti, would it?"

"Yeah. How'd you know that?"

"Sure, I can give you that lift."

The pieces of the puzzle were starting to fit together. In the middle was Meg, around the edges were Rick Mathis and the late Tommy Leary. That funny feeling I was having was getting even funnier.

Chapter 13

Who knew they had mansions in Syracuse? Certainly not me. But that was where the Montgomerys resided. And when you're wealthy, even the weather seems to cooperate. The day before the city was hit by an early summer deluge, a downpour that resulted in local flooding and at least three traffic fatalities. But on this night, the night of the party the Montgomerys were throwing for Meg, it was as if all was right with the world.

From the crowd that gathered at the Montgomerys it looked like Meg had been totally embraced by a family and a community that had once shunned her. She was the prodigal daughter, saved from damnation. And me, I was the savior.

The three-story brick house was lit up brightly against the clear night sky by a series of strategically placed floodlights, as if it were something out of *The Great Gatsby*. Music filtered out onto the street, a street lined with expensive cars, parked by car jockeys dressed in sharp matching outfits. They took my car from me and handed me a ticket stub, as if it would be difficult locating my modest heap amongst the other high-priced automobiles.

As I approached the house I spotted giant banner draped across the front of the house.

Welcome Home, Meg

Were they kidding? What did they think this was,

some kind of college homecoming queen celebration?

Well, maybe for them it was. For me, it was just plain embarrassing and more than a little unsettling.

The real party was out back, in the spacious yard that looked to go on forever.

I was seriously underdressed, wearing a simple, knee-length black dress, with a scoop neckline, and a pair of medium heels that I didn't think would sink too far into the still slightly damp grass. I hit one of the two bars set up on opposite sides of a large swimming pool, then drifted around, looking for Meg. I needed to get her alone talk to her.

It wasn't easy. The crowd was filled with people I knew and who knew me. Standing off to the side, a glass of champagne in his hand, I even spotted Sam chatting with our station manager. But Meg was nowhere in sight.

I strolled along the edge of the party, continuing my search for Meg. I spotted Rick first, talking to a couple of rough-looking biker types, guys who definitely stood out in this tony crowd. Finally, I spotted Meg, a drink in her hand, looking very happy, dressed in an elegant outfit that looked like it had been appropriated off the cover of *Vogue*, amidst a crowd of well-wishers.

I made a beeline for her, coming up from behind and putting my hand on her elbow. She looked up.

"Trish, I'm so glad you could make it."

"We have to talk," I said.

"Well, this really isn't the time. Can't it wait?"

"No," I said firmly.

Her face turned to steel. It was a look I hadn't seen before, a far cry from the Meg I'd interviewed in prison, the Meg who was tearfully begging for help.

She turned back to her guests. "Will you excuse us, please? I'll be right back." She handed her drink to one of her friends. "We can talk inside, in the library."

"Fine," I said.

"All right, Trish," she said, as we entered the cavernous, book-lined room in the back of the house. "What's so important that you had to drag me away from my guests?"

"Close the door," I said.

"I don't see why..."

"Close the damn door."

She did.

"How do you know Rick?"

"I told you. His sister..."

"That's a load of crap. How well do you know him?"

"Not that well, not that it's any of your business."

"So you're sticking to your story about knowing his sister in prison?"

"I didn't actually say I knew of her. She was in another cell block..."

"So you never actually met?"

"Not in person."

"What if I were to tell you Rick doesn't have a sister?"

"I'd say you were mistaken."

"He doesn't. And I checked the prison log. The only one he ever visited was you. Not only that, he was friends with Tommy Leary and he may have had something to with his murder. He may also have had something to do with murdering Jeffrey and the twins."

"That's ridiculous..."

I heard the sound of the door opening. I looked up and there was Rick.

"Hey, there you are. I was looking all over for you."

I watched Meg's face. The sweetness was suddenly replaced by one of menace. She paused a moment and then, speaking to Rick, as if I weren't even there, whispered, "She knows."

I looked at Rick. He mirrored her expression. I could see he didn't know whether to come forward or just stand there. I knew? What did I know?

And then something that had been hanging out in the back of my mind wormed its way to the front.

They were in it together.

"It's okay," Meg hissed. "I'll handle this."

Rick stared at her, then me and then back to her again. He looked like he wanted to say something, but instead he just left, closing the door behind him.

"He did it. He murdered them. And you knew about it all along."

She smiled. Her eyes focused like lasers, so intense that shock waves were sent through me. I could feel the power in them, the anger, the hatred. And I knew. I knew what those eyes could do. I knew what was inside her.

"Rick had nothing to do with it," she said in a voice no more than a whisper.

My mind went blank for a moment. Then it hit me. "Oh, my God," I said. "You did it, didn't you?"

Her face slowly morphed into a half-smile.

"When Jeffrey found out about Rick and me, he said he was going to leave me and take the kids. He'd make sure I'd never see them again, that I'd never get a penny from him or his family. I never meant to harm the girls. They were everything to me. They were my life. I didn't expect them home till later. But when I saw them, when they came home early and saw what I, what happened. I had no choice. You can see that, can't you? What kind of life would they have had knowing what I'd done? What would happen to them if I went to prison for it? How could I have lived knowing what they knew?"

"It's all about you, isn't it?"

"I did what I thought was best for everyone..."

"Best? Are you crazy? You are, aren't you? You're absolutely mad. You're a monster. You used me..."

"No, Trish, we used each other. You got a great story out of it. You got a new career. And I got my freedom. We both got what we wanted."

"The lie detector..."

"Oh, that was easy. All you have to do is convince yourself you're telling the truth..."

"You're a sociopath."

"Don't you just hate labels?"

I was stunned and confused, but not too stunned and confused to want to know more.

"How does Rick figure into all this? I don't see you and him walking off into the sunset together."

She laughed. "No. That's not going to happen." She moved closer to me, close enough so that I could smell the perfume she was wearing, Chanel No. 5. "He's in it for the money. And he loves me. But I don't care about that."

"He set up everything for you, didn't he? Roche. The evidence in Leary's place...You planned everything and used him to get it done."

She shrugged. "I don't know why you're so hung up on that word, Trish. Everyone uses everyone else. You get out of life what everyone else puts into it. If you're smart, that is."

She moved closer to me and ran her finger along my arm. I felt the chill. And I felt the electricity. I wanted to run and hide. I wanted to get away from this monster as fast as I could. But I couldn't move. It was as if she'd given me some drug that paralyzed me.

"Why are you telling me all this?" I asked, as she kept slowly, seductively running her finger up and down my arm. I wanted to grab her hand and push it away, but I didn't. I couldn't.

"Because I like you, Trish. Because I think we're very much the same. Because I know this will be our little secret."

"Are you serious?"

"Of course I'm serious. Why wouldn't I be serious? We're partners, Trish. Don't you understand, we're in this together? Your whole career is riding high because of me, because of my innocence. If I fall, you go down with me."

I didn't know what to say, so I said nothing. But she wasn't finished.

"Besides, what do you think would happen if it came out that you were single-handedly responsible for letting a murderer go free? No matter what happens, Trish, I'd still have my freedom. I could never be retried—that'd be double jeopardy. But you? You wouldn't have much of a career left, would you? You certainly wouldn't be the media darling you are now. And I know you, Trish. I know you wouldn't want to give that up for anything in the world. You'd rationalize away what happened. It wouldn't be your fault. A jury let me off, not you."

She stopped. She smiled. I wanted to slap that smile off her face. I wanted to grab her by the neck and...

"My advice to you, Trish, is to leave it be because if you do, we both come out winners. And if you don't... well, I don't think you want to even think about the consequences of that."

"What if I can't? What if you're wrong about me?"

"I suggest you try. And try hard. Because if you don't, well, let's just hope it never comes to that. Besides, I don't think I'm wrong about you."

She reached out and grabbed my hand and pulled me closer. Then, suddenly, she lunged forward and kissed me full on the lips, her tongue slipping into my mouth, gently caressing mine. I stumbled back, in shock and disgust. I wiped my lips with the back of my hand, trying to erase her taste from on me, from inside me.

She stepped back, smiling. "We're not so different, Trish. You and me. We're tied together forever. More than friends, Trish, so much more."

I couldn't get out of that room fast enough. My heart was beating so rapidly I thought it would burst out of my chest. I couldn't catch my breath. I needed fresh air so I rushed outside, past the revelers, finally finding a place near the side of the pool where I could be alone, where I could pull myself together before getting the hell out of there. A few moments later, my heart still racing, I looked up to see Meg appear on the back porch. I heard the tinkling of glasses and suddenly the din of the crowd shrunk to silence, the music stopped abruptly.

"Hi. In case some of you don't know me personally, I'm Meg Montgomery, and I want to thank all of you for making me feel so welcome. The last four years I've spent in prison have not been easy ones, as you can well imagine. But it was nothing compared to the shock of having my loved ones, my babies, taken away from me. The grief was and is overwhelming. I think about them every day. They are with me every day. All I can do from now on is try to dedicate my life to their memory in a way, I hope, that would make them proud. I know my transition back into society is going to be that much easier because of that...and because of you. And I just want to give special thanks to my good friend, Trish Sullivan...Trish, where are you?"

Oh, my God! That bitch! She was singling me out. I wanted to disappear. To shrink into nothingness.

"There she is," someone shouted, pointing in my direction.

"Trish, please, come up here. I want to thank you in front of everyone."

I shook my head as I slowly backed away. There was no way she was going to get me up there, in front of everyone, cementing this sick idea that we were tied together. Forever. The thought of it made me want to throw up.

"Well, folks, hard to imagine, what with her being on TV practically every night, but it seems Trish is a little too shy to come up here. But that's all right. We all know who you are, Trish, and we all know how instrumental you were in my getting a new trial and ultimately being able to stand here, a free woman. In any case, I want to thank you so much for coming. And I love you all so very much. Now please, y'all just have fun."

Mrs. Montgomery approached her from the other end of the porch. She put her arm around Meg and said, loud enough for everyone to hear, "Welcome home, dear."

There was applause. The band started up again.

Meg hugged her mother-in-law and I saw her staring over her shoulder at Rick. She nodded slightly and he looked over in my direction. Our eyes locked. His face was grim, serious, dangerous. Finally, he released his hold on my eyes, raised his hand slowly till it was at his side, and cocked his fingers into a mock pistol. I did not need an interpreter to understand what he was saying.

I was no longer glued to the spot. Without looking up, I made my way down the front lawn, toward the valet. I gave him my ticket and waited impatiently for him to bring me my car. I did not want to see anyone I knew. I did not want to talk to anyone. I just wanted to get out of there.

My car pulled up. I handed the kid a five. Just as I was getting in I looked up and saw a familiar face get out of a car that had just pulled up. It was Leo Ames, the man who claimed to have heard Tommy Leary brag about committing the murders. Just as he was taking his ticket from the valet kid, I saw Rick striding down the front lawn. At first I thought, *he's coming after me.* But he wasn't. He walked right over to Leo and whispered in his ear. They both scanned the area. Just as their eyes lit on my car, I slipped into the driver's seat, hoping they wouldn't spot me. But they did. I started up the engine, backed up the car, and got the hell out of there.

Chapter 14

As soon as I got home I had a drink. And then another. I wanted my mind to shut down, but it would not. It kept racing. No matter what I did, no matter what I tried to think about, it all came back to Meg. She was laughing at me. They were laughing at me. I had helped set a monster free. What could I do? They had me boxed in. I had to speak to someone, someone who could help give me some perspective, some advice. I picked up the phone and dialed Sam. But as soon as he answered, I hung up. What could I say to him? If I told him the truth, he'd fire me. Not because he wanted to, but because he'd have to. And then what? Where could I possibly find another job?

And then there was Meg. That smug, conniving, murderous bitch. She was going to get away with it. She had gotten away with it. I started to feel as if I'd murdered those children myself. I was as much a murderer as she was because without me she would be where she was supposed to be.

What could I do? How could I fix this? Could I fix this?

I had another drink. Anything to help me get to sleep because maybe, just maybe, when I woke up in the morning it would all be gone. None of it would be true. None of it would have happened. Meg Montgomery really was innocent and I'd done the right thing, a good thing.

Maybe.

Maybe.

I slept in fits and starts and when I woke up it was still dark. The clock read 3:30 a.m. My head ached. I popped a couple of Tylenol. I went through the motions as if it were morning. I got up. I had a cup of coffee and a bowl of cereal. I stared at the wall. I got dressed. I would go to work. I would go somewhere. I would drive and that driving would take me somewhere. Maybe the office. Maybe I'd just hit the thruway and head east then south, into New York City. Why? I don't know. I don't know because I wasn't really thinking straight.

I got in my car. I turned on the ignition. All this happened, but honestly, if you asked me I don't remember any of it. I just know that it happened because when I looked into the rearview mirror I saw a car parked behind me. And in that car was a man. And that man was Rick Mathis. At four o'clock in the morning Rick Mathis was sitting in a parked car in front of my house.

I panicked. I locked all the doors. I pulled out of my spot, my eyes glued to the road ahead. Because maybe I was hallucinating. Maybe no one was sitting in that parked car. And maybe that no one wasn't Rick Mathis.

When I reached a red light several blocks from my house I looked in the rearview mirror and the car was there. And yes, Rick Mathis was in that car.

I hit the gas, darting into the intersection, running the red light.

I drove around Syracuse, with no particular pattern to where I was going. I would see a street and turn onto it, then turn onto the next one. I did this till I was practically lost. But I wasn't lost. I was still with me. And so, I thought, was Rick Mathis.

Almost an hour after I began this pointless journey, I found my way back to my house. I looked for signs of life, but at five in the morning, in Syracuse, there were no signs of life. I parked my car. I ran to my front door. I went inside. I double-locked the door. I went straight to the window and peered outside. No movement. Nothing. And then, just as I was going to go back into my room and try to get some sleep, I saw a car cruise by slowly. It was the same car. It was Rick Mathis's car. And yes, he was in it.

With the aid of an Ambien, I was able to get a few hours' sleep. Even so, I was up by seven-thirty. I went into my study, found Meg's file, and began, one by one, tearing up all the papers and photos. I put them in a plastic bag, tied it up and put it in the kitchen, by the rest of the garbage.

I went into the bathroom to wash my face. When I looked into the mirror I saw an unfamiliar face. And yet it was my face. I closed my eyes but when I reopened them and looked into the mirror again, it was still my face the one I did not at first recognize.

I called in sick. I did not want to face myself so how could I face those people?

At one o'clock the phone rang. It was Sam.

"Trish, you okay? Jackie said you were sick."

"A touch of stomach flu. Must have been something I ate at the party."

"We can get someone else for tonight's eleven o'clock."

"No. I'm fine now. I'll be there.

"You're sure?"

"Yes, Sam. I'll be there."

I would be there because finally, after hours of pacing back and forth through my apartment I'd come up with a plan. It was a plan borne out of desperation, a plan that was bound to fail, but it was something. A possible way to make things right. A possible way to undo what I'd done.

I hung up the phone and called Mark.

"Hey, Mark, it's me. Everything all set for tonight?"

"Yeah, why wouldn't it be?"

"No reason. I just wanted to make sure. So I'll see you at the Social Club, right?'

"Right."

Somehow, I got through the rest of the day. Maybe it was because I'd made a decision. At nine o'clock, I began to get ready for work. I rummaged through my jewelry box and found the same lucky, moon-shaped earrings I was wearing the day Knightly pulled me over. I put on a pair of jeans and a dark sweater and then packed the outfit I was planning to wear on camera that night into a garment bag.

A few minutes after ten, I arrived at the Meg's house, the one she'd retrieved from the Montgomerys. I noticed Rick's car parked out front and I parked across the street, a few cars down, and crouched down in the seat, in a position where I could see the entrance to the house.

I had less than half an hour and unless Rick left, I'd had to give it up. But for once, things were working out for me. At precisely ten-oh-five, Rick emerged from the house, got into his car and pulled away.

I grabbed the garment bag from the back seat, folded

it over my arm. I patted my purse to make sure the gun was still there, a gun I'd owned and had a permit for. A gun I'd purchased because a colleague had said I might need one for protection, a single woman alone in Syracuse, a prime candidate for stalkers. I reached the front door and picked up the welcome mat. Just as I'd hope, the house key was still there. I unlocked the door and stepped inside. The downstairs was dark, but up the stairs I could see a light. I took the gun out of my purse and started up the stairs, as quietly as I could. I could hear the sound of the TV.

Hugging the wall as close as I could, I made it up, one step at a time, slowly, methodically, and with each step I got bolder, knowing that yes, I was going to go through with it.

Finally, I made it to the top of the stairs. I quietly dropped the garment bag to the floor, took a deep breath and moved into the lighted bedroom doorway. There was no one there, but I could hear the sound of running water coming from the bathroom. Good, I thought. She would come out preoccupied, totally vulnerable, totally unaware that she was going to die.

I moved to the bed and picked up a pillow, then stepped back to where I'd stood before. I aimed my pistol at the doorway. Minutes passed, at least it seemed like minutes though it was probably only a few seconds. The sound of running water stopped. I felt a lump in my stomach. My hand shook. But I did not lower it. The pistol remained aimed at the bathroom entrance.

Finally, Meg, naked, her face buried in a towel, came out. She held the towel to her face for a moment as if she knew someone else was in the room but didn't want to see who it was. Finally, she dropped it and looked up. At first, she looked confused, but a moment later that expression changed. I swear it changed to a look of amusement.

She remained there, frozen, for a moment, her face slowly turning into a smile, as she stared not at me but at the gun in my hand.

"I knew you'd come for me," she said finally.

I had no words.

"You really think you're going to do this?" she asked, her voice firm, sure of itself.

I did not answer. The time for talk was over. I was not her. I was me. And I was prepared to watch her die because with her death would come freedom for me.

She spread her arms out wide, as if she were getting ready to fly or as if she were going to embrace me. She was stunningly beautiful. An unworldly kind of beautiful. That something so beautiful could be so monstrous was a perverted kind of miracle. Still smiling, she took a step toward me then another. I did not hesitate. I took one step back, raised the pillow so that it enveloped the barrel of the pistol then fired once, then again.

Almost simultaneously the smile disappeared from Meg's face and was replaced with a baffled look, as if she did not expect what to me seemed inevitable. Almost immediately after the sound of the muffled shot droplets of blood flew through the air, some landing on me.

The bullets had struck Meg in the chest. She fell back immediately from the impact. I heard the thump of her body hit the floor. Then the room was silent, the smell of gunpowder in the air. I stepped over to her and heard what I knew to be her dying gasp. Her body jerked and then was still.

I knew she could not possibly be alive.

I went into the bathroom, turned on the shower, stripped and stepped in. The steaming water felt good as it soaked my body. I soaped up, then rinsed. When I was finished, I dried off with the same bath towel that Meg had used earlier, changed into the other clothes I'd brought with me, putting the soiled clothing and the used bath towel into the garment bag. I would wash them all and then destroy them.

When I'd finished, I picked up Meg's phone and dialed 9-1-1. When the operator answered, I whispered, "Help...there's someone in the house...help...please." I gave the address and hung up.

I wiped the phone clean then laid it on the floor beside Meg's hand.

I turned off all the lights, looked around to make sure I'd left no sign of my being there, then left the house.

I drove to Onondaga Lake, jumped out of the car, made sure no one else was around then tossed the gun into the water. I got back into the car and drove to the Little Roma Social Club where I saw Mark sitting in the van, smoking.

I parked the car, approached the van and tapped on the window. He rolled it down.

"Cutting it a little close, aren't you?"

"I'm here, aren't I? How we doing on time?"

"A minute thirty," he said, getting out with his camera.

I checked myself in the van's side mirror.

"Let's go," he said. "You look great."

I took my place in front of the Club. Mark handed me the mike, plugged the earphone into his ear while I plugged one into mine, and aimed the camera at me. With the fingers of his left hand he counted down five, four, three, two one. I heard Corey, the evening anchor say, "Here's Trish Sullivan, reporting live outside the Little Roma Social Club on today's developments."

"Thanks, Corey. Well, it looks like Anthony Alcante's luck has finally run out. Mr. Alcante, reputed head of the Conigliaro crime family, was arrested at two p.m. today on murder and racketeering charges, stemming from an eight-month undercover FBI investigation. Rumor has it that Vincent Palma, better known as 'Sonny,' Mr. Alcante's trusted bodyguard and a reputed soldier in the Conigliaro crime family, has agreed to testify against his boss in exchange for a grant of immunity."

As I was reporting, back in the studio they were showing file footage of the earlier arrest.

"Here's Mr. Alcante this afternoon outside the Roma Social Club, site of today's arrest."

While the audience was being shown the file footage, I absently scratched my right ear and I realized my earring was missing. I quickly touched the other ear, thinking maybe I'd forgotten to put them on, but that one was there. Oh, my God, I must have dropped it at Meg's. Or maybe it was in my car. I prayed it was in my car.

I was jolted out of my head by Mark, who poked me and gave me the wrap it up sign.

"If, uh, convicted, Mr. Alcante could spend the rest of his life behind bars. This is Trish Sullivan, back to you, Corey."

"Are you okay?"

"Yes," I said, handing Mark the mike.

"Well, you look like shit and you zoned out there for a sec. Maybe you're not over what you had. Go home. Get some sleep. And good work, Trish."

"Thanks. Yeah. I've gotta get back to bed."

I sat in my car and watched Mark drive off. I got back on the road and when I got to a relatively deserted spot along the highway, I pulled off the lone earring and tossed it out the window, into the woods.

I drove around a little longer then headed in the direction of Meg's house. When I got there, a few police squad cars were parked out front, along with an ambulance. It looked like the aftermath of a late night frat party. Several people were standing out on the sidewalk. A group of cops were milling around, as one in uniform directed traffic.

I parked across the street, flashed my Press card, and got as close as I could to the front door. After a few minutes, Knightly came out of the house.

"What's going on?" I asked.

"Your pal Meg got herself whacked."

"Oh, my God. You're kidding."

"Even I don't joke about something like that."

"What happened? Robbery?"

"No forced entry, nothing appears to have been taken, so I'd have to say no."

"You mean someone she knew killed her?"

"Or someone she let into the house."

"Any likelies?"

He shook his head.

"How did you find out?"

"She called nine-one-one. Said someone was in the house."

"Did you find anything?"

"We're dusting for prints now, but I can't tell you anything else, Ms. Sullivan. You'll have to wait for the release, like everyone else."

A technician walked out with bagged evidence. I could see it, through the plastic baggie. The earring. My heart started pounding. Stay calm, I told myself. Stay calm.

The cop holding the bag passed by Knightly. "Whatcha got there?" he asked.

He held up the bag. "An earring."

"Where'd you find it?"

"Behind the toilet, in the chick's bathroom."

"Probably hers," said Knightly, "but log it in."

Another uniformed cop came up to Knightly. "We found the boyfriend. Name's Rick Mathis. We took him down to the station."

"There's your likely," I said, as nonchalantly as I could manage.

"We'll see," said Knightly. He turned to his partner. "That's a wrap for me. We'll let these boys do their job and figure out what we have in the morning."

Chapter 15

I couldn't sleep that night either. I'd thought of everything, but that damn earring. I knew it wouldn't take long before Knightly realized that he'd seen it before. On me. And then...

I had to figure something out. Something.

The murder was the lead story on the morning news and by evening it had been picked up on the national news. I stayed as far away from the coverage as I could and Sam agreed, saying I was too close to it to report it with any kind of objectivity. All I knew was what I read in the papers and what we reported on the news.

Trish was dead. She'd been shot twice, point blank range. There seemed to be no forensic evidence. There was no mention of the earring. I figured if Knightly did peg it to the murderer it would be something they'd hold back, that little piece of information they use to nail the killer, something they don't want the public to know.

The funeral was two days later. I didn't want to go but I knew I had to. And so, dressed in black, as if I were in mourning which I most certainly was not, I stood away from the crowd of mourners, most of whom had never met Meg but were drawn by her notoriety.

The service was quick, and as they lowered her coffin into the ground, I began to move back to my car. As I reached out to open the door, I felt a hand on my shoulder. Startled, my body jerked forward. It was Knightly.

"Hello, Ms. Sullivan."

"Hello, Detective Knightly."

"Nice funeral, huh?"

"Yes."

"Nice turn out. Especially for a woman who killed her husband and two kids."

"You still think she was guilty?"

"I know she was."

"So, who do you think killed her?"

"You knew her better than I did, who do you think did it?"

"You're the detective."

"Yes. I am." He pulled something out of his pocket. It was a photo. Of the earring. My heart began to race, but I did my best to remain calm—it was like the feeling I had when I first went on air. I felt like I would have a heart attack, but I learned how to feign serenity, as if being on camera was the most natural thing in the world.

"Recognize this?

"Yes. I do. It used to be one of my earrings."

"We found it at the murder scene."

"That doesn't surprise me."

"Why would that be? I mean, finding one of your earrings in the murder victim's house, not far from where we found her body."

"Because when she admired them I gave her my pair."

"Really? When was this?"

"A few weeks ago. I don't remember exactly when."

"Yeah, well maybe you can try."

"It had to have been before last Saturday because I remember her saying she wanted to wear them at the party. That they would mean something special to her because they were a part of me and it was because of me that she was a free woman."

"That's very sweet. Seems you two were like, what, sisters?"

"You think?"

"Did she wear them that night?"

"I can't be sure. Maybe."

"It's kind of interesting because you see this earring is for pierced ears. And although she did have pierced ears at one time, four years in the can without earrings, the lobes closed up."

"Obviously, she was planning to have them re-pierced, but she probably never got around to it."

"I guess that could be it. But you know, it's kinda strange we only found the one earring."

I shrugged.

"I guess we'll never know for sure, will we? By the way, you wouldn't happen to know where we can get our hands on that other earring, would you? We searched every square inch of her house and all we found was the one."

"I lose earrings all the time, kinda like socks in the dryer. Who knows where they wind up? I'm not quite sure what you're getting at, Detective."

"Oh, I think you do, Ms. Sullivan."

I stared him down.

"You're not suggesting I had anything to do with her murder, are you?"

"You tell me."

"What possible motive could I have? And besides, do you think I'd do something so stupid?"

"Lots of smart people do stupid things. And as for motive, I don't know. Maybe you were jealous she had a boyfriend because you wanted her all for yourself. Or, it is what you guys call sweeps, isn't it?"

"So this is a joke to you?"

"Murder's not a joke, Ms. Sullivan."

"I don't think I'm going to answer any more of your questions."

"That's probably a good idea. Maybe you'd better get yourself an attorney." He turned and started to walk away.

"Wait," I said. "I'll give you one more question. What is it you want to ask?"

"Where were you at eleven the night she was killed?"

"I was doing a remote on Tony Alcante's arrest, so I was on camera at the Little Roma Social Club. That should be easy enough to check out."

He smiled. "Except you didn't get on air till approximately eleven-twenty. I had a little chat with your cameraman. Mark, right? He said they had to put the weather on ahead of you because they were afraid you weren't going to show on time. And I timed it. From Meg's house to the Social Club is less than five minutes. Plenty of time for you to have killed her, called nine-one-one, and showed up to do your little report."

"That's ridiculous."

"Is it? Well, maybe so. In the end, it don't matter. The way I see it, she got what she deserved. I'll be in touch, Ms. Sullivan."

* * *

Back at the office, Jackie unloaded the news on me.

"The D.A.'s office subpoenaed a copy of last Wednesday's broadcast. Wonder what that's all about."

"I have no idea," I said, hoping she'd drop it there, and she did. But I knew. He was going to see what earrings I was wearing. I rushed to the studio and asked if they kept a copy. They had. I took a look. I freeze framed it a couple times and sure enough, there it was, me wearing the earring. But because of the way I wore my hair, you could only see one of them.

A few minutes later, as I sat at my desk trying to look busy, my mind racing all over the place, Mark stopped by.

"That cop came to see me yesterday and asked a whole lot of questions. Wanna tell me what's going on, Trish?"

"I have no idea."

I didn't have a story for the evening news, so I asked Sam if I could cut out a little early, telling him I wasn't feeling all that well. I wasn't home more than ten minutes when there was a knock at the front door. It was Knightly.

"Mind if I come in to talk to you for a few minutes?"

I hesitated a moment. He was the last person I wanted to see. But I didn't want him to get any funny ideas about me, so I said, "Sure. Can I take your coat?"

"Nah. I'm not staying that long."

"Something to drink?"

"I wouldn't turn down a cup of coffee."

"I'll make some. Donut with that?"

"Very funny."

"Make yourself at home."

"I will." He plopped down on the couch, as I went into the kitchen to start a pot going. A moment later, I was back.

"Grapevine has it that you'll be outta here soon."

"What grapevine is that?"

"The one that says you got yourself a job down in the City."

"It's not definite yet."

"It will be. You're good."

"Thanks. But I'm sure you didn't come all the way over here to congratulate me."

"You'd be right about that."

I heard the pot whistle. I excused myself, French pressed both of us a cup of coffee, and returned to see Knightly checking his phone.

"Anything important?" I asked.

"Nothing that can't wait."

"So?" I said, handing him his cup.

"Thanks. So, remember those earrings I asked you about? As I recall you said you gave them to Meg a week or so before her murder. Is that correct?"

"It is."

"The reason I ask is we took a look at that news report you did he night she was murdered and you'll never guess what we saw."

"What would that be?"

"Well, you know that earring, the one that was missing? Well, it turns out you were wearing it. Approximately one half hour after she was found dead. What do you think about that?"

"Oh, you mean these?" I said, sweeping my hair from

behind my ears to reveal a pair of the moon-shaped earrings.

Knightly turned white. His face twitched. He put down his cup. I could practically see his mind working.

Finally, he spoke.

"How could you give her a pair and still have a pair?"

"When I like something, Detective, I always buy two of them. You want to take a look in my closet? I've got doubles on pretty much everything. It's part of the business. We mix and match all the time and when I find something I like, something that fits well, I don't want to take a chance I can't find it again."

"So you went out and bought yourself another pair to cover your tracks, did you? You wouldn't happen to be able to tell me when and where you bought them, would you?"

"You know us women, Detective, we're buying stuff all the time. I just don't remember where I got these. Sorry."

"Tell you what, Ms. Sullivan, I'm gonna do some checking around and if I find out you purchased them after she was murdered and not before, which I'm damn sure is the case, then I'm gonna come back here and take you down. You can be sure of that."

I shrugged, trying hard to suppress a smile. "You do that, Detective. But you're not going to find what you're looking for. Tell the truth, Detective, you're not actually sorry she's dead, are you? After all, you thought she was guilty all along."

"I still do. And you know what, I'm going out right now and dance a fuckin' jig on her grave. Because she did it. You know it and I know it."

I smiled.

He smiled back at me and at that moment I knew. I knew that he knew that I'd done it. But I knew more than that. I also knew that he wouldn't do anything about it. That he wouldn't take it any further. That in his mind justice had finally been carried out. We were partners now, Knightly and me. We had both gotten what we wanted. Knightly had gotten his pound of flesh and me, I would get out of Syracuse.

And in the end, was there that much difference between us?

ABOUT THE CONTRIBUTORS

Ross Klavan's darkly comic novel *Schmuck,* was published in 2014. His original screenplay *Tigerland* (starring Colin Farrell, directed by Joel Schumacher) was nominated for the Independent Spirit Award. He's written screenplays for InterMedia, Walden Media, Miramax, Paramount, A&E and TNT. As a performer, his voice has been heard in dozens of feature films including *Revolutionary Road, Sometimes in April, Casino, In and Out,* and *You Can Count On Me* as well as in numerous TV and radio commercials. In other lives, he was with the NYC alternative art group Four Walls and was a reporter covering New York City and London, England.

Tim O'Mara has been a NYC public school math and special education teacher since 1987. His first three mysteries featuring Brooklyn schoolteacher and ex-cop Raymond Donne—*Sacrifice Fly, Crooked Numbers,* and *Dead Red*—were published by St. Martins/Minotaur Books. His fourth Raymond novel, *Nasty Cutter,* will be published fall 2016 in England by Severn House Publishing, and later in the year in the U.S. You can reach Tim at www.timomara.net.

Charles Salzberg is the author of the Shamus nominated *Swann's Last Song,* and the sequels *Swann Dives In* and *Swann's Lake of Despair* which was a finalist for two Silver Falchions, the Beverly Hills Book Award and the Indie Excellence Award, as well as *Devil in the Hole,* which was named one of the best crime novels of 2013 by *Suspense Magazine.* He teaches writing for the New York Writers Workshop, where he is a Founding Member. Henry Swann returns in *Swann's Way Out,* which will be published in early 2017 by Down & Out Books. Find out more at www.charlessalzberg.com.

OTHER TITLES FROM DOWN AND OUT BOOKS

See www.DownAndOutBooks.com for complete list

By J.L. Abramo
Catching Water in a Net
Clutching at Straws
Counting to Infinity
Gravesend
Chasing Charlie Chan
Circling the Runway
Brooklyn Justice

By Trey R. Barker
2,000 Miles to Open Road
Road Gig: A Novella
Exit Blood
Death is Not Forever
No Harder Prison

By Richard Barre
The Innocents
Bearing Secrets
Christmas Stories
The Ghosts of Morning
Blackheart Highway
Burning Moon
Echo Bay
Lost

By Eric Beetner (editor)
Unloaded

By Eric Beetner and
JB Kohl
Over Their Heads

By Eric Beetner and
Frank Scalise
The Backlist
The Shortlist

By G.J. Brown
Falling

By Rob Brunet
Stinking Rich

By Mark Coggins
No Hard Feelings

By Tom Crowley
Vipers Tail
Murder in the Slaughterhouse

By Frank De Blase
Pine Box for a Pin-Up
Busted Valentines
and Other Dark Delights
A Cougar's Kiss

By Les Edgerton
The Genuine, Imitation,
Plastic Kidnapping

By A.C. Frieden
Tranquility Denied
The Serpent's Game
The Pyongyang Option (*)

By Jack Getze
Big Numbers
Big Money
Big Mojo
Big Shoes

By Richard Godwin
Wrong Crowd
Buffalo and Sour Mash (*)

(*)—Coming Soon

OTHER TITLES FROM DOWN AND OUT BOOKS

See www.DownAndOutBooks.com for complete list

By William Hastings (editor)
*Stray Dogs: Writing
from the Other America*

By Jeffery Hess
Beachhead

By Matt Hilton
*No Going Back
Rules of Honor
The Lawless Kind
The Devil's Anvil*

By David Housewright
*Finders Keepers
Full House*

By Jerry Kennealy
Screen Test

By Ross Klavan, Tim O'Mara and
Charles Salzberg
Triple Shot

By S.W. Lauden
Crosswise

By Terrence McCauley
The Devil Dogs of Belleau Wood

By Bill Moody
*Czechmate
The Man in Red Square
Solo Hand
The Death of a Tenor Man
The Sound of the Trumpet
Bird Lives!*

By Gary Phillips
*The Perpetrators
Scoundrels* (Editor)
*Treacherous
3 the Hard Way*

By Tom Pitts
Hustle

By Robert J. Randisi
*Upon My Soul
Souls of the Dead
Envy the Dead* (*)

By Ryan Sayles
*The Subtle Art of Brutality
Warpath*

By John Shepphird
*The Shill
Kill the Shill
Beware the Shill*

By Ian Thurman
Grand Trunk and Shearer

James R. Tuck (editor)
*Mama Tried vol. 1
Mama Tried vol. 2*

By Lono Waiwaiole
*Wiley's Lament
Wiley's Shuffle
Wiley's Refrain
Dark Paradise
Leon's Legacy* (*)

(*)—Coming Soon

59324001R00193

Made in the USA
Charleston, SC
02 August 2016